HONEYMOON FOR ONE

PORTIA MACINTOSH

Boldwood

First published in Great Britain in 2019 by Boldwood Books Ltd.

Copyright © Portia MacIntosh, 2019

Cover Design by Debbie Clement Design

Cover Photography: Shutterstock

A CIP catalogue record for this book is available from the British Library.

Paperback ISBN 978-1-83889-077-3

Hardback ISBN 978-1-80426-170-5

Large Print ISBN 978-1-83889-656-0

Ebook ISBN 978-1-83889-075-9

Kindle ISBN 978-1-83889-076-6

Audio CD ISBN 978-1-83889-078-0

MP3 CD ISBN 978-1-83889-350-7

Digital audio download ISBN 978-1-83889-074-2

Boldwood Books Ltd
23 Bowerdean Street
London SW6 3TN
www.boldwoodbooks.com

For my incredible family

1

MY WEDDING DAY

Your wedding day is the start of a life-long journey, and, like any other journey, it requires a lot of planning.

First, and most importantly, you need to know where you're going and how you're going to get there. Are you on a one-track path to growing old together or are you planning on making stops at pets, babies or house moves?

On a real trip you're going to want insurance, but on the life-long journey of marriage, assurance is what you need. Are you doing this with the right person? Will they stand by you for better, for worse? For richer, for poorer? In sickness and in health?

When your plans are all in place and it's time to set off on this wonderful, wild adventure, the only thing left to do is pack – but pack light.

Unfortunately, on this non-stop flight to a happy ever after, ex-boyfriends will not fit in the overhead storage, no matter how much you dissected the relationship. All baggage must be destroyed before boarding – you absolutely cannot bring your baggage into a marriage.

Before you tie the knot, customs will confiscate any and all contra-band still on your person, not limited to, but including flirtatious What-sApp threads and other miscellaneous weaponry.

I'm travelling light today. All I have with me is my something old (a necklace my grandma left me in her will), my something new (the sapphire studs in my ears), and my something borrowed (a handkerchief from my mum, which I'm going to keep in the pocket of my wedding dress, because you'd better believe I had my wedding dress made with sneaky pockets). My something blue is (apparently) my best friend, Ali, who is currently lying on the chaise longue at the bottom of my bed in my hotel room.

'Oh, Lila,' she says dramatically. 'Are you sure you want to do this?'

I smile at myself in the mirror. Most best friends are supportive, attentive maids of honour. Ali is showing me her love and support by constantly questioning whether or not this is the right thing to do. I wouldn't have her any other way though.

'I'm pretty sure,' I tell her. 'I made sure I was sure before I spent thousands of pounds on a wedding and a honeymoon.'

'Well, yeah, I figured,' she replies. 'But... I don't know, I don't think I thought you'd go through with it.'

I laugh.

'And yet here we are,' I say, smiling at her.

'Daniel is... you know, he's fine,' she says.

'Fine,' I repeat back to her. Just what a bride wants to hear on her wedding day.

'Yeah, he's fine... he's maybe just fine though?'

My best friend hasn't waited until my wedding day to say this, she's been telling me for years that Daniel was just too boring to settle down with. I think this is a 'speak now or forever hold your peace' type conversation, not that the latter sounds remotely like something Ali would do.

'I know you think he's boring,' I tell her. 'But, maybe "boring guys" are the ones you settle down with? Take that playboy banker you met last weekend – you wouldn't marry him, would you?'

'Well, someone clearly did,' she points out. 'There was a wedding ring in his hotel bathroom.'

'Was?' I dare to ask.

'Yeah, I flushed it down the lav,' she says casually. 'I really don't appreciate being lied to.'

Ali is a real force to be reckoned with.

'I know you're only being semi-serious with the whole talking me out of getting married thing,' I start. 'But honestly, I've thought this through. I love him, we're happy together – OK, things might not be wild, but I know in my heart that it's time to put sexy playboy bankers behind me.'

'Well, that's what I do with them,' Ali says with a wiggle of her eyebrows.

I know that Ali just wants me to be happy, but I did consider all of this before agreeing to marry my fiancé, Daniel Tyler, and when I say I considered it before agreeing, I mean I literally asked him for a moment, before I gave him my answer. The reason for this is because marriage is something I take seriously. My parents, both sixty-five years of age, have been married since they were nineteen. I might be thirty-one, but I want to marry once, and for life. I had a blast in my twenties, Daniel and I moved in together when I was twenty-nine and now, comfortably accepting of the fact I am in my thirties, I finally feel ready to tie the knot.

When some women say they have been planning their wedding for years, what they really mean is they've been dressing up in net curtains as kids and trolling Pinterest for flower arrangements as adults. Well, I really have been planning weddings for years... sort of. Not my own wedding and I'm certainly not a wedding planner.

I'm a rom-com author and although the weddings I work with may be fictional, I haven't just planned a lot of them – I've ruined a lot of them too. I've written ten books now, so it's pretty safe to say I've considered every possible triumph, every little hiccup and every epic fail my romantic yet devious mind can conjure up.

So, yes, while I have researched flowers, cakes and dresses, and tweaked them accordingly (pockets! Honestly, this is going to be a game changer), I don't just know what this wedding needs, I know what it doesn't need too. Obsessing over what flavour frosting to have is rather silly – that's just the icing on the cake. What you should be worrying about are the things that are out of your control.

I have essentially reverse-engineered every single wedding I've ever written, to make sure that my real wedding is perfect. It's kind of a genius move.

I know for a fact that Daniel's Auntie Susan and his Auntie Carole hate each other – and I mean hate each other. I also know that Ali would flip out if she knew that Alex, her ex-boyfriend, had been invited to the wedding. But thanks to my choice of venue – and, more specifically, room – they'll probably never see each other. I know that neither of his aunties likes to dance and I've put them at opposite ends of the room, with multiple pillars blocking their view of each other. The same strategy will work for Ali and Alex, although I have had to get a little creative with some balloons to keep him out of her sight. So, he might not have the best view of the speeches, but he'd thank me if he knew it was saving him from having to pick pieces of his jaw out of his salmon. And then it's only a matter of time. Once Ali has had enough to drink, and my girl drinks, she won't even recognise him – hell, she'll probably try and flirt with him.

There's a knock on the hotel door. I glance over at Ali, who looks back at me expectantly.

'Erm, can you open it?' I ask her.

She pulls a face, like a lazy teenager who doesn't want to tidy their room. You'd never know she was a hugely successful literary agent (although not mine, I hasten to add).

'I'm in my underwear still,' I point out.

I've had my hair and make-up done, now I'm just waiting for my mum to turn up with my dress. Ali is completely ready; she isn't going to flash anyone if she answers the door. Although I suspect she might if they were hot.

'Fine, fine,' she replies, carefully pulling herself to her feet in her bridesmaid dress. She looks absolutely smoking in the bright red dress she selected for herself to wear today. Her long blonde hair extensions cost more than my mobile phone, but I can't help but marvel at how real they look. My own real long blonde hair definitely looks real, but not in the way you'd want it to – it's more like the kind of real where a little sunshine or rain will make it fizz up like a bath bomb, which is why I've opted for one sleek-looking fishtail plait today.

During the wedding planning stage there was this whole conversation, involving some of our friends, about whether or not it was appropriate to wear a bright red dress to a wedding – especially if you were a bridesmaid. I just wanted my bridesmaids to be happy and if Ali wanted to wear a red dress, then I wanted her to wear a red dress too. I'm sure I should be in tears, worrying about my wedding aesthetic, or that my friend might upstage me, but I'm not. I'm just happy.

Ali reluctantly opens the door. She lets in my mum and my sister, Mandy. They both look as if they've just stepped off a roller coaster.

'What's wrong?' I ask, turning around on my dressing-table stool.

'Something has happened,' my mum says solemnly.

'What?' I prompt. A dramatic build-up is a plot device, not an appropriate way of delivering bad news in real life.

Mandy steps to one side, to reveal my three-year-old niece, Ruby, standing behind her.

Ruby is my flower girl. She also insisted she wanted an up-do like her mum, so I had her golden blonde curls wrapped around a flower crown. I say 'had' because her crown appears to have vanished and her curls look so wild, I don't know how we tamed them in the first place.

'Oh, my God,' I shriek, before placing one hand on my chest and the other over my mouth.

'Sis, I'm so sorry,' Mandy starts. 'I left her in the gardens with June, but I suppose she was too busy swiping on bloody Tinder to keep an eye on her, and she got attacked by a bloody bee!'

'It was on my head,' Ruby explains sheepishly.

June is our nineteen-year-old cousin. I don't think she's looked up from her iPhone since she was fourteen. A terrible choice for a babysitter, for sure.

'You all need to relax,' I say, giving up my faux-devastated act. 'It's fine, Ruby looks beautiful as she is. I don't care if she has a flower crown – she's a kid, I'm surprised she kept it on this long.'

'Lila Rose, what have I told you about being sarcastic?' my mum ticks me off as she recovers from the fright.

I keep telling them all not to worry so much. I have all the bases covered. Nothing is going to go wrong today. I'm certainly not going to have a meltdown because a three-year-old can't keep flowers in her hair.

'Don't you mean Lila Tyler?' my sister says.

'Lila Tyler,' Ali says mockingly. 'Lila Tyler, Lila Tyler.'

OK, I admit, it isn't an ideal married name, and I've always been so fond of Lila Rose because it's not only a beautiful name, but it sounds as if I was born to be a romance writer. But if Lila Tyler is what my new name is going to be, then that's what it's going to be. I may as well get used to it.

'Well, crisis averted,' I say. 'Is it time to put my dress on yet?'

I am so excited to finally be able to wear my dress. Other than a few times trying it on, putting my hands in the pockets, dancing around in front of the mirror, I really don't feel as if I've been able to enjoy it yet.

'Yes,' my mum replies. 'Sorry, it's in my room. I'll go fetch it.'

'And I'll break a brush in this one's hair,' Mandy says, nodding towards Ruby.

'I want my flowers,' Ruby says.

'You get them for the ceremony,' her mum tells her.

'No, my hair flowers. I want my hair flowers.'

'Then you shouldn't have taken them off and left them in the garden,' Mandy replies.

Ruby pouts.

'Well, I can't have a moody flower girl, can I?' I say playfully. 'I'll go get them for her.'

'You're getting ready,' Mandy says. 'Don't be crazy.'

'It's fine,' I insist. 'She wants them.'

And I want everything to be fine, so if Ruby wants her flowers, I'll go get them, and if it's easier if I do it myself, then I'll do it. There really, really isn't any need for things to go wrong today.

'Thanks,' my sister says. 'She was by the fountain.'

I grab my black tracksuit from on top of my bed, hop into my trackies, zip up my hoodie and head downstairs to retrieve Ruby's crown from the large angry bee that allegedly coerced her out of it.

I chose the Victoria Hotel for my wedding – a stunning, (unsurprisingly) Victorian building, tucked away in its own private woodland – because it was close to London, but easily accessible from the north of the country, with lots of rooms so Daniel's family and friends could travel down from Yorkshire and stay the night. Seriously, I am leaving no room for complaints, from either side of the family.

I walk down the spiral staircase, stroking the silky smooth wooden bannister. Not because I need to, but because I want to drink up every last drop of today. I want to remember every sight, every smell, every touch. I've hired two photographers, both with different areas of expertise, to ensure that every shot is accounted for, that I have a memento of every moment. I'm only doing this once, so I'm going to make it count.

It's July, so the delphiniums in the garden are blooming, in various shades of pinks and purples. I considered including them in my bridal bouquet, but I remembered reading that they were toxic to humans and while I had no intention of eating them, something about carrying something so poisonous down the aisle on the happiest day of my life just put me off.

Sure enough, by the large, stone fountain, I spot Ruby's flower crown, lying on the floor. I pick it up and examine it and, thankfully, it's absolutely fine. I say thankfully, not because I care, but because Ruby does. I've done everything I can to make sure today is as close to perfect as possible, so I'm pretty confident nothing important can go wrong. Any small thing that goes wrong, I'm not going to worry about. I'm not going to let it ruin my day.

It's such a lovely day today. Warm, but with a slight breeze. Of course, that's why I picked today, but you can never be sure with weather forecasts, can you?

I take a moment to admire the gardens. They always smell so much better in the summer, don't they? And the colours are amazing. The flowers, the fountain – I love the noise of the fountain, the gentle rushing of water. I'm about to take a quick photo with my phone when my ears pick up on another noise, a raised voice, coming from inside the hedge maze. I'm right by the entrance, so I edge closer towards it.

As I walk closer, the voice sounds more familiar. It's Daniel, my fiancé...

2

It's impossible to write fiction without bringing a little bit of real life into it. Writing about what you know is always going to benefit your work and, as soon as you realise this, you stop writing about the things you've experienced and start looking for experiences to write about.

It's pretty much the same with dialogue. As soon as you notice there are some great things to be overheard, while sitting on the train or using a public toilet, you realise that you can gather some brilliant material, just by observing human nature, listening to conversations, watching people with all the concentration you'd lend to a gripping David Attenborough documentary.

I often lose my nose in other people's conversations, but today I don't feel so bad about it. It's my fiancé's voice I can hear – doesn't that make it my business? Perhaps it's an invasion of privacy, to listen in on someone you know, but he's supposed to be getting ready and...

'I can't believe you're doing this.'

A female voice snaps me from my thoughts and my ethical hesitations are carried off by the breeze.

'I *have* to,' Daniel replies emphatically. 'How can I not?'

An ice-cold sensation pumps through my veins.

I'm so close to the neatly trimmed hedge, I can feel the short, sharp branches scratching at my body through my hoodie.

I can hear their voices perfectly now, but I need to see. I peer around the corner, just enough to catch a glimpse.

Only a few metres inside the maze, Daniel is pacing back and forth. He looks so good, in his wedding suit, but his face tells a different story. All the colour has drained from his face and he's frantically scratching at his hipster beard, just as he always does when he's anxious.

Standing in front of him is our friend Eva. She's wearing a floor-length, pleated maxi dress in a fiercely saucy shade of red – I imagine this is because I made such a big deal of saying red was an acceptable colour to wear to a wedding, she'll be trying to prove a point. It's split from the neck to the navel and I don't think I've ever seen her dress quite so sexily. I don't imagine her dress is supposed to be floor-length, but at around 5 ′ 2″, everything must be too long for her. Daniel has always been disappointed he never quite made 6′. Still, he towers over her. As he paces back and forth in front of her, she just stands there, hugging herself.

I'd say Eva was more my friend than Daniel's – she's more of a frenemy, if I'm being honest. She used to go out with Daniel's friend Paul. After they broke up, when Paul moved to Canada, she somehow stayed in our friendship circle. Neither of us are that close to her though. Definitely not 'fraught-looking conversation, hidden in a maze less than an hour before a wedding' close.

'What did you think was going to happen?' he asks her.

'I thought... well, I don't know what I thought,' she replies. 'But I didn't think *this* would happen.'

'I'm about to get married,' he reminds her.

I'm sure she knows or she wouldn't be here in that trampy dress. I catch myself. There's nothing wrong with her dress. I'm just getting defensive because I can't get my head around why she is *here* with *him*, *now*.

'Don't marry her,' she says.

My eyes narrow angrily as my mood darts from one end of the spectrum to the other, from Buddhist to barbarian. I want to grab her by her fiery red hair and drag her into the fountain. Who the hell does she think she is, telling *my* fiancé not to marry me? But as much as I want to confront her, I can't, because I want to hear everything she has to say first.

'I said I would leave her for you, months ago, but you told me not to,' he snaps back.

What?

'Because I wasn't going to tell you to leave her. It wasn't my call. You should've just left her,' she replies.

'Eva, this wedding has been booked for months. I can't just cancel it – we'll still have to pay for everything. Why are you telling me this now?'

'Because I love you and I can't let you marry her,' she replies, folding her arms. 'I won't let you marry her. I know it was only supposed to be a bit of fun at first but...'

I urge myself to exhale, but I can't. I can't breathe, I can't move, I can't scream at them...

'I love you too,' he replies. 'But I can't back out now.'

Tinnitus deafens me. All I can hear is a screaming in my ears – a sound I wish I could make myself, but I can't. I feel as if I'm going to pass out, but I can't. I can't afford to look away. I need to see this.

As Eva takes him by the hands and pulls him in for a kiss, I'm not really sure why, but my immediate response is to take my phone from my pocket and snap a picture. I check the shot, to make sure it's in focus – I do everything but put a bloody Instagram filter on it. Well, I did say I wanted to capture every last second of today, didn't I? This is one hell of a Kodak moment.

Eva, the scarlet woman, grabs my fiancé's arse as they kiss, and finally my fight or flight reflex kicks in. As I flee the scene I drop Ruby's flower crown (it hardly seems important now) and place my hands over my mouth, to stop me crying until I'm out of earshot, and to stop me throwing up all over the flowers.

I run through the hotel without any of the care or attention I left it with, barely fifteen minutes ago. I unlock my phone and the picture is still there on my screen – it doesn't matter, it's all I can see. I see it in the art on the walls, in the pattern of the carpet. If I blink, you'd better believe I see a freeze-frame of the two of them together.

I call Ali and ask her to get rid of my mum and sister. I simply tell her that we need to talk. By the time I get to the hotel room, I've stopped seeing them kissing and started imagining them in the bedroom together, tearing off each other's clothes, her flinging him onto the bed before climbing on top of him, her long red hair cascading down over his body as she leans forward and...

'That lying, cheating bastard,' I rant as I burst through the door.

'Don't worry, your three-year-old niece has left the room,' my friend jokes awkwardly. Ali is the wild one, the one constantly caught up in drama, the one who has a weekly (if not biweekly) meltdown, over some man or other.

'That liar! That fucking liar...' I continue.

Ali grabs me by the shoulders and sits me down on the bed.

'Talk to me, girl.'

'Daniel...' I start, but then I get that sick feeling again. It rushes up from my stomach, burns up my oesophagus and reaches my mouth, but by the time it leaves my lips the only thing that pours out of me is emotion. I scream and I cry – and it's an ugly cry, none of that 'single tear on the cheek' movie bullshit. Wailing, sobbing, eyes pouring, nose running. I'm just a gross, ugly mess and the only thing stopping me from completely falling apart is my best friend, blindly rubbing my shoulder and wiping my nose. She still has no idea what's going on.

'Daniel is cheating on me,' I sob. 'He was, he maybe still is...'

'I'm sorry, Daniel is mugging *you* off?' she asks in disbelief. 'He's been punching since the day you met. You are an absolute babe.'

I squeeze Ali's hand. A compliment like that, from someone as gorgeous as Ali, goes a long way. If I told you Ali was a Playboy bunny, you wouldn't have a hard time believing me. I think she's in her late thirties, but she doesn't look it. I tried to look at her passport once and she didn't speak to me for a week. From her ridiculous hair extensions to her absolutely massive fake boobs to her lip fillers, Ali has spent a lot of time and money on her look and it's flawless. I am not quite so perfect.

I hate to be a cliché, and I really wish I could say that I hadn't done this, but I went on a very strict diet in the run-up to my wedding. My hard work paid off though (apart from going down a cup size, to which Ali immediately said she'd give me her surgeon's card) and I felt sure I was going to walk down the aisle as the most confident version of myself I have ever been. It hasn't stopped my fiancé cheating on me though, has it? Now, my self-confidence is so low, it's downstairs in the lobby.

'Who the hell would have an affair with him?' Ali asks, quickly adding, 'no offence.'

'Fucking Eva,' I tell her.

'Eva?' she squeaks. 'She's honestly the stupidest bimbo I've ever met.'

She is stupid. When she was with Paul, we all got together for a game night, and Eva was so certain that Wales wasn't a part of the United Kingdom.

'And didn't Paul move to Canada, just to get rid of her?' she continues.

'Well, it seems like she got over him, by getting under Daniel,' I reply.

'That bastard,' she says. 'How did you find out?'

'I just... happened upon them in the gardens, having a sneaky chat. They went into the maze to get some privacy I imagine, but they barely went inside. Absolute morons.'

'They were probably worried they wouldn't be able to find their way out,' she says with a half-smile.

'They said they were in love with each other,' I start weakly, my voice still wobbling. 'She said she wasn't going to let him go through with the wedding, he told her he had to. Then they... they kissed.'

Ali wipes my eyes with a tissue.

'What are you going to do?' she asks me.

'I'll tell you what I'm not going to do,' I start, substituting a little of my sadness for some anger. 'I'm not going to marry him.'

'Well, that's fortunate,' Ali says with a smile. 'Because your make-up is fucked.'

I can't help but laugh, and it feels good, despite the painful feeling from the sucker punch to my chest.

'I can't face anyone,' I whisper.

'And you don't have to,' Ali replies.

'Can you take care of it? Can you tell people the wedding is off? I... I don't even know where to begin.'

'This isn't my first rodeo,' she says. 'I've called off a few weddings in my time.'

She really has.

'Thank you,' I say. 'I just want to get out of here, but I don't know where to go. I can't go home, back to the house… What happens with the house?'

'Don't get ahead of yourself,' Ali insists. 'We can sort all of that.'

'I just want to get out of here, out of London…'

'You need a holiday,' Ali says.

'I've already bloody paid for one, haven't I? My stupid honeymoon that isn't going to happen now.'

I cock my head as a wild idea occurs to me.

'I could still go on honeymoon,' I say.

'What, like a make-up holiday?' she asks. 'Because I don't think that's a good idea.'

'No, I could go on my own,' I say. 'I could go, chill out, try and work out what I'm supposed to do now – I've put off writing my book, because I've been so caught up planning this wedding. I could treat it like a sort of writer's retreat.'

It was never my intention to write on my honeymoon. I have been neglecting my work in favour of planning and (almost) executing my wedding, but safe in the knowledge that I have a few weeks after we get home to finish my book before my deadline. It would be a pretty full-on few weeks though, so I may as use this bonus free time to write without the clock ticking in my ear.

Ali smiles widely.

'So, you're just going to go to Italy on your own?'

'Why not?' I reply. 'I planned this whole wedding – including the honeymoon. The tickets are at home, the hotel is booked in my name, because I booked it, because… now that I think about it, he hasn't wanted any say in any aspect of the wedding planning. I thought he was just being a typical bloke, not really caring about silly wedding stuff…'

'Bastard,' she says.

'Yep.'

My wedding dress, hanging on the wardrobe next to us, catches my eye. My absolutely jaw-dropping, Vera Wang wedding dress. I didn't want anything too big and poufy, but I did want something special. My white dress is strapless and fitted, right down to the thigh. The bottom third is handcrafted, with over seventy yards of bias-cut organza tiers, ruffled into a rosette shape at the front and the back. It is just the right amount of poufy and I'm absolutely devastated I'm not going to get to wear it.

'I'll put it somewhere safe for you,' Ali says.

'No you won't, you'll take it home and take photos in it,' I joke.

'Maybe I'll do both,' she replies. 'Are you really going to go to Italy on your own?'

'I think I am,' I reply. Am I? 'Can you cancel things here but, maybe make sure I have enough time to get home, get my bags and go?'

'I can't think of a job I'd be more perfect for,' she says as she hugs me tightly. 'Maybe Tom Hardy's wife.'

'You'd be great at that,' I tell her. 'And you're an amazing friend.'

'And you are going on your honeymoon on your own,' she squeaks, unable to believe the words coming out of her mouth.

'I am,' I say, unable to believe the words coming out of mine.

I am, though. I am going on my honeymoon, completely on my own.

3

The first thing I do is tear down the 'Welcome Home Mr & Mrs' banner that is hanging above our front door. At best it's bloody embarrassing, at worst it's serving as a sort of weird celebration of my heartbreak, which I just don't need right now.

I cast my mind back to when we bought this house, two years ago. We'd been together for a couple of years so I (thought) knew we were happy together, but this was my first big, real, adult thing, and I was terrified.

I wouldn't say my twenties were the finest example of maturity. I met Ali through mutual friends when I was twenty-one. I believe she was twenty-eight at the time, but she says she's twenty-eight now and, as her best friend, I will always swear it's true. I had a few friends, but I didn't have a best friend. I know that sounds kind of immature, but I don't mean it like that. I mean, I had plenty of people who I could call friends, people I could hang out with and have fun, but I didn't have that one special person I could rely on, who I could tell anything to. No one I could count on in times of crisis, like needing a shoulder to cry on when you catch your lying, cheating, bastard fiancé kissing one of your least favourite friends inside a maze on your wedding day. You know, pretty standard stuff.

Before I met Daniel, we used to spend almost all of our time together. We rented a flat together, we'd shop together, lunch together – we'd enjoy wild nights out and girly nights in. Of course, all that had to change when I met Daniel – it's just all part of growing up, right?

Making more time for my boyfriend meant less time for my friend, but no less than your average person would have taken for their friends. And while Ali didn't mind that I had a boyfriend, she did mind that it was Daniel. I figured they just weren't really each other's cup of tea. Ali is a wild-child party girl with a penchant for short skirts and shorter relationships. Daniel works in recruitment and spends his spare time playing golf or watching football. Perhaps I should've trusted my friend's judgement when she said he wasn't right for me. That just because he was safe and didn't mess me around, he wasn't a smart choice for marriage. But life isn't a rom-com. I didn't expect to have everything in common with him, or for him to come home from work with massive bouquets of flowers, or to whisk me away on romantic weekends. That's not reality, is it? I just loved him, and that was all that mattered to me. It doesn't sound as if Dear Daniel was as content as I was; he had to go out and find more.

I stuff the banner into the wheelie bin and push it to the end of the drive. As I get there, I curse myself. Why did I do that? I mean, I know why I did that, and it was definitely on autopilot, but I did it because in the back of my mind I know that I'm going away and that the rubbish collection is this afternoon, and that Daniel will forget to put it out, because he clearly forgot this morning.

I shake my head as I walk back towards the house, a house that was supposed to be my dream house.

We bought our cute little semi in the suburbs with big ideas. We were going to extend it, which would usually come up when we talked about having babies, when we'd talk about what names we liked and laughed about what kind of parents we'd be. Daniel said he'd turn one of the rooms into a massive office for me, where I could hang my book covers on the walls and glide around on my ergonomic desk chair to reach the different ends of my massive desk. We haven't got round to it yet, because after we bought the place (spoiler: buying houses is expensive) and started doing up the rooms we already had, like the kitchen and the bathroom that were both in desperate need of work, my office wound up quite low down the to-do list.

I pause for thought.

We hadn't got around to doing my office yet, not haven't. I forgot to change the tense because in all the crap buzzing around in my head, I temporarily forgot that, as well as no longer having a fiancé, my home situation is going to drastically change too. One of us needs to leave, and I don't want to give up my home that I've been working so hard on, but then again, I don't know if I can handle the financial burden of a house still in need of renovations, a mortgage, all the bills – not on an author's salary, which cannot be predicted from one month to the next.

Inside the door, our suitcases are waiting for us. I look at Daniel's suitcase with all the disgust I'd give to the man himself. I begrudge every second I spent booking this honeymoon for him. Every trip to the shops to buy him the things he needed. I'm so pissed off that I packed his case for him. Not just because I'm realising that I did everything for this wedding, but because of the implication. I thought he was just lazy or out of his depth. Instead, it seems as if he just really, really didn't care. That he was too caught up in Eva to even think about what the rest of our lives together was going to look like.

I turn my nose up and snub his stupid suitcase, heading into the dining room (where my tiny work desk is squashed in) and retrieve my laptop and charger. I place them inside my carry-on bag, just in case I need a distraction on my solo flight. Then I head into our newly finished bathroom – and when I say newly finished, I mean the grouting around the bath wasn't even dry when I wanted to have a bath last week.

Looking in the mirror gives me a fright. Who is that person staring back at me? That sad-looking woman with the bright red eyes (they're usually green, I swear), with make-up smeared all over her face and snot still running from her nose – because, honestly, I don't even know what to do about it, it just keeps coming and coming.

People always tell me that I don't look my age. I've always wondered whether it's just down to the unique sense of style that may be exclusively mine. I have a real fondness for strange accessories – kooky stuff that you don't find on the high-street, like necklaces with a doll's eye hanging from the chain (which actually closes when you lie down) or earrings made to look like fairground fish in bags of water. It's hard to look your (nearly) thirty-two years of age when you have fairground fish earrings.

I'm an above average 5´ 6″ and thanks to my pre-wedding diet I managed to rein in my curves a little, which left me feeling more confident, but still suitably 'thicc', as the kids say. I was so full of confidence this morning, so excited to have my picture taken in my beautiful dress. Now I'm just looking at this crying monster in the mirror and wondering whether, without the make-up, the long blonde hair and all the distracting accessories, I really do look my age, whether the little lines I'm starting to notice around my eyes are beginning to show, whether my natural boobs are lower than they used to be. God, I could look in the mirror and find fault with myself for hours right now if I had the time.

I grab a face wipe and begin to remove the 150 pounds face I had carefully applied by an incredibly skilled make-up artist just a couple of hours ago. At some point, during my initial hysterics, I have turned myself into a Picasso portrait. I have eyeliner on my chin, lipstick on my forehead – the oh-so-subtle shimmer that was applied to my eyelids has somehow bred, covering every inch of my face, making me look like a sad red disco ball. My hair still looks flawless, at least, with my beautiful, long blonde fishtail plait still in place, hanging down from one side of my face. So not a complete waste of money, hey?

I wipe as much off as possible before applying a bit of foundation. It's not that I care at all what I look like right now, but I do actually want them to let me on an aeroplane. I don't want to look unstable or as if I have some kind of highly contagious infection that makes your eyes explode, your nose run and your face turn bright red and blotchy. The foundation is a resounding success – now I look one even colour and depressed.

A text comes through from Ali, asking me to let her know when I've left so that she can break the news to everyone there. I tell her I'll be out of here in five minutes and ask her to break the news gently. Not for Daniel's sake, but for my family – especially my mum. I ask Ali to explain to my mum that I'm okay and to tell her, and only her, where I'm going.

As I lock my phone again, that's when I notice the engagement ring on my finger. Suddenly it feels tight, heavy even. It's a reminder of what I've lost that I just don't need. Actually, it's not just the reminder I don't need, it's the ring. What do I need an engagement ring for? I take it off and stuff it into my jewellery box for now, to be returned to its purchaser at a later date.

As I leave my bedroom I eyeball my bed suspiciously. My bed – my super-king, super-comfortable mattress that I pushed for. Daniel didn't think we needed a super king, he said upgrading to a king was enough, but there isn't a huge amount of difference between a double mattress and a king mattress, so I eventually talked him round. As soon as it arrived he agreed with me that it was one of the best things we ever bought, but now all I can think about is whether or not he and Eva slept together on it. I don't think even Daniel would stoop that low.

On my way here I called up the taxi company and asked them if they could send the car a little earlier, and to our house instead of the venue. Well, I'd have to be crazy to pay for a taxi to the train station when I've got one pre-booked that I've already paid for. What with the suffocating wedding costs, that there is no way I can get refunded, that I haven't dared to think about yet. My plan is to go to the station, catch the train to the hotel (one of Daniel's only real contributions to the wedding was where we could cut corners and save money – that should have been a red flag) and hide myself away from the world until tomorrow, when I can hop on a plane and escape my mess of a life for a while, just until I figure out what to do.

I head for the door and grab my case, placing it outside on the kerb, ready for my taxi to come and pick me up and take me away from all of this. I'm about to lock the front door when Daniel's suitcase catches my eye again. I pop back inside, grab it, and drag it out to the bottom of the drive where mine is.

It doesn't take long for the white Mercedes C-class to show up, covered in white balloons, with 'just married' emblazoned across the back window. I puff air from my cheeks. I just had to tell them – when I booked it – that this car was to take us from our wedding reception to our honeymoon. I don't suppose the driver questioned the reasons why I brought the journey forward by so many hours or why I wanted picking up from my house instead, and I'll bet the car was just all ready and waiting to go.

'Hello, love,' the driver says as he steps out. 'Congratulations.'

He hasn't looked me in the eye yet, as he has busied himself rushing around the car to open the boot, so he doesn't know what a gigantic case of emotional baggage I'm going to be for him.

'Thanks,' I reply. I don't really know what else to say.

'So we're going to the... Oh.'

He's noticed my face.

'Yep.'

'And, the, erm...' He looks so awkward, I feel sorry for him. 'The, erm... the other passenger?'

'Just me,' I say, putting on my bravest of faces, reaching for my suitcase.

'Let me get that for you,' he says as if he wants to help me – really help me – but this is the only way he knows how. I am, after all, a complete stranger, and he has no idea what has gone on – he's assuming it's bad though, and he'd be absolutely right.

I'm really hoping that the hotel is the last place Daniel will think to look for me, if he even tries to look for me, so I'm probably safe there. I can hide away in my room or prop up the bar or eat something real with calories and fats for the first time in months.

The taxi driver comes back for Daniel's suitcase.

'Oh, no, not that one,' I say.

'You leaving that one there?' he asks, confused.

'Yeah.'

'What, with the bins?'

'Yep,' I reply. 'That one is trash. It's got to go.'

4

A latte, an M&S sandwich, a bag of crisps, a bottle of water, two McDonald's cheeseburgers (the single ones, I hasten to add), fries, a share bag of Maltesers and, oh, I don't know, maybe five porn star martinis. That's everything I've had to eat and drink since I ran away from my wedding – if I'd had it beforehand, there's no way I would've been able to run away at all.

In defence of the amount of alcohol I have consumed, it is important to note that I have consumed it over the course of many hours and I have eaten a lot of food with it.

In defence of the amount of food I have eaten, I needed a lot to soak up all the alcohol.

In defence of all of the above, I am miserable, I've been on a diet for months, my life is falling apart, and I have nothing better to do.

Isn't it amazing how a thing or place can hold so many memories?

The boutique hotel, 22 Hampton, is where Daniel and I had our first night away. It's in London, so not exactly a million miles from home, but at the time we were both living with roommates and wanted our first time to be something special. I'm not really sure how it came about, but we decided to wait for a little while before getting intimate. Well, neither of us were just looking for something casual, so we were happy to get to know each other first... or maybe it was just because we had roommates and we didn't get much privacy. I do have a tendency to remember things in a (not necessarily accurate) positive light.

So we went out for dinner, drinks and then Daniel brought me back here so that we could finally spend the night together.

I remember the first time I came here, falling in love with the mismatched furniture and the exposed oak beams. Industrial girders and gears still hang from the ceiling in some of the rooms – apparently this place used to be a mill of some kind. I remember reading about it in absolute amazement the first time we came here. I would drink it all up every time we stayed here in the early days. By the time we were a little deeper into our relationship the only thing we'd drink up would be the complimentary bottle of white wine before we ripped each other's clothes off, and by the time that urge died down we were already living together. Amazing, really, that once we moved in together and could have sex as much as we wanted, we didn't exactly jump at the chance whenever we could. I suppose I just figured that, you know, when you're in a loving relationship, these things die down. Turns out Daniel's fire wasn't put out, it was just being ignited by someone else. For God knows how long!

I do feel safe here, because only Ali knows where I am. Luckily I booked this place as a wedding present for Daniel. I had this stupid idea that the first place we had sex as a boyfriend and girlfriend should be the first place we had sex as husband and wife. The only person here for me to have sex with tonight is myself – I think I'll pretend I have a headache. I'm sure I will in the morning.

I don't even feel all that drunk, I suppose because it's been a dragged-out, half-hearted drinking binge. All I feel is bloated, and as if I want to brush my teeth.

It's a shame that I ate and drank so much on my way here, because someone went all out in the room, making it perfect for a wedding night. Champagne chilling in the fridge, chocolates on the sideboard, rose petals scattered everywhere, essential oils and fluffy robes. I could've saved myself some money in the railway station and just eaten and drunk too much in here by myself.

I suppose I could have another drink, or...

I'm pulled from my poor judgement-making by my phone ringing. I've blocked Daniel across all platforms – Eva too – so that I don't have to listen to any poor excuses. There is nothing either of them can say to me that will make me feel any better right now. Still, I eyeball my phone suspiciously for a moment before glancing at the screen and realising that it's my mum.

'Hello,' I say, casual as ever.

'Lila, are you okay?' my mum asks.

'Oh, you know,' I reply, putting my brave voice on. 'How are you?'

'Oh, darling. I've got Mandy here too – can I put you on speaker?'

'Sure,' I reply. 'Hi, Mand.'

'Lila, are you all right?' she asks.

'I'm just... I think I'm still in shock. I can't believe it. Sorry for disappearing. Ali said she'd take care of things. I just wanted to get away.'

'We completely understand,' Mum says. 'Don't worry about anything. Ali was great. We've got all your things here and there were lots of presents. They're here with me.'

Oh, God, I'd forgotten about all the presents.

'Can you guys return them for me? I don't want people to think I'm keeping them.'

'Of course we can,' my mum replies. 'Don't worry about anything like that. We're worried about you. Ali says you're going on honeymoon on your own.'

'I am. But honestly, Mum, I think it will do me good. It's the best place for me. I can relax and work and try and figure out what to do next.'

'There's plenty of time to think about what happens next,' Mandy tells me. 'You just focus on having a nice time, I suppose.'

'Has Daniel spoken to either of you?' I can't help but ask.

'No, he scarpered pretty sharpish after everyone found out,' my mum says. 'Your dad was furious – I've never seen him so mad. I think Daniel was scared.'

'Spineless,' Mandy chimes in. 'That's what he is. Absolutely spineless.'

'That's one word for him,' I exclaim.

'Have you heard from him?' my mum asks.

'Nope,' I say. 'Although I did block him, so he couldn't if he wanted to. I suppose I'll unblock him at some point, when my head stops spinning, hear what he has to say for himself.'

I say that because it sounds right, but I never want to hear his voice again. The thought of Daniel calling me makes me feel physically sick, because I absolutely don't want to talk to him. The thought of him not trying to call though... somehow that seems even worse. I can't stop questioning how much he could've cared for me, if he was able to cheat on me for God knows how long (I'm scared to think about that too), so it does seem like a possibility that he might not have tried to call at all. The only comfort I have right now is the control I have over the situation. The fact that *I* left *him* is all I have.

'Are you sure you want to go on your honeymoon alone?' Mandy asks.

'I just thought it would be better than being at home facing the music,' I say. 'Getting to enjoy my honeymoon is the least I deserve, right?'

'Of course,' my mum replies. 'Just keep in touch, let us know you're okay.'

'I will. I'm so sorry about all of this.'

I feel emotion creeping into my words, causing my voice to crack.

'You have nothing to apologise for,' my mum insists firmly. 'Now go and have some fun, okay? We love you so much.'

'Love you, sis,' Mandy calls out.

'Love you both too,' I reply. 'Thank you.'

Wow, somehow I feel even worse for hearing their voices. I know that I should probably feel comforted, hearing from people who love me, but I love them too, and hearing them so upset makes me even more furious at Daniel. Cheating affects more than just the two people involved; the ripples stretch far and wide. Hearing my mum so upset shifts me from sadness to anger again. Daniel is lucky I've got him blocked, just in case he did try to call right now.

I grab my phone from my bag and look up where I'm headed on my solo honeymoon for the millionth time. At first, I would be looking it up constantly, um-ing and ah-ing about whether or not it was the right place to book. Then, after I booked it, I would gaze at the website longingly at least once a day, marvelling at the stunning pictures, counting down the seconds until it was time to go. Now I'm just looking to see how dumb an idea going alone might actually be.

Just off the coast of Naples is a private island called San Valentino – or Valentine Island, as the English website and brochure call it. The Italian name is much better, isn't it? Such a beautiful, sexy-sounding name. Unfortunately, it doesn't sound quite so great in my North London accent, so I've just been calling it by its English, touristy title, Valentine Island.

Valentine Island is a luxury, five-star resort designed for couples who are madly in love – the website says it's perfect for honeymooners, which is why I booked it. It calls itself 'the most romantic place on earth', but so does every review I have read too, so it must be something special. It's supposed to have action-packed activities, if that's the sort of thing you're into, or it can be the ultimate place to chill out with your significant other. Perfect for some hardcore relaxing, in a hot sunny country.

Oh, it's going to be so romantic, when I show up on my own. I can eat on my own, sleep on my own... the only person I have to talk to is myself, and as for honeymoon sex – supposedly the best sex of your life – well, we'll see how good that is with myself, won't we? I suspect I'll have a headache again then too.

I've never even been on holiday alone before, never mind on honeymoon. Alone. To the most romantic place on earth. Now that I'm here, with my bags packed, waiting to fly off on my own, I do wonder whether or not this is a good idea... but I can't exactly go home, can I? Not when I'm not ready to face Daniel yet.

5

DAY 2

I was a bloody good girlfriend/fiancée. It might sound big-headed of me to say as much, but I was.

I have been loyal to Daniel since the day we met. I haven't cheated on him – I haven't even been tempted. I've done everything I possibly could for him, even turning myself into a regular Cinderella, taking care of all the cooking and the cleaning. Not because he made me, or even expected me to, to begin with, but because he had the busy office job with the early starts and the fixed hours, and I worked from home. I could do my work at any time. I could take breaks to empty the washing machine or clean the windows whenever I wanted to. If I had work that needed doing, I could do it whenever, whether it was during the day or at night, after Daniel went to sleep. And let me tell you something, while I might have been Cinderella, that Disney shit is absolutely false: cute little critters do not come in and help you tidy. In fact, since we moved to the suburbs, the closest thing we've had was a fox in the kitchen, and it did the opposite of tidy up.

So I'm sort of like a housewife, but one with a full-time job. Except, when you work from home, even if people know you work from home they still don't actually think you do any work at all. They think you sit around, watching TV, drinking tea, or that you go out and shop and get your nails done. Sometimes, people are actually baffled that my house could possibly have a thing out of place, because I just have so much free time in it, apparently. As though books just write themselves.

Perhaps it's my age, gender, occupation and very specific personal taste, but I think Carrie Bradshaw has a lot to answer for. Throughout the entire *Sex and the City* TV and movie universe, she lived the high life on a writer's wage, while seemingly never really putting all that much time into it. I used to have a weekly column in the local newspaper, and it pretty much allowed me to buy a takeaway a week. Her local area might be larger, but she's enjoying a lot more than a Deliveroo in her life. Perhaps a Mr Big is the key – when I asked a fellow writer when I was first starting out if she had any advice for me, she simply told me to 'marry well'. But sadly, I don't have a Mr Big, all I have is a Mr Big Fucking Liar, and I don't even technically have him any more.

I wasn't just a good partner to Daniel, I was a great one. I'd always do my best to make him things he liked or buy him little presents, just to show I was thinking of him, but all just in the most normal way, not in an over-the-top way. I suppose the fact that it was so subtle sometimes might be why it so often went unnoticed.

I would always go all-out to make his birthday special and I'd plan his Christmas presents months in advance. Naturally, I treated our wedding and our honeymoon with the same care and attention. I wanted to make it absolutely amazing for him. I wanted to take every little fantasy I'd ever played out in my fiction, and every hint of what he might like from his words, to come up with something truly special.

Look at where all that hard work has got me. Seriously, if there were ever an argument for doing the bare bloody minimum, my situation right now would be it.

The reason this is on my mind right now doesn't have as much to do with Daniel's lack of gratitude as you might think. It has more to do with the fact that, in an attempt to make this honeymoon truly magical, I did everything I could to make sure that it would be perfect, and now I'm facing having to go through it all on my own.

A tall, good-looking man boards the plane and sits down in the seat next to me – the seat that was supposed to be for Daniel. I did tell the airport staff that Daniel wouldn't be flying, and they said something about it freeing up the seat for the waitlist. At least someone gets to sit in it, I suppose.

'*Ciao*,' the man says as he sits down next to me.

He looks a little bit like a younger Joe Manganiello, but without the beard.

'Hello,' I reply.

It's like something out of a rom-com: a heartbroken woman who has fled the scene of her wedding, only for a handsome stranger to wind up sitting on the plane next to her. If there was any justice in the world, we'd fall madly in love somewhere over the Channel.

Once we are up in the air, things get a little awkward when an air hostess brings us two glasses of champagne.

'Here we are,' she says. 'You two let me know if I can get you anything else, okay?'

You can somehow just detect that she is talking to us as if she thinks we are together.

'Oh, we're not together,' I insist quickly.

'Okay,' the air hostess replies, baffled. 'Well, I will still assist you both, if either of you needs anything.'

Perhaps she wasn't talking to us as if we were a couple at all, and I wonder why I got so defensive.

'You don't want her to think I am your boyfriend?' the man asks with a chuckle. He has a strong Italian accent, but his English is perfect.

'Oh, no, it's not that at all, quite the opposite,' I reply, embarrassed. 'I had hoped it would be a seat for my husband.'

'Oh, er...' I cringe as I watch him agonise over his wording. 'This is, er... I'm not looking for a wife. I have a boyfriend, back in London.'

I don't know what is more embarrassing: that I entertained, hypothetically, for a second, that the first handsome stranger I met might fall in love with me and be the answer to all my problems, or the fact that this poor gay guy thinks I just went from insisting he wasn't my boyfriend to telling him I want him to be my husband. I down my drink anxiously.

'Oh, no, you are going to laugh when you hear this,' I begin to explain. 'I called off my wedding today.'

The man's big brown eyes widen. I realise that this partial explanation may have only made things worse. Now he probably just thinks I want to marry him because I'm on the rebound.

'Wait, I can explain this better,' I say. I take his untouched drink from him and knock that back too. When, oh, when will the mortification end today? 'I was *supposed* to be getting married today, but I caught my fiancé kissing one of our friends. It sounded like they'd been having some sort of affair, God knows for how long.'

'I'm sorry, that's very bad,' he replies.

'It is,' I agree. 'So... I don't know why but I thought it would be a good idea to still go on my honeymoon, but on my own.'

I can see a wave of relief literally wash over the man as he connects all the dots, and realises what's going on. First, his tense posture relaxes, then the anguished look on his face melts away.

'So this seat was supposed to be for your husband...'

'Yes! But no husband means spare seat – so were you on the waitlist?'

'Yes,' he replies. 'I'm travelling home for a wedding. My brother is getting married. I am sorry to hear about your wedding.'

'Well, if this hadn't happened to me, then you wouldn't have been able to take the ticket, and you'd still be stuck in London. So, at least something good has come out of it,' I say.

'That's a good way to see things,' he replies. 'But I am still sorry for you.'

'Thanks,' I say. 'Well, I'm done embarrassing myself for the day – why don't you tell me about you?'

'I'm Angelo, I'm twenty-one,' he begins. 'I'm an art student, in London. I met my boyfriend, Liam, while studying. He is so wonderful!'

I smile. It's weirdly nice, to see someone so in love. You'd think I'd be jealous, being so miserable myself, but it's comforting to see that real love is still alive and well in some people. It's only the people who I know who are sick – and me now, of course – and, at the risk of Angelo catching my bitter cynicism, I decide it best not to talk any more about my love life.

The air hostess notices our empty glasses and tops us up. It's probably best I pace myself for a while now.

'So your brother is getting married, you said?'

'Yes, Antonio. He has known his girlfriend since school. They're very happy together. It would have broken my heart to miss their wedding and I missed my flight earlier. I read the wrong time. Antonio is my twin – we're like two halves of the same person. I'm his best man. It would have ruined his day.'

'So I did something good today,' I say with a smile.

'Yes, *bella*, you did something very good.'

I sit back in my seat, able to relax, just a little. I don't take out my laptop as I had planned. I just don't feel in the mood for writing romance right now. Anything I try to write, it's going to come out all bitter and horrible – the best I could hope for is sarcasm, which isn't really the most romantic tone out there.

'It's very brave, to go on honeymoon alone,' Angelo says, finally at ease enough to enjoy his free champagne. 'You are a brave woman.'

'Hmm, I don't know about that,' I reply. 'Just between us… I'm not doing this because I'm brave, I'm doing it because I'm scared. I'm scared to face my fiancé – or ex-fiancé, or whatever. I'm scared of what happens next. I don't want to talk to him about what we do with the house, or how we split our Blu-ray collection, or who gets the expensive mattress we've just bought, which I honestly think he's going to have to physically fight me for because I love it.'

Angelo laughs.

As that sentence went on, I could feel it getting more and more tragic, and my words becoming more and more emotional. A U-turn into a joke (that is based on something real, as all good jokes are) was my only option.

The truth is that, while I am scared of all those things, there is one thing that scares me even more. It's the thought of talking to Daniel, and of some little part of me thinking we can work this out because maybe things aren't so bad… but he said he loved her, and if he loves her, does he even love me? Can he even love me? And if he doesn't love me, well, I couldn't take him back even if I wanted to, could I?

'You should just forget about him,' Angelo suggests. 'Have a nice time. Napoli is beautiful. You can see the sights, eat good food, go dancing…'

'I erm, I'm not actually stopping in Naples,' I reply. 'I'm catching a boat there, to San Valentino.'

I blush a little, saying Italian words to a real Italian, knowing I probably butchered them.

'Oh, you're going there?' he replies.

'Yes...'

'I've heard all about it,' he continues, an unsure look on his face.

'Is it nice?'

'It's nice for a honeymoon,' he replies with a shrug of his shoulders.

'Oh.'

'You can still have a great time,' he tells me. 'It's summer, and there is plenty to do, even without a man. And it's mostly tourists, so lots of people who speak English – you won't be alone.'

'Thank you,' I reply.

I don't know how much of what he's saying is true and how much is designed just to make me feel better, but I appreciate it either way.

I suppose all I can do now is try and make the best of it, even if I am headed to the most romantic place on earth, absolutely, completely, 100 per cent alone.

6

After clearing up the misunderstanding on the plane, things didn't seem quite so unbearable. The same went for my time at Napoli airport, where I had Angelo on hand to be my translator.

We made our way through the airport together where we eventually found Angelo's parents, brother and a few other family members waiting to greet him. He introduced me to everyone but no one else spoke English. His mum did give me a kiss on both cheeks and, not only did she thank me for helping her son, but she invited me to the family wedding (something Angelo had to translate for me). I did consider it, for a moment. It felt like something from one of my rom-com novels, like the kind of scenario where I would meet the love of my life, but I realised the reality of it would probably be awkward. I wouldn't know anyone or speak the language. People would ask me questions about why I was there and it would be a whole mess of awkward-to-explain.

Before they left, Angelo did offer to help me find the transportation to the island, but I told him I'd be fine by myself.

But then, all of a sudden, after all the noise and the wedding excitement, I felt very much alone – all alone – in a foreign country, where I don't speak the language, and I kicked myself for being stupid enough to go on holiday by myself. I felt as if you'd need to be a reasonably strong and comfortable person to go on holiday alone, but to do so after having your heart broken, well, you'd have to be an idiot.

Still, I didn't panic, because that would've only made things worse and, after a few conversations with some very kind bilingual people, I worked out how to get the car service, that would take me to the boat, that would take me to Valentine Island.

I do feel a little better now that I'm on the boat, not just because I feel safe and as if I know where I'm going, but because Ciara, our island guide, is Irish. I had a quick chat with her before we set off. She told me that she used to work in Magaluf until she heard about a job on the boat here. Desperate to swap rowdy young people for romantics, she accepted, but it turns out she's never actually been off the boat. She ships people over, telling them tales of the island, how it came to be and what it's famous for, as well as showcasing all the different activities it has to offer, but she's never set foot on dry land there. If it hadn't backfired so spectacularly for me with Angelo, I might have asked her if she wanted to join me.

I had hoped the boat trip wouldn't feel quite so weird, but it does. I was hoping I would just blend in with the other holidaymakers, but the seats are all in pairs, and the seat next to me is empty. Everyone else here is with their significant other, with their head on their shoulder or their hands intertwined as they listen to the tour guide or gaze out of the window – not that there's anything to see at this time of night. Just wide open space, like the seat next to me. Still, on the plus side, I did get two glasses of champagne, instead of one. Result for the single girl. I'd say I'm winning but it kind of feels like, metaphorically speaking, everyone here is playing chess with their partner, and I'm playing draughts with myself. So I'm not exactly winning really, am I?

It's still quite warm, even though it is dark now. That's the south of Italy in July for you, so I don't know what else I was expecting. It did cross my mind to come when the weather was slightly cooler, but as far as weddings in jolly old England go, I didn't want to take any chances with the climate there, so July felt like the safest choice.

I cannot believe I had more control over the weather than I did over the groom on my wedding day.

It's late when we finally arrive on the island. We are ushered from the boat and up a dimly lit path towards the grand hotel building. It feels as if the panoramic sound of the waves pushing against the beach is nudging me towards the floodlit building, but I can't help but hang back just a little. I feel as if there is strength in numbers, but I am here alone.

I hover outside the entrance, allowing enough time for all the other loved-up couples to check in before me, because the idea of checking in alone, with a queue of couples gagging to get to bed behind me, is just that little bit more than I can handle today, after everything that has gone on.

I step into the huge hotel lobby, with its sky-high ceilings and gleaming marble floors. It's an ultra-minimal open space, but it's so full of plants I feel as if I'm still outside. The ambience of the room must shift with the clock because the lights feel romantically low, and the ceiling is lit up with twinkling lights, made to look like little stars in the night sky.

I don't know why I worried about other people hearing me; it's as though I was expecting one desk with a naff red-roped queue leading off behind it. Instead, there are multiple desks, all attended by attentive-looking staff. I head straight down the middle, not wanting to look as if I'm playing favourites.

'Hello,' I say, testing the waters to see if he speaks English. I exhale pure relief when he does.

'Hello, *signora*,' he replies. He detects my nerves. 'Don't worry, almost everyone here can speak English, to our English-speaking guests.'

That's such a huge relief. I did notice, on the boat, that everything was said in a handful of languages, but English was first. I suppose that's great for me, but I almost feel guilty, speaking a language that many people take the time to learn. All I have under my belt is an F in GCSE French. If you'd like me to describe my bedroom or order something from a bakery, I'm your girl, but if you're after a real French conversation, well, my vocabulary is severely lacking in... *je ne sais quoi*.

'How was your journey?' he asks.

I just stare at him blankly. I must look as if I've been dragged through a hedge backwards, and cried all the way.

'It was great,' I lie politely. 'Thank you. I have a booking under Lila Rose.'

He checks his computer.

'Ah, the Tylers,' he says happily. A second later it occurs to him that I'm standing here alone. 'Is Mr Tyler with you?'

'Mr Tyler got held up at home,' I lie, because, first of all, this poor bloke doesn't want to hear me banging on about my private life and, second of all, I'm suddenly worried I might get the boot for being single. 'He'll be joining me later.'

'Not a problem, Mrs Tyler,' the man replies. 'If I could get a signature, *per favore.*'

'My name is still Rose,' I tell him politely, hoping he'll get the hint.

'I see,' he replies. 'Here in Italy, a woman keeps her maiden name when she gets married too.'

Oh, this poor bloke. I'm not going to spell it out for him – it would only make him feel bad. I just smile and nod.

'You are staying in one of our luxury villas, yes?'

'I am,' I reply.

'*Bene,*' he says. 'It's all ready for you. Savino will assist you with your baggage and show you the way.'

'*Grazie,*' I say– one of the only two Italian words I have managed to absorb. The other, of course, being *ciao.*

A small, twenty-something Italian man appears almost out of nowhere. The two exchange words in Italian. I have no idea what they're saying, but there seems to be some sort of misunderstanding.

'Apologies, Savino is still learning,' he tells me. 'He will take you now.'

Savino is wearing a cream shirt with a gold name badge, but I don't imagine I'll learn much more about him.

'English, only a little,' he explains to me as he leads me outside to a golf cart.

'That's okay,' I reply.

I don't feel much like talking. Not just because I'm in a bad mood, but because there's so much to take in here.

Valentine Island is even more beautiful than the photos, even at this time of night. Tiny lights illuminate the pathways that lead around the resort. One of the things that appealed to me the most was the claim that this place had everything. Multiple pools, beaches, trails, activities, sports, spas, shops, restaurants with cuisine from all over the world – and then there's the accommodation. When I made our booking, I spent a lot of time looking at different options. There were lots of different rooms in the hotel, where we just came from, but then there were the villas that we're passing now. I was leaning towards the villas, each of which contained three apartments, one on each floor. I liked the idea of having our own little living space, with a kitchen for cooking our own food (bought from the island supermarket – this place is a dream!) and a balcony for catching some private rays.

But then I saw the luxury villas. Not only were they much bigger than the standard ones, but they came with their own private pool – and you only go on a honeymoon once, right? Or so I foolishly believed when I booked it.

It's kind of hard to take the place in, so late in the evening, with my sore, bleary eyes. I think I'll just get a good night's sleep, and then explore tomorrow.

We head uphill, to where the luxury villas are. A driveway encased in greenery leads up to a beautiful, long white building with a terracotta-tiled roof. Somehow finding the perfect balance between modern and rustic, the walls are brilliant white, with climbing plants creeping up them and around the arch windows and their white shutters.

To access the villa, you pass through the leafy-green-covered veranda archways, where Savino unlocks my door before ushering me through.

Walking through the door leads us straight into a gorgeous open-plan living area. Immediately there is a kitchen/dining area, with glittering white worktops and a square dining table with just two chairs, one on each side.

Savino shows me up the stairs first, to a mezzanine bedroom. One side of the bedroom is completely open, looking down over the living space. The other is nothing but glass, looking out over an infinity pool, which looks out over the beach. I have a view of the sea that I imagine goes on for miles and miles, because right now, once the beach lights stop reflecting on the water, all I can see is a black-looking ocean, only illuminated slightly by the moon.

The bed, much to my annoyance (although it is a lovely touch) is covered with rose petals and chocolates. There's a little fridge next to the bed with a bottle of bubbly in it and two glasses on the bedside table. If it's just for me, I probably won't need one glass, let alone two.

Back down in the kitchen area, a few steps lead down to a lounge space, where there is a large cream corner sofa, with one side facing the flat-screen TV on the wall and the other facing the bi-folding doors that look out over the pool. The entire back of the villa is nothing but glass; I can't wait to see it in the daytime.

'Bathroom,' Savino says bluntly, gesturing towards a door. 'And, er, *piscina.*'

'Pool?' I say as he opens the door that leads to the swimming pool, just a small patio's distance away.

'Yes, pool,' he replies. 'Only your pool.'

Having my own private pool is like a dream come true. Well, think about it. You can do whatever you want, swim laps, drift around on a lilo – it doesn't matter, because you're not getting in anyone's way and no one is getting in yours. And then there's the added bonus that it doesn't matter what you look like. You don't need to suck your tummy in as you walk to the pool or frantically try to make sure your bikini top stays in place as you climb out, because no one is watching. It's just you, your infinity pool and the horizon.

I fantasise about being in the pool, watching the sunset over the ocean. I'd daydreamed about doing this with Daniel when I probably should have been writing my book. I hope it isn't ruined for me now.

Before Savino leaves, he realises he is still clutching my suitcase, so he places it down in the lounge area. I plonk myself on the sofa next to it.

It's quiet in here. Really quiet. Maybe too quiet, for my particular set of circumstances. I desperately wanted to escape from my life earlier, but now that I'm here, with it being so late and the villa being a little out of the way... I feel so alone. Not just here, but when I eventually go back to my real life too.

As I unzip my suitcase, something immediately catches my eye. My mind darts back to the airport, when a lady who worked there asked me if I packed my bag myself. I said yes because I did. I feel so, so fortunate that no one looked inside, because it would seem my dear friend Ali snuck a honeymoon present in there for me – I imagine when she stopped by to put the banner up. I'm starting to regret leaving her that key to water my plants – oh, wait, she won't be using it now.

I remove the massive purple dildo from my suitcase and stand it on the table. It's made of soft plastic and yet it's so hard and heavy. It stands erect on the table, at maybe eight or nine inches. I know Ali well enough to know that this was probably her idea of a joke. I don't think she looked at me, and then at Daniel, and thought, Yep, they'd appreciate an emasculating big, purple plastic dick on their honeymoon.

Here alone, it just makes me feel sad – which sounds weird, but I can imagine what was going through Ali's head when she planted it in there, and then I imagine what Daniel would have said when we found it. There's no way he would've found it funny, which would've made me find it even funnier. Mostly it just makes me miss my friend.

I snap a photo of my new purple friend sitting pretty on the coffee table, and text it to Ali with the caption:

Got here safe, it's a gorgeous place. Thanks for the present – what the hell am I supposed to do with that? haha x

I only have a chance to remove a beach towel from my case before a reply comes through.

Do you need me to send you a diagram? Haha! Glad you got there safe. Stop moping and have some fun! x

Moping is exactly what I'm doing right now; she really does know me so well.

I quickly toss my phone to one side, not wanting to see another word, well-meaning message or photo from the wedding.

I pick up the resort guide from the table and have a flick through. It's only the same information I've looked at on the website a million times, with a handy little map for finding your way around, but reading about the twenty-four-hour bar is something I didn't already know.

It is late... after 10 p.m. now... I could go to the bar? Not because I desperately need a drink – I think I've had enough for one day – but because it's something to do. Something other than crying myself to sleep upstairs.

I look down at my tracksuit and wonder whether I can go to the bar like this. It's not exactly a scruffy hoodie and baggy bottoms, it's a bizarrely sexy Victoria's Secret tracksuit, made from impossibly soft black material. And I've still got my wedding hair in, which will go a long way to making me look presentable. As for my face, well, it's probably best I don't look at it. I haven't cried in a while, so my eyes probably look fine, and my foundation will still be perfect, because it changed my life when I started spending good (read: too much) money on make-up. I'll just be rocking a sort of... unnatural natural look, that's all.

Or I could go to bed. I probably should...

Actually, no, sod it, I'm going to check out the twenty-four-hour bar. I'm not going to waste another second crying over Daniel bloody Tyler.

Not tonight, anyway.

7

If I had to walk the streets of London at this time of night, I'd be terrified. I'd have my phone clutched tightly in one hand and my rape alarm in the other, ready to make some noise and call for help at the first sniff of danger. Here, though... I have never felt so safe walking around on my own.

I suppose it's the fact that it is a private island. The only people on the island are supposed to be here. Staff are paid to work here, and anyone staying at this place isn't going to need to mug me for the few Euros I have in my handbag, because if they can afford to stay here, they're not going to be resorting to petty crime any time soon. Unless they're like me, with an expensive wedding that is still largely to pay for.

The easy-to-follow map has led me straight to the twenty-four-hour bar, which is inside the main hotel building. Sadly, it is completely empty.

I'm just about to leave and kick myself for trailing down here when a man in a white shirt emerges from the toilets.

'Oh, is the bar open?' I say.

'It sure is,' he replies. 'It's always open.'

The barman has a strong, west-coast American accent. I love how diverse the staff are here; they seem to have acquired people from all over the globe.

'Great,' I reply, taking a seat on a bar stool. 'Can you make me a porn star martini, please?'

'I can,' he replies with a laugh.

I didn't mean to imply he couldn't.

'Sorry, of course you can. Thank you.'

The man seems puzzled by my awkwardness.

What is it with me and making a fool of myself in front of gorgeous men? First, it was Angelo on the plane, now it's this guy here. It's as if I forgot how to talk to men while I was in a relationship, and now, now that it sort of matters how men perceive me (well, only if I ever want another one, and the jury is still out on that), it frustrates me, just how weird I'm coming across.

'Why not?' the man says, heading behind the bar.

I feel as if I must've caught him about to take a break or something, but he's started making my drink now, looking around behind the bar for the various tools and ingredients.

'What's your name?' he asks me.

'Lila,' I reply. 'What's yours?'

The man smiles.

'I'm Freddie.'

Freddie is tall, maybe 6′ 3″. He looks quite broad too, which makes me wonder what's going on underneath that shirt of his. I can tell, as he shakes my drink, that he must be quite muscular – muscles he must've got throwing around something much heavier than a cocktail shaker. He has a mess of brown hair on top of his head, which he pushes out of his eyes with the back of his hand. Interestingly, despite being tall, dark and handsome, he has the most vivid blue eyes I've ever seen.

Freddie finds me getting lost in his eyes. As he gives me a cheeky smile, I notice the dimples that form in his cheeks.

This might be my broken heart and booze consumption talking, but he is possibly the most gorgeous man I've ever seen in real life. He seems to ooze charm and warmth and there's just something about his nature, I don't know, I feel as if I know him.

'One porn star martini,' he says, placing it down on the bar in front of me.

The cocktail is such a vivid pink colour, while the little shot of champagne sparkles next to it.

'What do I owe you?' I ask.

He just smiles and laughs.

'It's on me,' he replies. 'I think I'll join you for one, if you don't mind?'

'I'd be glad of the company,' I admit.

Freddie walks back around the bar with his drink and sits down next to me.

'So, how do you drink yours?' he enquires curiously.

At the moment the answer is 'quickly and *en masse*', but today isn't a usual day.

I watch as Freddie squeezes his passion fruit into his drink. He pours his shot of champagne in before giving it a stir with his finger. He looks at me, waiting for an answer, as he lightly sucks the fruity alcohol off his fingertip. Perhaps I'm thirstier than I realised.

'I, erm...' Pull yourself together, Lila. 'Not like that. I drink mine separately. A porn star martini is like ordering a drink that comes with a free mini drink. Usually, my best friend and I use our shots to toast something before knocking them back.'

Today, at the airport, I was toasting alone. Here's to me, free of my bastard fiancé. Here's to my holiday, which I don't have to share with anyone. Here's to the rest of my life, which it looks as if I'm going to be spending all by myself. I soon stopped toasting myself, when I realised that, with each drink, the toasts were getting bleaker.

'A free mini drink.' Freddie laughs to himself. 'I've never heard that before. I like it.'

I smile, suddenly feeling a little nervous for some reason. Then I realise I'm self-conscious, because of my scruffy outfit.

'Sorry, I bet not many people walk in here like this,' I say, gesturing down at my tracksuit.

'Not many people walk in here at all at this time,' he replies. 'Couples are all in bed – after such busy days, I don't suppose anyone wants a middle of the night martini. Your hair looks really nice.'

I am blindsided by his compliment.

'Oh, this?' I say, suddenly even more self-conscious as I run my hand gently from top to tail of my long, blonde fishtail plait. 'I was at a wedding yesterday. I feel kind of daft with it now. I look like Elsa from *Frozen*.'

Freddie cracks up.

'Well, you know what to do, don't you?'

'What's that?'

'Let it go.'

I stare at him, a combination of amused and puzzled.

'Like the song, from the film...'

'I know that,' I laugh. 'I'm just surprised you do.'

'Erm, thirty-two-year-old men can enjoy *Frozen* too,' he points out.

'I'll be thirty-two next,' I reply. I don't know why I tell him, like it's *so* amazing to have our age in common, so I quickly get back on topic. 'You know what, I will let my hair down.'

First I remove the hair grips that have been keeping the hair around my hair so neatly in place. Then I unfasten the clear plastic elastic band from the bottom and let my hair unravel – as my life has.

As I tszuj my newly freed hair, I realise that the plait has left me with some sort of crimped effect. I run my hands over it, but I can feel how big and eighties it must be looking.

'Oh, God, that was a mistake, wasn't it?' I say. Freddie just chuckles. 'Should I have left it in?'

'Yeah, probably,' he teases. 'You still look beautiful though.'

I can feel my cheeks flushing so I turn my attention to my drink, finally taking a sip.

'Oh, wow,' I blurt. 'This is the nicest one I've had over the past couple of days.'

And I have had many.

'Have you had many?' he asks with a laugh.

I feel as if he's reading my mind and it sends a strange tingle through my body.

'Erm, no,' I reply. 'Just a couple.'

'Well, I'm glad you like it,' he replies. He sips his. 'Oh, yeah, that's pretty nice. It's been a while.'

'You don't make many of these?'

'Not any more, no.'

It surprises me that they're not more popular here. Back home, it's still one of the cocktails *du jour*, even with the espresso martini hot on its heels. I'm starting to think I use a lot of casual French, for someone who doesn't think she remembers much French... and is in Italy.

'How did you get so good at it?' I ask, not really expecting an answer. Freddie has one though.

'I learned from the second best, who learned from the best,' he explains. 'I used to work at a bar in LA, called Dionysus. Hugely popular bar over there. The owner, the man who trained me, was taught how to make them by the inventor. He said it was such a simple drink, but so easy to mess up, if you didn't do it right.'

'Well, you do it right,' I say. I realise I'm drinking it quite quickly but it's not like earlier, because I was drowning my sorrows, it's because it genuinely tastes incredible.

'I wish I could make cocktails,' I say. 'Instead of having to pay 12 pound a pop for them in London bars.'

'It's really not that hard, once you know what you're doing,' he tells me. 'Would you like me to show you?'

'What, now?'

'Sure, why not?' he replies. 'It's been so quiet in here through the night this week, I guarantee no one will come in.'

'Erm, okay, sure,' I reply excitedly.

'Okay, let's do it.'

There's a real spring in my step as I follow Freddie around to the business side of the bar. This is the last thing I thought I'd be doing tonight.

'The Negroni is one of my favourite cocktails,' he starts. 'So I figure, when in Rome – or reasonably close to it, I suppose – why not make something Italian?'

'Sounds great.'

Freddie glances around the bar, looking for the things we need. It's strange – for someone who makes such amazing cocktails, it takes him a little searching to find everything.

'Okay, so, we're making a Negroni Sbagliato,' he explains. 'The

Negroni is pretty strong, and you seem to like sweet drinks, so we'll give this a shot.'

'Sounds even better.'

Freddie places bottles down in front of me.

'Campari, sweet vermouth, champagne,' he says. 'Follow my lead.'

I watch Freddie closely, doing exactly as he does, only with much less confidence and potentially zero style.

'So, what do you do?' he asks me.

'I write books,' I reply.

'Oh, nice. What genre?'

'Contemporary romance,' I say. 'Rom-coms.'

'Nothing like *Edge of Eden* then?' he asks.

'No.' I laugh. 'Everyone always asks me if it's like that – it's that or *Fifty Shades of Grey*. My books aren't exactly PG, but they certainly aren't mucky books.'

'Mucky books?' He chuckles. 'I love your accent, Lila. There's something so attractive about the English accent.'

'Are you sure?' I ask. 'I can imagine American ladies finding Hugh Grant swoonsome, but... I always thought I sounded a bit "apples and pears".'

I can't think of a better way to describe a strong London accent.

'I don't think I'm going to get all your jokes, am I?' Freddie asks, bemused.

'You're not the first person to say that, don't worry.'

'I got that one,' he replies with a laugh.

We hold eye contact for a moment, exchanging smiles. I can feel him, drawing me in, deeper and deeper.

'So, what's next?' I ask, snapping us out of it.

'Where are the oranges?' he asks himself as he hunts around.

We garnish our drinks with a wheel of orange. They look incredible, they smell amazing – I wonder how they taste...

'Let's give them a go,' he says.

I reach for my glass, but Freddie stops me.

'No, no, you drink mine, I'll drink yours,' he says.

I look at him with all the discomfort you'd give someone you suspected of spiking your drink, but what I'm actually worried about is a barman trying a drink made by me, an amateur. Not that it matters – I'm not trying for a job here. But there's just something about Freddie, something I like... something that makes me want to impress him.

'Erm,' I say hesitantly.

'I can tell you if you did a good job,' he says. 'It sounds like you've been drinking indiscriminately all day – you won't be a very good judge of quality, will you?'

Oh, God, I like it when he teases me.

'Come on,' he insists, nudging his drink towards me.

'OK, fine, but if it's horrible, please pretend it's nice. It's my first time. You don't want to knock my confidence, do you?'

'I'll be gentle,' he assures me.

As I slide my drink towards Freddie, he reaches for it at the same time and our hands collide. He lets his hand linger on mine and it feels really good... until my brain ruins it for me.

I just realised, all of a sudden, that while I've been here I've completely pushed Daniel out of my head. I feel so weirdly guilty, for being here with this guy, feeling happy and flirty, when I know I should technically be celebrating my wedding night right now. I'm doing the opposite, and enjoying it? That doesn't seem right.

I quickly snatch my hand away and take an over-large gulp of my drink.

'Ooh, that's nice,' I say. 'I've probably had enough for one day though. I should get to bed.'

'Okay,' he replies. 'Where are you staying? I can walk you back.'

'No, don't be daft. You stay here.'

'There's nothing here for me,' he replies. 'It's no trouble.'

'No, no, I'm fine,' I insist, standing up, edging towards the door. 'Thank for the drinks.'

'You're welcome,' he calls after me.

As I walk up the hill, towards my villa, I mentally kick myself for feeling guilty, and being loyal to Daniel when it's the last thing he deserves. He might not have cared that we were in a relationship, or that it was our wedding day, but I can't just shut those things out of my head – not for more than a few minutes at least.

As delicious as those cocktails were, I've definitely had too much to drink today. Extenuating circumstances, your honour, but I still feel sick, and I'll still feel hungover in the morning.

I let myself in and plonk myself on the sofa.

'What the hell are you looking at?' I ask the big purple dildo.

It doesn't reply.

I feel so comfortable on the sofa, I don't want to get back up. Instead, I grab the beach towel I removed from my suitcase earlier, and pull it over me. I can't face sleeping in that bed tonight, not with all that romantic crap on and around it. I'll clean it all up tomorrow and I'll try to do better. I just need to get through tonight and I'm sure, in the morning, things won't seem quite so bad.

I hope...

8

DAY 3

I don't know what hurts more, my head or my stomach.

I open my eyes and immediately answer my own question – it's my head; my head hurts the most. It feels as if I've been hit with a blunt object, like a...

I notice the dildo on the table. It probably would make an excellent weapon, but I think I'll take my chances without it. What the hell am I supposed to do with it? Other than Ali's suggestion, I have no idea. I need to dump it somewhere. Perhaps I could put it in the bin, but it's so big, I'm sure the maid would see it. Best case, I look like a pervert. Worst case, I look as if I've had a really big row with my significant other and snapped. I'm not a million miles away from such a spree, if I'm being honest. Daniel is lucky he's in England and I'm here.

This place is stunning, but with the ocean-facing wall being made entirely of glass, it's like a greenhouse – even with the terrace door that I forgot to close last night. Once I put the air conditioning on, I'm sure I'll feel much better but, right now, the heat is making me feel sick.

I look at my phone. It's 10:30 a.m., and it's so warm already so I kick off the towel that I've been using as a blanket all night.

From where I am I can see my private pool, glistening in the sunshine. I'll bet the water is so lovely and refreshing right now. Maybe a swim would make me feel better. It would definitely cool me down and it might even distract me for a bit. Then maybe I'll be able to get some work done.

I wonder what one of my strong, female lead characters would do in a situation like this. Something liberating, to show what a strong single woman she was. Like, I don't know, taking all her clothes off and jumping into the pool, like a sort of baptism before she started her life again, a much better version of herself.

I wish I had the guts to do something like that. I can't even imagine how good it must feel. Thinking about it, I do have my own private pool. There's no risk of indecent exposure, no one to see my bloated tummy after all the crap I ate yesterday... I can have a 'strong woman' moment if I want one. You know what, I think I will. Balls to it. I'm going to do it and it's going to feel amazing.

I take off my tracksuit and my underwear. As I pull my hoodie off, I realise just how big my hair is. I must've looked so funny last night.

I hover by the sofa for a moment, staring at the pool, trying to talk myself into going for it, because I'm definitely getting cold feet.

But, really, why wouldn't I just do it? I'm going to do it. Yes, I am. I'm going to do it right now. I'm still standing here though, shifting my weight from one foot to the other.

I'm doing it!

I run towards the pool, with a level of athleticism I haven't shown since never. By the time I reach the edge of the pool, I couldn't stop if I wanted to. I jump in – I don't know if it's head first or feet first. I don't suppose it's either. It doesn't feel like a very graceful manoeuvre, but I've done it, and I'm so proud of myself.

As the icy cold water hits every inch of my body like a million tiny knives, I kind of wish I hadn't bothered. I don't feel liberated, I feel as if I'm going to get hypothermia. But as soon as I come up for air and swim towards the edge of the infinity pool, I finally take in the incredible view of the beach and the ocean, low down on the ground below me. Everyone looks so small from up here, and I feel a million miles from anyone. It's just me and my pool, and it's amazing.

'Good morning, Lila.'

I turn around and see Freddie, standing next to the pool, holding a fishing net. He looks so good, I want to bite my lip. His body is ripped with muscle – muscle everywhere, muscles on his muscles! I don't think I've ever seen anyone with a body like this in real life. Given that he isn't wearing anything but a pair of small, tight swimming shorts, I can see a lot.

And then I remember what I'm wearing. Nothing.

'What the hell are you doing?' I ask.

With absolutely zero grace I scramble closer to him, so I can hide my nakedness behind the wall of the pool. If I can just hang onto a little bit of my dignity, that will be great.

'I'm fishing mosquitos out of the pool,' he replies. 'What does it look like I'm doing?'

'Like... like you're being a pervert,' I reply. I'm not sure if my face is red with anger or embarrassment – I think it's a bit of both.

The last thing I expected to see out here was the barman from last night, cleaning my pool. I suppose he does a few different jobs here, and I know that he needs to make a living, but shouldn't he be cleaning the pool when no one is planning on using it? I don't care how fit he is.

'I'm being a pervert?' he says. 'I'm not the one skinny dipping!'

'Are you allowed to talk to me like that?' I ask.

Freddie just laughs and takes a seat on a sunlounger. He lies back and places his hands behind his head. I am momentarily distracted by the bulge of his biceps, which look even better without a shirt on them.

I squeak in disbelief.

'And now, what, you're sunbathing?'

'You're smart,' he says sarcastically.

'What do you think your boss will say when I call up and say the barman is sunbathing by my pool?' I ask.

Freddie's face falls for a moment. Hopefully the threat of me calling his superiors will send him packing. He shuffles towards the end of the sunlounger.

'Lila... do you actually think I'm a barman?' he asks.

'Erm, yes,' I reply, only now I'm not so sure. 'You served me a drink in a bar.'

'You asked me to.'

'Because you're the barman.'

'Nope.'

'What?' I say. 'I'm so confused. So, you're the pool boy?'

Freddie laughs so hard he falls back onto the sunlounger.

'Oh, Lila, you're killing me,' he says. 'I'm a guest too. I'm staying in the suite next door to yours.'

Oh, God. Oh-h-h-h, God.

I look over at the villa. I hadn't really processed just how big it is, in relation to how much smaller my living space is. It is *one* villa, with multiple suites inside. Well, it was dark when I got here and, after my first post-wedding drink, I'm not actually convinced I was fully sober for another second of it. Looking at the building now, I'd say there are maybe three separate suites in this one old villa. And there are three ladders into the pool, one outside each set of bi-folding doors.

'The porter told me this was my private pool,' I say.

'It's the villa's private pool,' he tells me. 'The three suites share it.'

'Oh... my... God, I am so embarrassed.'

Still leaning on the side of the pool, I place my head in my hands.

'It's funny,' he insists. 'Don't worry about it.'

'I'm mortified,' I reply.

I thought I'd hit rock bottom yesterday, but I hadn't. This is rock bottom. It has to be.

'Can I grab you a towel?' he asks.

'Yes, please. There's one on my sofa.'

Freddie dashes inside my part of the villa to grab it for me, and I hear him roar with laughter. What's so funny in there?

Oh, God. Oh-h-h-h, God. No, please, God no. He's seen the dildo – I mean, how could he bloody miss it?

He walks out with my towel, with the biggest grin ever plastered across his face. I want to slap it off.

He holds the towel out for me.

'Here we go,' he says, stifling a laugh.

'Close your eyes,' I say.

Freddie does as I ask, so I hurry out of the pool, snatch the towel from him and wrap it tightly around my body, before dashing towards my apartment.

'Hey, at least the water made your hair less massive,' he jokes. Today his teasing just pisses me off.

I don't reply.

'Hey, Lila,' he starts, following me towards my door.

'Just leave it,' I say.

'Sorry, I just thought—'

'Please, just go away,' I snap.

'Okay, fine,' he replies, taking the hint. 'I'll leave the two of you alone.'

Freddie retreats back to his portion of the pool area. I close my door behind me.

I can't believe I thought he was the barman – but why did he make me a drink, if he wasn't? And he didn't just make me a drink, he made a drink, a real one, an amazing one. He knew what he was doing.

I plonk myself back down on the sofa and place my head in my hands. So this is rock bottom. I've had a few false starts, but this is the one. This is my lowest point. Things can only improve from here.

One thing I know for sure though: I never, ever, ever want to see Freddie again. I don't think I could look him in the eye.

9

I watch the text cursor flashing on the blank page of my Word document. I've been staring at it so long, I'm convinced my heartbeat has fallen in sync with it. I realise it is probably quite slow for a heartbeat, but that's what it feels like. It feels as if I'm giving up, as if my heartbeat is about to grind to a halt. It's going to down tools, just as my brain has. I think they're going on strike, after everything I have put them through over the last couple of days. Between the heartbreak, the over thinking, the binge drinking and the overeating, my poor body has been through so much.

After my embarrassing pool incident with Freddie, I thought it best to hide away and get on with work. I've drunk lots of water, and I had a salad brought to my suite for lunch, which my body feels much better for. There is just one problem though... my book, or lack thereof.

My book is due in around five weeks – two of which I am here for. While I admit I have been neglecting doing my work, because things got so crazy in the run-up to the wedding (although, in hindsight, not as crazy as they could have been), I do actually have two thirds of a novel and the plan was to write the final third after my honeymoon. But I can't do it; I just can't. How the hell am I supposed to write a love story, when I think love is stupid/possibly doesn't exist? There's writing fiction and then there's completely making things up, and I cannot flog the happy ever after I have always believed in, when I'm not all that sure it exists any more.

So, I'm starting again. I don't have much choice. There's no way I can finish writing the love story I started while I was all loved-up and happy. Every romantic thing I wrote, I wrote with Daniel in my head. My mindset has totally changed. There's no way I can just pick up where I left off – the tone will be completely different.

I dropped my mum a text message to let her know that I'd arrived here safe, promising to call her in the morning. It's the afternoon now and I'm sure she must be worried about me. I can't put off talking about what happened any longer, as much as I'm trying to bury my head in the sand by working – or trying to, at least.

'Hello,' my mum answers after one ring. I feel guilty, as if she's been waiting by the phone for me to call.

'Hi, Mum,' I say with a faux-cheery attitude. She sees straight through it.

'Oh, love, are you okay?' she asks.

'Oh, I'm fine,' I say, continuing to play it down. 'Just taking things a day at a time.'

'Still got him blocked?' she asks.

'Yes,' I reply. 'Although I might unblock him, maybe see if he tries to call, see what he has to say for himself now I'm over the initial shock.'

Well, I'm not exactly over it, but I'm a little calmer at least.

'His mum says he's gone into hiding,' she continues. 'She gave me a call to apologise. She was mortified. Couldn't stop apologising. He doesn't get his lack of manners from his mum.'

That's so like Daniel, to just hide from his problems. After chatting with my mum for a while, I decide that I will unblock him, giving him a chance to call, but I doubt he will, not if he's hiding. I wonder if he thinks giving me space will allow this whole thing to blow over.

I massage my temples for a moment before I begin staring at my screen again. Less dwelling, more keeping myself distracted. That's what I need.

My eyes are pulled from my blinking cursor by something else, dancing in front of my window. It looks like a pole with... white underpants on the end.

I pull myself up from the sofa and go check it out. When I get to the door, I realise it's Freddie. I think he's making a gesture of peace.

I feel my cheeks trying to tug my mouth into a little smile. I open the door.

'Can I come in?' he asks.

'OK,' I reply. 'But leave your pants outside.'

Freddie raises his eyebrows but resists a cheeky comment.

I sit back down on the sofa. Freddie sits next to me.

'Oh, are you writing your next book?' he asks, nodding towards the screen.

'Trying,' I say. 'It's not going all that well. Story of my life at the moment.'

Freddie is wearing a rather short pair of shorts, which show off his muscular legs. On his top half, he's wearing a low-cut white vest – I'm not sure when the trend of men showing their 'cleavage' kicked off, but I'm as confused by it as I am secretly delighted. As always, his hair is messy and he's wearing the same pair of black Ray-Ban sunglasses as this morning. The glass is mirrored, so when you try to look into Freddie's eyes, all you see is yourself. There's just something so mesmerising about his eyes – the fact that I can't see those glittering blue pools of his puts us on more of a level playing field.

'I just wanted to apologise, for earlier,' he begins. 'And last night, I guess. I thought maybe you were being cute, asking me to make you a drink. I didn't realise you thought I was the actual barman. But it was just a silly misunderstanding and I don't want you to feel bad about it, okay?'

'Okay,' I reply. 'Thank you.'

'And I'm sorry if I embarrassed you today. I don't really know what happened...'

'I'm going to say that was all me,' I respond.

'You and your friend,' he says, nodding towards the dildo.

'I really need to move that,' I say with a deep sigh. 'It's not mine. Well, I suppose it is. It was a sort of joke honeymoon gift, from my best friend.'

Freddie's face falls for a second before he smiles bigger than ever.

'You're on your honeymoon? Congratulations! It should have occurred to me, that you'd be here with someone,' he says. 'I'm here by myself. I think I forget that it's supposed to be for couples.'

'You're here alone?'

'Yeah.' He laughs awkwardly. 'I was after some solo time and, well, a place full of loved-up couples seemed like a really great place to be left alone.'

'That actually makes a lot of sense,' I reply. 'I'm here by myself too – less by choice though, more like my wedding was supposed to be a couple of days ago but it never happened, so I thought I'd come on my honeymoon alone.'

'Wow,' he says. 'I'm sorry things didn't work out.'

Freddie takes his sunglasses off.

I stare at him for a few seconds.

'You look oddly familiar,' I tell him. 'Do you ever get told you look like anyone? I can't quite put my finger on it.'

Freddie laughs.

'I just have one of those faces,' he explains, before quickly switching back to our previous topic of conversation, not even detecting (or perhaps just ignoring) my attempt at a subject change. 'I can't believe you're here on your own too.'

'I'm sure it happens,' I reply.

'It really doesn't,' he says. 'I got talking to someone who works here – they told me no one comes here alone. Why would they? It's a place designed for couples. I didn't think I'd notice, other than there being couples everywhere, but it's amazing how apparent it is.'

I shrug.

'I have a lot of work to do anyway. I don't suppose I'll notice,' I tell him. It's partially true, and partially a big old hint, to get him to leave. We might have cleared the air, but I'm still so, so embarrassed, and I feel so uncomfortable right now.

'Do you want to go for a drink or something to eat?' he asks.

'Are you inviting me by default, because I'm the only other solo person here?'

'No, I told you, I came here to be alone,' he replies, sounding almost hurt at my suggestion.

'If you'd come here and my husband had been with me, would you have asked us both to dinner?'

'If I'd seen you both naked, then yes,' he jokes. 'Lila, I'm only asking because we're both here by ourselves, and it sounds like you've had a crappy few days, with a big shock...'

'I'm fine,' I lie. 'Really, I am. I just want to get on with my work, and to be left alone. Surely you understand, if that's why you're here?'

'Okay, yeah,' he replies, standing up. 'I completely get it. Well, I'm just next door, if you want me.'

'Thanks,' I reply.

Freddie takes off, leaving me to my blank document.

I hope I wasn't too hard on him by telling him I want to be alone, but even if I weren't still absolutely mortified by everything that has happened so far, it feels so weird and wrong to even be entertaining dinner with another man – on my honeymoon, too. I mean, I know it isn't technically my honeymoon, even if it was supposed to be, but unsurprisingly, my new status is taking a lot of sinking in.

Why hasn't Daniel called me? That's what I can't get out of my head. He's unblocked now, so why isn't he trying my phone non-stop? If he called me, it would make me feel sick, I'd panic, I wouldn't answer, I never want to speak to him again... but why hasn't he called? Why doesn't he care? How can our four years together mean so little to him that he could ruin our wedding and then not call me, not to apologise, or explain, or even just make sure I'm okay?

I know that Freddie is gorgeous and it's a very odd coincidence that he is here on his own too, but how can I go for dinner with him, with all this on my mind, and with all this work to do?

It's a nice idea, but I think I just need to keep myself to myself. I'm sure Freddie will be fine – after all, he did come here unaccompanied too. The thing I can't help but wonder though, is... I know why I've come here on my own, but what is Freddie running away from?

10

DAY 4

Today is a new day, and the first proper day that I have left my suite during the daylight hours. The sun is shining, there isn't a cloud in the sky, and there's a wonderful breeze.

I might not be loved-up, but I have fallen in love with Valentine Island this morning. I got up early, had a shower, put on my gorgeous new cream sundress and a brave face, and left the safe confines of the villa to explore the island.

In the glorious light of day, I can see that the top part of the driveway to the luxury villas is lined with white columns. Neat green hedges sit on top of them, forming archways. With the warm sun gently beaming down on me, my mood feels lifted. I weave in and out of the columns for fun, high on the smell of sea air. There's just something about feeling the sun on your shoulders and filling your lungs with the salty scent of the ocean that instantly relaxes a person – you can't beat it.

On the right-hand side of the wall is an army of trees, the start of the island's massive forest, where you can bike, hike or just lose yourself in nature. On the left is where the built-up part of the island is.

I reach the first viewing point, a third of the way down the road. I'm still quite high up, so from here I can see everything. Between where I am and the ocean, I can see the villas, the restaurants, the swimming pools and tennis courts. I can see the beach, which already looks alive with people.

As I near the main 'town' part of the resort I hear a strange noise. A sort of squeaking sound, coming from the bushes. I move towards it cautiously, but when I peer inside the bushes and see what was making the noise, I melt. Not even the hot summer sun could cause me to melt so effectively – not like kittens! Lying in a little pile on the floor are four tiny little kittens. Tabby cats, with adorable white noses and cute little white tummies. They can't be very old, and I imagine they're strays. Someone has placed a little brown saucer next to them. I imagine it had food for the mum on it when they placed it down, but it's all gone now. It's comforting to know that someone is looking after them, even if their mum isn't around. They are sleeping now, so I don't touch them. I leave them in peace and go on my way. I don't think I'll be able to resist coming back to see them when they're awake though.

I notice a place called Sabatini, which must be one of the many Italian restaurants that the island boasts. The feeling of walking into an air-conditioned room, after being outside in the hot sun, is a real rush. The gentle sensation change, from your head to your toes, is a real wave of something inexplicably wonderful. I might start walking in and out of buildings, just to get that high.

The waiter who greets me seems a little taken aback that I'm here to eat breakfast on my own, but he shows me to a table. He asks if someone will be joining me, but I say no. He doesn't ask any questions.

I love how leafy and green everything is here, inside and out. Inside the restaurant, a variety of plants line the walls and hang from the ceilings. I love the way they smell; it makes the air seem so clean.

I order a cornetto – an Italian pastry, a little bit like a croissant, but much softer, which is filled with a really thick, really yellow creamy custard. It is absolutely delicious, and complemented perfectly by the cappuccino I wash it down with.

I can feel my stress and tension melting away. I'm feeling lighter by the minute, but I'll bet a massage would make me feel even better even quicker. I know that there is a spa inside the hotel building. I think a massage is just what I need, to usher me those final few steps into holiday mode. The right pair of hands will have no problem, working my worries out of my tight neck and shoulders.

I feel the cool air con as I walk through the doors, but this time it is accompanied by the gorgeous smell of cocoa butter. Now I really do feel as if I'm on holiday. I want slathering in it, from head to toe.

But as I talk to the spa employee sitting behind the front desk, I feel my stress taking hold of me even tighter.

'You only do couples' massages?' I reply in disbelief.

'This is a romance resort,' the girl behind the desk informs me. She is a young Italian girl, in a bright pink uniform. Her eyebrows are almost as severe as her fake tan – imagine, being orange with fake tan when you live in such a warm, sunny country.

'So you only offer massages for two people?'

'Well, yes,' she replies. 'Technically.'

'What if only one person wants a massage?' I ask.

'They are couples' massages,' she tells me again. 'People don't come to Valentine Island to do things without their partner. No one has ever asked before...'

I don't think this poor girl knows what to say.

'So, I can't just have both people massage me at once?' I ask.

'Are you sure you'd rather not come back with your partner?' she asks. 'Most partners are happy to accompany their loved ones.'

My partner couldn't even be faithful to me – that's pretty much rule one in the couples' handbook. Amazing, really, that there are people out there willing to do things they don't want to do, just to make their significant others happy. I could never get Daniel to do anything he didn't want to do.

I'm sure that, if I pushed for it, they wouldn't refuse me a massage, but it's the fact that she said no one comes here alone, people's partners love to come with them... I feel embarrassed, as if they're probably thinking my partner doesn't want to be here with me. Technically he doesn't and that realisation washes waves of sadness, anger and embarrassment over me. I give up and double back to a tourist information board I saw earlier. I might not be able to get a massage, but I'm sure there are plenty of things I can do.

Looking over the board, I realise that perhaps there aren't plenty of things for me to do. It really does seem to be the case that every single thing to do here is designed with couples in mind. Everything here involves two people, from the sports to the relaxation events. Even the yoga sessions show poses that involve couples – what am I going to do, turn up on my own and just pointlessly lie back with my legs in the air? That sounds like my sex life. No, thank you.

I hear the ringing of a bicycle bell, so I quickly move out of the way. Two men cycle past me on a tandem bike.

'*Buongiorno,*' one of them calls to me.

Bloody hell, even the bicycles are built for two.

You worry, in the real world, whether your worth as a person is attached to your relationship status. You know that it shouldn't be, but as women we are raised to believe that we need to find a man. I suppose we do, in a technical sense, for some reasons. If we want to have kids, for example, it is unfortunate but only men have one of the key ingredients. Of course, there are other ways to go about it if you are single, but it's nice to have a significant other, someone to make you feel loved and always have your back.

Being single isn't really something people aspire to be, it's what we are by default. It is human nature to want to find someone, and to feel disappointed if you can't, or if things don't work out. Naturally, you feel (wrongly) like a little bit of a failure if you can't find the right person for you. I can't make you feel better – you're not going to take relationship advice from someone like me, are you? Look at the mess I'm in – but I can promise you that you can feel worse. Come to Valentine Island, if you want to see how small and insignificant you are. Here, I'm too single to even ride a bike.

There are some things I can do here that don't require a significant other. I can go to the shops, buy loads of food, and go back to my villa and eat it.

I could've bloody done that at home though!

11

Obviously I forgot to turn the air conditioning on before I left the villa, so it's like walking into an oven when I arrive back. It's so warm in here, I'm surprised my dildo hasn't wilted.

I pull open the bi-folding doors. It's very warm outside, but it's even warmer indoors. There's no way I can sit in here, not until it cools down a little.

I slip off my sundress to reveal my bikini. One of the best things about being on holiday is taking a holiday from your bra too. I like to wear mine for as little time as possible while I'm away somewhere warm, and a bikini is a great way to do that.

Outside my villa's back door, I have my own little sunbathing area, sectioned off by trees, right by the pool, so I grab my sunglasses and my bag of food shopping and head outside to hole up on my sunlounger.

The hot floor tiles outside burn the bottoms of my feet as I literally hotfoot to my seat. Right as I get there, I notice Freddie swimming laps of the pool. I'm about to dash right back where I came from when he spots me.

'Hey, Lila,' he calls out.

'Hello,' I reply politely as I take my seat. Well, I can't go back inside now, or he'll know I'm avoiding him.

As I take out my drink and my bag of crisps, I notice him swimming towards my edge of the pool. When he gets close, he rests his arms on the side and his chin on his arms.

'What you got there?' he asks, nodding towards my lunch.

'Prickly pear San Pellegrino and San Carlo crisps.'

'Ooh, nice,' he replies. 'I haven't had potato chips in a long time. I've been on a diet.'

'Yeah, so have I,' I tell him. 'That's why I'm eating them now. The diet is officially over.'

'I'm on vacation, right? I should be allowed some chips.'

'Do you want some?' I ask.

I watch him ponder whether or not it's a good idea. A mischievous look spreads across his face. You can tell he wants to say yes.

'Don't let me lead you astray,' I quickly add. 'I only wanted one bag but they only sold twin packs.'

'You sound mad about that,' he says, furrowing his brow.

'Yeah, I wouldn't normally be mad about bonus crisps,' I admit. 'It's just this bloody place.'

'Well, you seem like you need a chat and I seem like I need some chips, so I will join you,' he says, before hurrying out of the pool like an excited little kid.

I wasn't technically asking him to join me, I was just going to give him some of my surplus crisps. I can't really bring myself to hurt his feelings, now that he's sat down on the sunlounger next to me.

'So, why are you so upset you got a good deal on some potato chips?' he asks as he opens the bag.

I catch myself staring at the droplets of water rolling down his body and I tell myself off. His eyes are up there, Lila. His cool, sexy blue eyes...

'It was just the last straw today,' I tell him. 'I got up earlier, I had a real spring in my step, I was excited for the day ahead.'

'And then?' Freddie asks between mouthfuls.

'I thought I'd get a massage, except I can't because I'm single,' I tell him. 'Thought I'd go for a bike ride but, nope, I can't, because I'm single. All the sports – not that I even want to play any – but they're all doubles sports, for couples!'

'I know!' he replies enthusiastically. 'This is exactly what I've been up against since I got here. All I can do is hang out here, swim, go to the beach, visit the bars. I wanted some peace and quiet, but I suppose I've got too much here.'

'We're worthless because we're here solo,' I tell him.

'We're not worthless,' he replies. 'But I take your point.'

'I thought I'd be able to go on my honeymoon on my own and have fun, but without my fiancé... I can't do anything. I'm starting to think that's going to be a theme, moving forwards.'

'What happened with your fiancé?' he asks, before adding quickly, 'If you don't mind my asking.'

'We were supposed to be getting married – in a matter of minutes actually. I was buzzing, nothing was going to get me down. My niece lost her flowers and I said I'd go and get them for her, rather than trust anyone else with it – I figured they'd get distracted or lost, or something. I didn't want to leave anything to chance, so I made sure I had full creative control over everything. I managed everything on the day... The only thing that wasn't my responsibility was Daniel, my fiancé. All he had to do was put on his suit and turn up. Oh, and I suppose be honest and faithful and not shag our friend.'

'Oh,' he replies.

'Oh indeed,' I say. 'So I went to find the flowers and, just by pure chance, there he was, hiding behind a bloody bush, talking with her, about how they loved each other and blah blah blah.'

I'm a little sick of going over and over it now.

'Lila, that's so awful. I am so sorry. What an awful way to find out too.'

'It was awful, but I feel so relieved I found out at all,' I reply.

'So no one had any idea?'

There's a thought. I hadn't considered whether any of our friends might know. I suppose Gerry, his best friend/best man could have been in on the secret. It makes sense that he would confide in someone and, now that I think about it, he must've provided him with a few cover stories from time to time. I wonder about the others in our friendship group. I'd bet my life there's no way Ali would've known; she has no time for cheaters, which I really appreciate. That's the way it should be, right?

Whatever consenting adults want to get up to is absolutely fine, so long as everyone is happy with it and no one gets hurt.

There's a sincerity in Freddie's voice. Halfway through that, I worried I might regret telling him as soon as I'd got the words out, but I'm glad I did. It's nice to talk about it, or perhaps it's not nice to talk about it, but it is just nice to talk to someone generally.

'Thanks,' I say.

'You get much work done?' he asks me, changing the subject.

'I did not,' I admit.

'I'm sorry,' he says. 'I'm not doing a very good job of cheering you up, am I?'

'No, but the crisps are,' I joke.

'It's nice to see you smile,' he says. 'That first night, when we met, you seemed so happy. You did think you were in with a bartender, though, I suppose.'

'Yeah, I'm sorry if I was a bit weird. That was my wedding day, actually. I came straight here.'

'Wow, so this is all still pretty raw, then,' he says. 'Tell you what, I was going to have another stab at seeing if you wanted to go for dinner with me, but I totally get why you might want to be by yourself now. So I'm going to leave you, and if you want some company, just shout, okay?'

'Okay, thanks,' I reply.

'And thanks for the chips,' he says, heading back over to his side of the garden. 'I'm going to need to swim for another hour now.'

I smile at him, even though he's walking away.

Freddie can't help but hide that he feels sorry for me – I'd feel sorry for me too, so I can't be annoyed by his pity.

It might be nice to have someone to have dinner with… but I just can't. I can't bring myself to go for dinner with a man; it doesn't feel right. And I know that he isn't romantically interested in me. I mean, look at him. He looks like a Greek god and I look like a Greek vase.

It just doesn't feel right… and the way I'm feeling now, I'm not sure it ever will.

12

This holiday is proving to be neither a fun distraction from my life nor a distraction-free writer's retreat. I'm not relaxing. I'm not getting any work done. I'm not really sure where I fall between these two opposites, but I'm not really having much fun.

I'd be lying if I said I hadn't had any fun... that first night with Freddie, to the best of my memory, was a lot of fun, and chatting with him earlier today was sort of nice, just to have some human interaction with someone who wasn't rejecting me from a spa or selling me crisps in bulk.

I'm not surprised I'm having trouble writing a romance novel, after everything I've been through. I've had the occasional bout of stress-related writer's block in the past – never anything like this though. What usually helps me is to relax, so I'm going to try and do a bunch of the little things I would usually do to try and chill myself out. I always work better when I'm chilled.

Normally I would just try a couple of techniques, but these are not normal circumstances, so I'm going to try every last thing I can think of – that I'm capable of doing alone, at least.

I've finally cracked open the welcome champagne that was left in the bedroom for my husband and me. Well, it's not as if he's really supposed to be turning up late, as I told the guy on Reception, is it? And I'm not exactly saving it for any gentleman company. So I've poured myself a glass, while I'm running my bath.

Booze – check. Bath – check.

The bathroom here is amazing, because of course it is, because everything here is amazing apart from their policy on single people.

The bath is taking a little longer to fill than your average bath, because this bath is huge. I'd imagine it was built with two people in mind, just like everything else. So I've got two people's amount of champagne in a bath big enough for two people – I finally feel like I'm winning again.

I dip a toe in to test the temperature of the water before placing my glass on the side, climbing in and lying back. The water is so deep, unlike in my bath at home. We recently got a new one – exactly the same size as our old one, because we only have so much space, but the new one doesn't have the previous occupier's neglect turning to mould around the edges. The problem is that, because it's relatively small, you just can't get a deep bath, and my boobs and my knees will always poke out of the water like desert islands. In this bath though... it's so deep, I could submerge myself if I wanted to. I'll settle for water up to my chin for now.

The previous titleholder of my entirely fictitious best bath awards was the one in our hotel room when we went to Thailand on holiday last year. Well, I say it was in our hotel room – it was actually on the balcony outside, which was just so surreal. It was as if you knew you were sitting in a bath, but you could feel the heat of the sun, and look out over the view, which boasted trees for days.

It was such a gorgeous holiday; I had such an amazing time. Until we got home, actually, now that I think about it.

We landed back in England late afternoon, which meant it was evening by the time we were home. We were so jet-lagged, I don't think I've ever felt exhaustion like it. I just wanted to go home and go to bed, but Eva was having a birthday gathering at her flat, and Daniel said we had to go. I made a case for not going, said we weren't that close, that she wouldn't care if we weren't there. Now all I can think about is whether they were carrying on back then, and if that's why he insisted we go. I just can't stop thinking about every single time I've seen them in a room together, trying to recall their body language or the conversations they would have. Now that I think about it, I don't think I've ever seen them interact, not properly. I've seen them exchange polite hellos and good-byes, but that's it. And now I realise how weird that is.

The only thing worse than me trying to picture what they were like when we were all together, is when I start picturing them together when I wasn't there. They must have been getting together so often when I wasn't around. I'm not even sure when he could've been spending time with her – I honestly never felt as if he wasn't there. He'd go to work, he'd play golf... I suppose Eva could've chipped into his golf time, which he deserves some credit for. The man who plays the world's most boring sport managed to find something even more boring to do instead – Eva. Daniel thinks he's so smart, and perhaps he is, to have found a way to do whatever he wanted while I blindly trusted him, but Eva is such a bimbo. What did they actually do, when they spent time together? What did they talk about? They probably just had sex, didn't they? Which makes me feel sick to my stomach. It's not as if he wasn't having sex with me, so he must've been finding the time to have sex with both of us. Eva wasn't just cutting into his golf time, she was cutting into his me time too. All those times he came home too tired to have sex, and I never suspected a damn thing. I feel like an idiot.

As my stress levels creep back up, I have another sip of champagne and squeeze even more of the yummy, fig-scented complimentary bubble bath into the water.

I just need to stop torturing myself with the specifics, because they're not making me feel better, and they're never going to.

After forty minutes in the bath, I decide it's no use. If the world's best bath isn't making me feel better after this long, it isn't going to help. Draining my glass hasn't helped me all that much either but, after the other day, I don't plan on getting drunk for a long time.

I wrap myself up in one of the big fluffy dressing gowns hanging in the bathroom, and head back upstairs.

I look through my suitcase, which I still haven't unpacked. I probably won't unpack it, because I'll only be packing it again. And when I arrive back home again, I probably won't unpack it for ages then either. Did you even go on holiday, if you don't leave your suitcase on your bedroom floor, unpacked, for six months?

Something in my case catches my eye and I feel as if I've seen a ghost. It isn't a ghost though, it's the white lace lingerie I bought for my wedding night. A figure-hugging, semi-sheer white lace bodysuit. When I tried it on, before I bought it, I felt so good in it, so confident. I was almost as excited to wear it as I was my wedding dress, and now I feel like such an idiot.

Disappointed, having recently spent so much money on white shit that I won't get to wear, I decide to put it on. Why can't I just wear sexy underwear? Why do I have to have a man for that?

I shrug off my robe and step into my bodysuit, before looking myself up and down in the bedroom's full-length mirror.

I look good, right? I mean, I'm nearly thirty-two, so I can't do much about time. I can't make my D cups be perkier (not without a bank loan and the help of Ali's surgeon) and those little stretch marks on my hips are there now, they're not going anywhere... but I still don't look bad. I feel great for losing a bit of weight. I feel as if I'm in pretty good shape... so what was wrong with me? Why wasn't I enough for him? I'm looking myself up and down and, while I can't see what is so wrong with me, suddenly it's hard to see what is right. I'm just a normal grown woman. I'm not a cute little thing like Eva. Is that what men really want, a cute little bimbo? Talk about unrealistic body standards for women – am I supposed to have my lower leg bones removed and beat a few of my brain cells out with them?

I plonk myself down on the bed, where my laptop waits expectantly. I still haven't written a word.

If I can't write something romantic, maybe I could write something sexy? Sex usually comes before romance anyway, and I do feel sexy in this. Perhaps if I could just get the ball rolling...

I do have sex scenes in my books, I just don't usually get into them getting into it. I'll have some descriptive kissing, maybe some clothes will start coming off, but as soon as stuff is about to happen – oh, sorry, dear reader, that's the end of the chapter. I just can't bring myself to write it.

I stare at my screen with my hands hovering over my keyboard. I'm trying to think sexy thoughts, but they're not really happening. I swear, this doesn't usually happen to me – yep, that old excuse.

I yawn, a combination of tired and bored of trying to write and getting nowhere.

I check my phone, to see if there is anything from Ali. We were texting earlier but she said she was getting an early night. Tomorrow she has a date with a man whose dad owns a department store (which she thinks is going to get her free shoes), who has been sexting her about his passion for practising tantra (which is why she's getting an early night).

I have nothing to do and no one to talk to... I suppose there is Freddie, next door. Handsome, sexy Freddie, with his muscles and his messy hair and his cheeky charm.

I look down at my underwear angrily – you're doing this to me, making me have impure thoughts.

I wiggle into a more comfortable position as the sleepy feeling starts to take over.

I suppose I should get my beauty sleep; after all, tomorrow I am sure I have a big day... of absolutely nothing.

13

DAY 5

I jolt upright in my bed. What was that?

The sun shining in through the bedroom windows tells me that it's morning. I wish I'd closed the blinds last night because it feels as if it is dissolving my eyes. As I wait for them to adjust, I hear the strange noise again. It's more of a screeching noise now. It sounds like it's coming from a woman – a woman in trouble.

I hurry on my dressing gown because, for some reason, I feel even more vulnerable, being so undressed.

As I creep down the stairs slowly, I hear it again. This time, I'd describe the noise as a squeal, sort of like a pig makes.

I notice, straight ahead of me, that the door is open, which makes me think someone has been in here while I was asleep. As I near the bottom of the stairs, I realise that someone is in here right now.

Savino, the porter who brought me here, is standing in the kitchen.

'Hello?' I say to him. His face falls.

'Lila?'

A voice from my not so distant past chills me to my core. It's Daniel's voice, there's no mistaking that. It surprises me that I'm pleased to hear his voice, and I'm touched that he's followed me to Italy. I think I'd been telling myself that, if he did turn up, I'd be throwing him into the pool, but now that he's here, maybe to apologise...

As I turn to face him I notice Eva standing next to him. They both have their suitcases with them.

'What... the hell... are you two doing here?' I ask as I slowly approach them.

I hear Savino frantically mumble something to himself in Italian before he scarpers.

'Lila,' he says again.

'You keep saying my name like you know me,' I start, with one of those truly terrifying angry laughs, the kind when your eyes widen and your face muscles tighten. 'Except you didn't seem to know who I was on our wedding day. And, funnily enough, you don't seem to recall who you're supposed to be on holiday with, because you're standing here with... her.'

I can't even bring myself to say Eva's name.

Eva remains silent. She's wearing a white maxi dress with a bikini top underneath, and she has a pair of sunglasses on her head – if that isn't the universal symbol of a woman on holiday, I don't know what is.

'I didn't know you'd be here,' Daniel says as his cheeks redden. 'You just disappeared and, well, after a few days, you didn't come back, and I knew this was booked... It seemed like a shame, to let the holiday go to waste.'

At first, I consider whether I'm just as bad as he is, because I had a similar thought, which is how I ended up here. But not only does Daniel not deserve to be here – because this mess is all his fault – but the fact that he's brought his bit on the side with him, on our honeymoon, that I booked... Oh, no, no, no, no, no. I don't think so.

'Lila, you just vanished,' he says.

'With good reason,' I reply.

I can feel the anger bubbling up inside me. I didn't think I could get any more angry or upset than I did at the maze on my wedding day, but him turning up here with her... it's like some sort of cruel joke.

'I realise we have our issues right now,' he starts. I don't let him finish.

'Issues?' I say. 'Daniel, you've been cheating on me for... how long?'

'That isn't a conversation for right now,' he says.

'Our problems are filed under more than "issues". I've never felt so humiliated.'

Daniel itches his beard anxiously. He is wearing the holiday clothes I bought for him, so I don't suppose the bin men took his suitcase, which is a shame.

'Well, you certainly levelled the playing field at the ceremony,' he says, starting to sound defensive. Eva places a soothing hand on his forearm, which makes me want to rip hers off. 'That was pretty humiliating.'

'Well, I wasn't going to marry you, was I?'

'The way you called things off though...'

'Daniel, I saw the two of you together, in the maze, talking, confessing your love for each other, kissing... Do we have to do this with her here?'

He ignores the last part.

'I was stood there, waiting for you to walk down the aisle. The music played, the bridesmaids walked down the aisle, everyone took their places. "Here Comes the Bride" started playing, but no bride came.'

'Ali said she'd told you,' I reply.

'She told me eventually. But first, she let me worry. She acted like she had no idea where you were, told me you were right behind her moments ago. She knew how worried I was and she just let me panic... until she announced, in front of everyone, that you weren't coming. When I asked why she told everyone that I was having an affair with Eva – she named her! She pointed her out!'

Man, that sounds like Ali.

'Oh, my God, Daniel, Eva, I'm so sorry, that must've been a pretty sucky day for you. If it's any consolation...' I raise my voice '... it was worse for me!'

'Lila, she called me out in front of my family. My parents, my gran! She called poor Eva a slut in front of everyone – she burst into tears.'

I shrug. Probably don't shag other people's fiancés, if you're such a delicate little flower you can't handle the fallout. The same goes for Daniel. I imagine it was horrible, for his gran to hear what he did, and to find out like that, but if he hadn't done it, it wouldn't have happened. They were playing a dangerous game. They asked for this. Both of them.

Absolutely unbelievable that he has the balls on him to bring his bit on the side on our honeymoon, and then have a go at me because it was embarrassing when people found out.

'I was still going to marry you,' he says. Eva doesn't even flinch at this remark; she just stands there, smug, like the cat that got the cream.

'Why, though?' I ask.

'Gorgeous, you wanna go for a swim? The water is great,' Freddie says to me as he walks in from the terrace, through the backdoor that Daniel and Eva must have opened.

What the hell?

Freddie appears to be wearing nothing but a towel. He's all wet, as if maybe he just stepped out of the shower. He walks over to us and, when he reaches me, he kisses me on the cheek.

I just stare at him as he runs a hand through his wet, shaggy hair. I swear to God he flexes his biceps as he does so, and not in a natural way – he's literally flexing on everyone in the room.

Daniel looks as taken aback by this as I feel. Eva looks positively dumbstruck.

'Who are your friends, gorgeous?' Freddie asks me.

I realise that he's talking to me, but I have no idea what he's talking about. Christ, he must be some sort of sociopath. He's acting as if we're a couple or something – and it seems as if he really believes it. I know I haven't been a single girl in a long time, but I didn't realise that giving a man a bag of crisps meant you were a thing. The rules have clearly changed *a lot* since the last time I played the dating game.

Freddie gives me another meaningful squeeze. As he releases me I notice both Daniel and Eva staring down at my body. I look down to see that my robe has opened, and my sexy white lingerie is on show. I quickly tighten my belt.

'Who are you?' Daniel asks him, unable to hide his jealousy.

'Great to meet you, buddy, I'm Freddie,' he says.

'You're Freddie Bianchi,' Eva says, stunned.

How the bloody hell does Eva know his name? Has she tried to shag him *too*?

'That's me,' he replies.

'Who?' Daniel asks, even angrier now that it appears Eva knows him.

Freddie Bianchi, I'm sure I know that name, he's...

'I'm such a big fan,' Eva tells him. 'Huge!'

'Who the hell is he?' Daniel asks her.

'Freddie Bianchi,' she says, as though the repetition of his name will trigger something in his head. 'You know, from the *Edge of Eden* movie.'

Oh, my God. That's who he is!

Edge of Eden was the first book in a series of erotic novels that absolutely exploded – so much so they made a movie of the first one. I haven't read the books or seen the movie, but I vaguely recall seeing a movie poster of a small blonde woman and a towering, muscular hunk of a man standing over her. I seem to think he looked a bit different on the posters, as if his hair was darker, or slicked back, or both...

'Yeah, that's me,' he says with an awkward laugh.

'What are you doing here?' Eva asks him.

'Lila and I met on the plane,' he tells them. 'I don't know what it was but we just fell for each other. Couldn't keep our hands off each other, could we?'

Suddenly something dawns on me... Freddie is acting. I imagine my nosey neighbour was outside and overheard our conversation. I told him all about Daniel yesterday so, if he was listening, he'd know how truly mortifying this moment was for me, before he stepped in. Is he really doing this just so I can save face?

'We couldn't,' I reply.

'We still can't,' Freddie says. He stands behind me and wraps his arms around my waist. As he buries his face in my neck, I can't help but marvel at what a great actor he must be. Even I believe him, and I know it's not true. 'So, introduce me to your friends, beautiful.'

'Well, this is my dear friend, Eva,' I tell him. Suddenly, I've found my confidence. I'm not an emotional wreck, on the verge of tears. I'm cool, calm, and rubbing every last bit of it into their faces. 'And this is Daniel.'

'Her fiancé,' Daniel says.

'Ex-fiancé,' I correct him. 'We had some issues.'

'Oh, *this* is your ex,' Freddie says. 'I've heard all about you, buddy.'

Daniel begins to pace. On his fourth length of the room, he notices the dildo on the table.

'What the...?'

'Babe, you need to see the movie,' Eva tells him enthusiastically, by way of an explanation.

Damn. I think I need to see the movie, now I know that Freddie is the star. I don't know much about *Edge of Eden*, only that it's an erotic tale about an S&M-loving lawyer who has an affair with a woman he's defending. I think she's on a murder charge or something – it's a tale as old as time.

I cannot believe I've been hanging out with a movie star all this time – I can't believe he's seen me naked! Oh, my God, I can't believe I ordered a drink from him. He's probably one of the most famous men on the planet right now, and I ordered a bloody drink from him. I mean, he did make me one, but even so...

'Eva, Dan, are you stopping for lunch?' Freddie asks them, dancing with me playfully. 'We usually go back to bed right about now but...'

We're interrupted by a hotel employee, bursting through the door with Savino close behind him.

'Please, allow me to apologise,' the man says. 'A terrible mix-up. We have never had anything like this happen before, where guests have been shown into a room where other guests are already staying. Mr Tyler called to advise that he would be arriving a couple of days late, and Mrs Tyler did say Mr Tyler would be joining later...'

Crap, I did say that, didn't I? I had no idea it would occur to him to actually turn up though, and to phone ahead and tell them to expect him.

I watch as his attention switches from the group to the sex toy on the coffee table. I need to throw that thing in the sea. He just sort of shrugs it off, as though he's seen some things before. He isn't about to be fazed by your run-of-the-mill dildo.

'As a goodwill gesture, we would like to show our new guests into a new room. We only want love, here at San Valentino.'

'Oh, super,' Eva says.

'I booked a suite,' Daniel insists, redirecting his anger to the hotel employee. 'I booked a suite, so I want a suite.'

'I booked a suite,' I point out.

'We do have one more next door,' the man replies. 'But it would need to be paid for...'

'Money is no object,' Daniel replies.

Eva beams. I'll bet she thinks she's landed on her feet.

'Don't you dare touch our joint bank account,' I warn him. 'Not so you can have a holiday with your mistress.'

The poor hotel employee looks as if he wishes he could be anywhere else.

'Actually my parents gave us money as a wedding gift,' Daniel replies. 'I'll use that.'

I seethe. What an unbelievable bastard. I don't know if this is the real him or just a knee-jerk reaction to the Freddie situation, which he seems to be taking surprisingly badly.

'Please, come this way,' he tells them. 'And you are all invited to dine in Ristorante Sabatini. Perhaps tomorrow evening.'

'Awesome,' Freddie says.

As Daniel and Eva are shown the door, he looks back at me, eyeballing us with a real resentment.

As soon as they're gone, Freddie quickly lets go of me. The show is officially over.

'I'm sorry, I hope I didn't overstep the mark,' he says hurriedly. 'I could hear him, from outside, and... I don't know, I thought maybe if I pretended we were together...'

'Thank you,' I say, wiping the tear that has escaped my eye. It hasn't escaped Freddie's attention though.

'Hey, do you want me to go?' he says. 'I can give you some privacy, check in with you later?'

'Thanks,' I say.

Freddie gives my shoulder a gentle squeeze before heading back outside.

Initially, seeing Daniel just made me angry. Then, when Freddie stepped in, I started to feel smug. But it wasn't a genuine smugness. I don't actually have a movie-star lover. Still, it felt great, having them both see me here with a genuine Hollywood movie star, and not crying my eyes out over a bottle of champagne and a jar of Nutella.

Now that they're being checked into the suite next to mine... I just feel sick. The thought of sharing a wall with them makes me feel sick, knowing they're together behind, hearing them on the other side...

I feel as if I have one foot in paradise, and the other in hell, and now all I want to do is go home.

14

DAY 6

You can always rely on your best friend for good advice, and Ali's advice regarding Daniel turning up was: 'Fuck him. Fuck him and fuck his dumb little bimbo too.'

I don't imagine she meant literally, but you never know with Ali.

She told me that under no circumstances am I allowed to abandon this holiday, just because they have shown up. She says that I was here first and that I should stand my ground.

I decided not to tell her about Freddie, because I imagine her advice would be exactly the same: 'Fuck him' – and this time she would mean it literally. Ali is a firm believer that the best way to get over a man is to get under another one, but I can't do that. Even if I thought it was a good idea, I don't think I'd be brave enough to try. I'm not exactly firing on all cylinders, self-confidence-wise, at the moment.

I text her back and tell her not to worry about me, and to enjoy her date tonight. There's no sense in both of us having no love life, is there?

Someone who isn't without a love life is Daniel, my ex – do I call him my ex now? I suppose it feels weird because we never formally broke up, but we absolutely have and, if there was any doubt in my mind, the fact that I can hear Eva squealing through the wall is all the confirmation I would need.

A knock on the front door jerks me from my thoughts.

I've been holed up here since yesterday, opening the door just once, to let in my room service last night, and even then I only opened the door for a few seconds, and only wide enough to yank the poor guy delivering it through the door before closing it quickly behind him. I figured that might seem a little weird, so I had the foresight to hide (not) my dildo, but only thirty seconds before I answered the door, so it's currently living under the sofa.

I haven't ordered anything this morning though (not yet), and obviously I'm not expecting any visitors. I'm tempted to pretend I'm not in, but this isn't actually my house.

As I open the door, the bright sunlight burns my eyes, causing me to squint. I've had the various curtains and blinds closed since yesterday, because I hated the idea of Daniel and Eva frolicking around out by the pool, looking inside and seeing me by myself or, worse, not even thinking to look in my direction because they're way too wrapped up in themselves.

'I didn't realise you were a vampire,' I hear Freddie say.

As I force my eyes open, I see him standing there in front of me, the sunlight causing a sort of angelic glow around his body.

'I didn't realise you were a movie star,' I answer. 'So we'll call it a draw.'

'I wasn't keeping it from you,' he tells me. 'At first, I thought you knew, and then, when I realised you actually didn't know who I was, it was kind of nice.'

I guess I can appreciate that, and I don't feel as if he was trying to deceive me, I just feel embarrassed for not realising it was him.

'Thanks for yesterday,' I tell him. 'You did me a huge favour. I had no idea they were going to show up. It was so embarrassing.'

'I feel like there's a conversation in that,' he says.

'There is,' I reply. I don't suppose he wants to hear it. 'Well, thanks. It's no fun being single on this island, but it's even less fun when your ex turns up.'

'That's why I'm here, actually,' he says.

'Oh?'

'Can I come in?'

'Yeah, sorry,' I say, stepping aside. 'Come in.'

'I did try the terrace door first,' he says as he passes me.

'Yeah, I'm hiding,' I confess. 'And, after yesterday, having it open feels like I'm inviting trouble.'

Freddie takes a seat at the dining table, so I sit opposite him.

'Well, how would you feel about coming out of hiding?' he asks.

'Not warmly.'

'You know how I did you that big favour yesterday,' he starts.

'Yes...'

'Well – and this isn't why I did it – but I've been thinking: we can help each other.'

'You got any exes turning up, who you want me to make jealous? Because you're not going to do that with me.'

I laugh awkwardly at my self-deprecating jokes. Ali always tells me off for making fun of myself. She says that women have enough to contend with, and enough people making fun of them, so we shouldn't be doing it with each other. I think she's onto something. Ali is unapologetically herself, and she's one of the happiest people I know. She doesn't care what people think of her, and she definitely doesn't need the validation of any man. If any man dared to dump her, it's not even like they'd need to be scared (even though she can be pretty scary) because she just wouldn't care. Ali doesn't want to be around people who don't want to be around her. I've always wished I were more like Ali, but I just don't have the balls. Perhaps now that I'm single again, and I'm going to have to thicken up my skin, I should try a little harder to be more like her – at the very least with matters of the heart.

'Nothing like that.' Freddie laughs. 'I really, really want a massage, but as you know I can't get one, because they're only for couples.'

'You want me to massage you?'

Freddie laughs even harder.

'No, Lila, I want you to come for a massage with me. Think about it – we can do all the couple stuff together. And the added bonus for you is that it will piss off your ex.'

Oh, God, he probably thinks I want to massage him now. I push the embarrassment from my mind and consider his proposal.

'He didn't like seeing us together, did he?' I say.

'When I hugged you, and your robe fell open – damn, I thought he was going to explode with anger.'

He really did. I've never seen such a fire under him.

'That was a nice touch, by the way. It's none of my business why you were wearing it in the first place, but...' I think he sees me wincing. 'No matter what you want to do, I think you'll enjoy screwing with him.'

'So, we're just going to pretend to be together, so we can do the couples' stuff?' I ask, to clarify, because I'm worried I've got the wrong end of the stick here.

'Exactly,' he replies with enthusiasm. 'Why should we suffer because we're single?'

I can't believe a movie star is lumping us together in the same sad, single slump. He really could have any girl he wanted. I suppose being here, surrounded by couples, there are no single girls for him to bag, other than me by some weird coincidence and, come on, he wouldn't look twice at me, and I'm not even getting into what leagues we're in as far as attractiveness goes (spoiler: we are not in the same league) but so far all he has seen is me being a nightmare, turning up with more baggage than Mariah Carey, bickering with my ex – who has already moved on. I am not at my most attractive right now and definitely only being invited to hang around with Freddie by default, but that's okay. I want to do all the fun stuff the island has to offer, and of course I want to rub Daniel's face in it a little. Well, that's what he's doing with me, staying here with Eva. If he were any kind of man, when he turned up and found out I was here, he would have turned around and gone home. Although I suppose if he were any kind of man, he wouldn't have cheated on me in the first place.

I have this weird reflex to try and steal him back. Not because I want him, but because I begrudge him being happy with his bit on the side. I can't believe he was going to go through with marrying me; that's what I can't get my head around. I think perhaps he wanted to have his wedding cake and eat it too, and Eva was going to let him. I wonder, if I hadn't rumbled him, how long he would've continued two-timing me. We'd be sitting here right now, living it up in paradise, without a care in the world. I'd be blissfully ignorant while he'd be sneaking off to call her.

Oh, the anger is rumbling inside me, just looking for a way to come out. You know what, a massage is exactly what I need.

'A showmance sounds like fun,' I tell him.

'Showmance? I like that,' he replies. 'Want to go for one now?'

I hesitate.

'You need to hold your head high,' he tells me. 'You deserve much better than him, and she's got nothing on you.'

'All right, fine, let's go,' I say with an awkward smile. 'You don't need to bombard me with flattery. I'll go get ready.'

'OK, cool,' he replies. 'Shall I open the curtains?'

'Sure,' I say. 'I'm ready to face the world now.'

Freddie opens the curtain to reveal Daniel and Eva in the pool outside. His movements catch their eye, causing them to peer inside. Freddie gives them a big smile and a wave, which Daniel ignores, but Eva reciprocates so eagerly she falls off her lilo.

I can't help but smile – at all of it.

Freddie turns around and gives me a wink.

'See,' he starts. 'This is going to drive him mad.'

15

Usually I'm pretty good at thinking things through. I might not be the most organised, or have the best ideas, but I do think about things and try to do my best.

Take my wedding – well, my attempted wedding – for example. I did absolutely everything I could to make sure that the day went well. From the seating plans to the food, to the location. I thought it through.

The same goes for my house. I could've insisted that the first room we decorated was my office – that's what Daniel said we could do, when he convinced me we should put in an offer. But then, when we actually moved in and realised we had to live there, I put my office on the back-burner in favour of having a decent kitchen and bathroom – because I can write on my laptop anywhere, but I can only use the bathroom as a bathroom, right?

I feel as if these examples were decisions and plans I made with a clear head and a positive mindset. They were all for the bigger picture, to make the rest of my life better.

Today, I don't think I thought things through, but today I wasn't thinking about the bigger picture.

Blinded by a need for revenge and a desire to enjoy the finer things of the island, I decided to couple-up with Freddie. In theory, this is a win–win situation, because I get to make Daniel jealous, and enjoy a massage.

In practice, I cannot believe how little I have thought this through. I've been after a massage in the hotel spa for days now, and with Freddie by my side I can actually get a couple's massage... but therein lies the problem. Freddie is by my side, right by my side.

All I thought about, regarding the couple's massage, was that I could have to be in a couple to get one. What I didn't consider was that a couple's massage involves us both being massaged at the same time and, so that we can be massaged at the same time, we are lying side by side, absolutely starkers.

We are lying face down on the massage tables, only small white towels covering our backsides. It was kind of awkward, when they told us to take our clothes off, because the two people who would be doing the massages gave us some privacy, but we didn't have any privacy from each other. We spent so long trying to work out exactly how we both got naked, without exposing anything to anyone, that the massagers assumed we were already in place and walked in on us awkwardly trying to lie down, without actually getting properly naked.

We were so awkward, in fact, that when they placed the little armrest between our tables, designed so that loved-up couples can hold hands while they have their massage, we had no choice but to do it, otherwise we would've looked even weirder.

So here we are, me and Freddie, a man I met only a few days ago, in this candlelit room, with romantic music pumping into the air and the sweet smell of cocoa butter filling our nostrils, holding hands as we're massaged.

The massage itself feels glorious, but the awkward situation with Freddie leaves me feeling stressed. I feel sorry for the masseuse working on me, because as fast as she is massaging my stress away, my brain is creating fresh stuff.

We have pillows positioned perfectly so that we can look into each other's eyes. I've mostly been keeping mine closed, but when I open them for a second, Freddie either smiles at me or cringes playfully. I suppose this could have been much weirder, with a different stranger. Thankfully we both know exactly where we stand in this fake relationship – awkwardly close together, but completely platonically.

Thankfully, we were told beforehand that this would be a silent massage. We were encouraged to hold one another's hand and stare deep into each other's eyes, but to try not to speak, instead focusing on the relaxing ambience and the love in the room.

I know I'm only here with Freddie because needs must, but if things had gone to plan I would be here with Daniel and, if I'm being completely honest, I can't imagine being here with Daniel.

I met Daniel four years ago, at a time when I was not expecting to meet anyone. It was just before I signed my first book deal, when I was struggling to get published. After you write your first book and begin the demoralising process of trying to find an agent or a publisher or both, you realise that writing the book might have been the easy part.

I've never been the type to think that everything will work out fine, just because I want it to. So I didn't exactly send my book out into the world thinking that I'd absolutely get a book deal, but I wouldn't have sent it if I didn't think it was good – great, even.

I sent it out and the waiting was agony... and then the rejection letters started coming through, and that felt much worse.

The first thing people tell you is that J. K. Rowling received a whole bunch of rejection letters before the first Harry Potter book was published, and now she's the first female billionaire author. I suppose, technically, that should have been comforting, but I know that for every J. K. Rowling there are a lot more authors who never make it, and I was worried about becoming one of those.

I think I had these fantasies about giving up the job I hated to become a bestselling novelist. I know now that it doesn't work like that, that it takes years and years of hard work and multiple books before you can do this gig comfortably.

Little did I know, just as I decided I was about to give up, I was just days away from signing my first book deal. Before I got the good news, I decided that I needed to get another job, so I made an appointment to see a recruiter.

With my degree in English and a few years working a social media job under my belt, I decided to try and find a copywriting gig. It might not be what I wanted to write, but it was writing that involved more than 140 characters.

I went into the meeting with the recruiter and I was sat down in front of this hipster-looking guy. He was skinny, with blown-back hair and a long shaggy beard. He was dressed in a suit that made him look fresh out of *Peaky Blinders*, as if perhaps he should be working in an overpriced barbers' shop and not a recruitment firm. Coupled with his South Yorkshire accent, that seemed so out of place amongst all the southerners, which only made him stand out and seem like someone from a bygone era even more. It was Daniel.

At first, he asked me questions about my work experience and my career goals, but then his questions got a little more personal. He started asking me what I did for fun and what my favourites foods were. I thought it was a little unorthodox, but I just went with it – after all, I really wanted to change my job, and Daniel was easy on the eye.

I didn't get the job, but I did get a date with Daniel. The good book news arrived a few days after our first date, and as things went from strength to strength with my work and my feelings for Daniel growing, I was on top of the world.

Daniel wasn't like the other boys, which I liked and found a little frustrating in equal measure.

I liked that he wasn't a 'lad lad lad' type. He'd never dream of going on a messy boys' holiday to Magaluf, coming back with a fiery red sunburn and a really bad case of chlamydia. Even though he enjoyed watching football, he was the furthest thing from a hooligan you could imagine, and the word 'banter' just isn't in his vocabulary. I never worried about him playing the field, juggling birds on Match, Tinder, Plenty of Fish and Bumble, serial dating a bunch of girls while he was dating me. I think that's why his affair has jarred me so severely, because you kind of expect the people you're dating to be dating other people in the early days, but Daniel just wasn't interested in anyone else and it wasn't long before we made things exclusive and official.

On the other hand, the thing that I wasn't so sure about with Daniel was his lack of explicit emotion. It took me a little while to realise we were actually dating. At first things seemed way more casual, with Daniel not exactly showing his affectionate side. I had to make the first move when it came to our first kiss – and when it came to the first time we had sex, weeks later, which was slower than you'd expect from your average male. Eventually, he did say his feelings out loud for me, but that touchy-feely, tactile side of things I usually love in a relationship never came. But that was Daniel. I figured he was just the silent type – your stereotypical northerner, not really wearing his heart on his sleeve.

So, I suppose, with Daniel never really being a fan of the mushy stuff, I knew that coming here was only going to be so romantic. I think I hoped that being on Valentine Island would bring out a bit more of his mushy side, but I knew at the back of my mind that I wouldn't get him to do anything like this.

I suppose, with that in mind, even if the wedding had gone ahead, I wouldn't actually have had anyone to do this stuff with and I'd be in the same position as I am now. And with a hubby in tow, there would have been no way I could've struck a deal with Freddie to coast through the holiday as a friendship couple.

Suddenly, I feel a little less stressed. Just as the massage ends.

The masseur and masseuse excuse themselves, so that Freddie and I can put our clothes back on.

'Well, that was weird, wasn't it?' he jokes, still lying face down on the table.

I make no attempt to move either.

'Just a bit,' I say. 'I didn't realise just how couply a couple's massage would be.'

'Well, now we know.'

'Now we know,' I reply, returning his smile.

'Would you like to get up first or second?' he asks.

'Hmm, first,' I say, unable to see a reason for either, other than getting my clothes back on as soon as possible.

Freddie buries his face deep in the cushion, so that I have as much privacy as possible. I hurry on my bikini, my jean shorts and my white Hollister crop top.

'Done,' I say as I let my bun down, allowing my long hair to fall around my face.

'That was fast,' he replies.

'Yeah, I learnt my lesson from earlier, when they walked in on us trying to hide behind towels.'

'I'll be quick, then,' he replies.

I dutifully turn around while Freddie gets dressed.

Facing the sideboard, where all the lotions are kept, I admire the candles sitting on top. In addition to the relaxing flicker of light coming from them, there's an absolutely delicious smell; I can't quite put my finger on what it is. As I lean close to take a big whiff, I find myself at eye-level with the mirror, and in the mirror I see Freddie, butt naked, from behind. He looks so fit and muscular, like a regular superhero...

I freak out at my accidental perving and jolt upright. As I do, my hair whips one of the candles over, which quickly causes a towel on the table to catch fire.

'Oh, fuck,' I blurt.

Freddie, who has hurried into his shorts, quickly soaks another towel in the sink and places it on top of the burning one to put the flames out. He is successful, but not before the smoke alarm on the ceiling starts going off.

'What happened?' he asks me, just as panicked staff members start flooding into the room.

'I, erm... I don't know,' I lie.

Well, I'm not about to tell him how hot under the collar he made me, am I?

16

Tonight, Freddie and I are going for dinner together... and I'm weirdly terrified.

With my break-up being so fresh, and so out of the blue, I haven't had much time to think about what happens next, but I suppose I'm going to have to go on a date with another man at some point, unless I want to die alone, which no one wants, do they?

In a way, going on a date with Freddie is a lot less pressure, because there is nothing romantic between us, so it's not as if I need it to go especially well. On the other hand, just because I don't need it to go well, doesn't mean that I shouldn't aim for that.

Take earlier, for example. If that had been my and Freddie's first-day date, it would have been an absolute disaster (or, if by some miracle we'd stayed together, one hell of a story to tell our grandkids). First of all, it was awkward. So awkward. From the getting naked in front of each other, to the forced hand-holding – and then there's the icing on the cake, you know, when I set the room on fire. I don't think I'd ever go on a second date with someone who caused a fire, just by being their awkward self, even if they were a movie star. Which brings me on to my next point...

Freddie is one of the hottest men in the world right now, in terms of both how famous he is, and how incredibly sexy he is. On the one hand, in the outside world, Freddie would never look twice at a girl like me – he wouldn't even end up in a room with a girl like me – so it's amazing that I've ended up at a candlelit dinner table with him. If you're going to have a trial-run first date with anyone, why not practise on the sexiest man alive, right? Not my words (although I am tempted to say it), the words of *People* magazine, in their annual Sexiest Man Alive feature.

While I was in the bath, getting ready for this evening, I did what any self-respecting girl would do. I did my due diligence on my date – even if it's not a real date. Normally I'd just type my date's name (or, in more recent years, Ali's date's name – because she isn't as security conscious as I am) into social media and troll through pictures of his ex-girlfriends and holidays. With Freddie, finding out what I want to know about him is the easiest thing in the world, because the Internet is full of everything you could possibly want to know about Freddie Bianchi, and the more I read, the more I want to know.

If there's one thing I know about the *Edge of Eden* books, it is that they have been responsible for the sexual awakening of many a woman. I low-key knew this when the first book blew up, and everyone and their aunt (literally, their aunt, which isn't a pleasant thought for anyone) couldn't stop talking about it, and what an incredible read it was, and how it has spiced up their sex lives. I've never really been into erotic fiction, so I've always given the series a wide berth, and then when the movie came out at the end of last year, I gave that a miss too.

I can forgive myself for not recognising Freddie. In real life, he doesn't bear too much of a resemblance to the character he plays – Edward Eden, a big-shot attorney with a penchant for justice and BDSM. Freddie looks like a cross between an LA surfer dude and a Muscle Beach colossus. He has longish, messy brown hair, a bit like Kit Harington from *Game of Thrones*, and a very laid-back dress sense. Edward Eden, on the other hand, wears a suit throughout the entire movie – in fact, the only times when he isn't wearing a suit, he's completely naked (at least that's what I read – I'm considering verifying this for myself). His hair is much darker – practically black – and always slicked back. He has this sort of moody, brooding look about him, whereas Freddie almost always has a loveable smile on his face.

I love that I'm talking about them as if they are two different people, when it's actually just one person acting. He must be a good actor, because when he walked into my suite yesterday and kissed me on the cheek in front of Daniel, I genuinely thought he'd hit his head in the pool or something.

'Well, it might suck that your ex turned up, but at least it scored us this dinner tonight,' Freddie says, across our candlelit table.

Oh, I'd kind of forgotten about this. Of course, this is our free dinner, and not just something Freddie has organised because – all together now – this is not a real date.

'Yeah,' I reply. 'The silver lining.'

'You look absolutely stunning, by the way,' he says.

I look down at my black Bardot cocktail dress, with the lace-up front. Another dress I bought just for my honeymoon, which I purchased with a particular fantasy in mind. One might argue that wearing it to dinner with a super-buff American movie star is way more of a fantasy than wearing it with your skinny northern husband, but it just reminds me of everything I've lost.

'You don't have to compliment me, no one is around,' I remind him, although I suppose it is a good habit to get into, for when we do have an audience.

'Maybe I meant it,' he says.

Maybe he did, but it's more likely he didn't.

At night, the vibe in Sabatini is completely different. The mood shifts, from cool and casual Italian coffee bar to a romantic Italian restaurant. Everything is the same, from the white marble tables to the leafy green plants all around the room. The only things that are different are the music and the lights. Impossibly romantic-sounding Italian music is playing, loud enough for you to hear, but quiet enough to allow for a decent conversation, and the lights are low – most of the light is coming from the candles on the table and the little fairy lights that hide in the leaves of the plants. With the way the tables are spaced out, with more distance than usual between them, and the lighting positioned just right, to make each table exist in its own little spotlight, it is easy to forget that anyone else is here. Until the waiter drops by, of course.

Speaking of the waiter, he places our starters down in front of us. Freddie is having Milanese meatballs, served in a tomato sauce with Gran Moravia cheese. As the waiter places it down in front of him, his eyes light up.

'This is actually the fourth time I've had these since I arrived,' he tells me. 'They're just so good.'

They must be, if he's so set in his ways with them. I wonder how long he's been here, and why he decided to come to Valentine Island, of all places, all alone.

I'm just a little jealous of Freddie's meatballs, until my Sicilian arancini are placed down in front of me. Hand-rolled risotto balls, made with mozzarella cheese and peas, coated in breadcrumbs, and served with a red pepper tapenade – they smell absolutely incredible. I can hardly wait for the waiter to leave before I am reaching for my fork.

'At least we can talk while we do this,' Freddie says.

'That's true,' I agree, although I'm a lot more enthusiastic about the eating than I am the talking.

As Freddie tucks into his meatballs something occurs to me.

'Are you Italian?' I ask him.

'Me?' he replies. He seems a little confused by me asking. 'Oh, no, you mean because of my surname? No, I'm not Italian. My real name is Freddie Wells.'

'Freddie Wells sounds like an actor's name,' I say between eager mouthfuls.

'It does,' he replies. 'Because it is – there is already a famous Freddie Wells. So, when it came to picking a new name, I decide to honour someone who had always believed in me, Miss Bianchi, my drama teacher.'

'Wow, that's really nice,' I say.

'Yeah, she was stoked when I told her. She's always been really proud of me. She says I'm her finest work.'

'Well, there's no one bigger than you right now,' I reply.

'You didn't even know who I was,' he says with a wild laugh, one that shows off his perfect white teeth, his cute dimples, and the twinkle in his eyes.

'I know... I'm so embarrassed.'

'Don't be,' he insists. 'I like it. Things have been so crazy... too crazy. No one knew who I was before the *Eden* movie and I knew that things would change, I just didn't know how much. I can't go anywhere. I can't do anything. Things like going for coffee or to the store for toilet paper – I can't do them, not without it making TMZ. Everyone wants to know what I'm wearing and who I'm dating, and I just couldn't take it any more.'

'See, being famous seems so attractive to plebs like me. But you make it sound awful...'

'It isn't awful,' he says. 'Or, at least, it isn't always awful. It's amazing, to finally have an acting role in a picture that people want to see. The money is great, and the special treatment isn't unwelcome... but I just needed a break. The press constantly trying to find out who you are dating – when you aren't dating anyone – gets pretty tiresome. They don't think you're single, they think you're hiding something. It's just too much sometimes, which is how I ended up here.'

I savour my last mouthful of arancini, devastated to be nearing the end of my starter, but excited for my main course. I feel as if I'm eating for fun now, and for the flavours, rather than because I want to get fat out of spite – because that would teach Daniel a lesson, right? (Wrong, it absolutely wouldn't.)

'So, why did you decide to come here?' I ask. 'To Valentine Island...'

'Why did you?' he replies, putting my question back to me.

'Erm, because I'd already paid for it,' I tell him. 'And because I wanted to get away, fast, and this was already booked for the day I just so happened to be wanting somewhere to escape to.'

'That checks out,' he replies. 'For me... I guess, I wanted to escape too, but I didn't really know where to go. I thought about trying to find a private island, but I just wanted peace. I didn't want to be all by myself.'

'I can just imagine you going full Tom Hanks in *Cast Away*,' I joke.

'Well, thankfully I wound up here, with you as my Wilson, rather than being stranded by myself, trying to crack open coconuts.'

I laugh.

'Why did you choose here specifically though? Didn't you know it was for couples?'

'I did, actually,' he replies. 'It's sort of like hiding in plain sight. I figured, everyone here is going to be too loved-up to even notice me.'

'How's that working out?' I ask.

'If I wear my sunglasses and keep my hair messy, I don't know, it's like most people can't quite place me, because they only know me from the movie. But then there are people like your, er, ex-friend, who can recognise me instantly.'

'Can I get you more drinks?' the waiter asks.

'Yes, can I have a porn star martini, please?' I reply.

Freddie orders a Peroni.

'I can't drink too many cocktails,' he tells me. 'They're too sweet.'

'If you're not actually a barman, how did you get so good at making them?'

'I used to be a barman,' he tells me. 'Right up until I landed the *Eden* role, I was still working bar jobs around my small roles. The small roles don't really pay.'

'And the big roles?' I ask casually, jokily playing it down.

'Yeah, they pay better.' He laughs.

'What's the first thing you bought?' I ask curiously. 'I've always wondered what the first big thing I spent money on would be, if I came into real money.'

'Ah, it's nothing cool,' he says, fidgeting with his cutlery as his cheeks flush.

'Oh, now I really want to know what it was,' I say excitedly.

My mind races, wondering what uncool thing he could've bought with his first big pay cheque. Perhaps he's a model-train enthusiast, or maybe he collects something not all that exciting, like stamps or coins.

'You sure you want to know?'

'Oh, I'm so sure,' I reply.

'I paid my parents' mortgage,' he confesses. 'Not exactly rock 'n' roll, hmm?'

I feel my jaw drop.

'I was expecting something lame,' I tell him. 'That's amazing. I'd love to do that for my mum and dad. I'd love to do that for myself!'

'Where is your house?'

'It's in London. Not the nice part though. You need to head out pretty far before you can find something affordable. We bought a fixer-upper.'

'You and your ex?'

'Yep,' I reply. 'Not sure what's going to happen with that yet. I'm scared to even think about it.'

The waiter saves me from a difficult conversation by placing our drinks down in front of us.

'Are you finished with the starters?' he asks. We say yes.

As the waiter clears our plates, I take a sip of my drink and he notices an expression on my face that I didn't realise was there.

'Is everything okay with the drink?' he asks.

'Oh, yes, sorry... it's lovely.'

He doesn't look convinced.

'Is everything okay with the drink?' Freddie asks.

I laugh.

'It's just... it's not as good as the one you made me,' I admit.

'It's nice to know I still have it,' he replies proudly, but then his face falls.

'What's wrong?' I ask.

He gestures to our left with a dart of his eyes. I look and see Daniel and Eva being seated next to us. Oh, wonderful! I wonder what the chances are, but these tables are the luxury tables, reserved for luxury villa guests. I can't believe he's here, with her, using money that was supposed to be a gift for both of us. I can't believe he kept the money; it should be returned, like all the other gifts.

While Eva seems quite preoccupied, trying to see through Freddie's shirt through willpower alone, Daniel stares daggers at us.

I notice Freddie waving at them and realise it's in response to Eva, who seems to think she's on waving terms with him now.

'I don't know what else to do,' he tells me through gritted teeth.

'It's fine,' I say quietly. 'Let's not let them ruin dinner.'

'Nothing is going to ruin my calzone,' he replies. 'It feels good, to take a break from clean eating.'

I quickly glance over at them but they're no longer looking over, they're looking at the menu and laughing together, something so simple, but it makes me so jealous.

'Hey,' Freddie says, trying to take my attention away from them. 'You okay?'

'I'm... fine.'

I don't sound remotely fine; you can hear it in my voice. I can't hide it.

'Hey, can I get a porn star martini, please?' Freddie asks the waiter.

I give him a puzzled smile.

'Everything is going to be okay,' he tells me as he reaches out to hold my hand. As Freddie caresses my hand with his, I feel a shiver of something run up my arm and down through my body, but then I realise he's doing it for Daniel and Eva's benefit – for the sake of my showmance – so I quickly nip my excitement in the bud.

'Thank you,' I mouth to him.

'I promise you, you are going to have an incredible holiday, no matter what,' he insists.

I smile.

'I hope so.'

The waiter places Freddie's cocktail down in front of him. He picks up the shot glass of champagne.

'Grab yours,' he says.

'My drink?'

'Yeah, we're toasting,' he replies. 'That's what you said you do, right? With your free mini drink.'

'Oh, God, that is what I said, isn't it?' I reply with an awkward laugh.

'You did, so come on,' he insists, raising his glass.

I do as he says.

'What are we toasting?'

'To us,' he says. 'And our honeymoon period.'

'To our honeymoon period,' I say.

I can feel my smile stretching so wide across my face, I'm worried it's going to run out of space. As Freddie rubs my hand I can feel my cheeks growing warmer – I hope it doesn't show.

I just need to remind myself that he's acting... and he's doing a great job too, because I've never seen Daniel look more jealous.

17

DAY 7

I have woken up in a remarkably good mood, which is not something I anticipated, given that I'm on my honeymoon without a husband *and* with my ex and his new bird in the room next door.

Last night Freddie and I finished our meal and left the restaurant as soon as possible. We had a one-course lead on Daniel and Eva, which meant we could get out of there before they did.

We enjoyed a nice slow walk back up to the villa, stopping at the viewing point halfway up the hill to take in the view. It doesn't matter what time of day it is, or what the weather is like, this place is always gorgeous, no matter which direction you're looking in.

As we got to our front doors my mood slipped a little, the thought of going inside alone and knowing Daniel and Eva would be coming back together weighing heavy on my mind. Freddie couldn't have been cuter though, doing a bit about getting me home before my curfew my parents set, and saying he'd better not kiss me, in case my dad was watching. It was the perfect (not real) end to a perfect (not real) date.

It was nice, walking with Freddie, getting to know more about him – more than you'd find out by watching his Jimmy Kimmel interview. OK, yes, I did look up a few of his interviews after I got home last night, just because I was curious and because I could.

I have to say, TV Freddie and real Freddie are pretty much the same person. Even when he's doing an interview, with adoring fans in the audience and a famous interviewer asking him about his massive success, he's still so down to earth. It's almost as if he doesn't know how to be a movie star yet, as if he missed the memo that says he's supposed to be an arsehole – a designer-clothes-wearing, model-shagging, egotistical arsehole.

So when I heard Daniel and Eva arrive home last night, I kept myself distracted with videos of Freddie for a while, and after hearing him talk about the *Edge of Eden* movie, I'm really tempted to watch it. Visually Freddie might look the part, but I can't imagine someone so sweet and a little shy playing the role of an S&M-loving playboy lawyer.

This morning I'm sitting outside on my terrace, catching some rays in my bikini. It's still early, so it's not all that hot and sunny yet, but I'm making the most of my alone time on the terrace.

I worked so hard, to look good in my wedding dress – and my honeymoon bikini – but it still doesn't feel like enough. Of course, as women, we're under a lot of pressure from Instagram and magazines, but I think most of the pressure comes from ourselves and this belief we have that we need to look a certain way. When was the last time you looked at a woman at the beach and thought to yourself: damn, she'd look perfect, if she just lost 6 lbs? No, me neither.

I suspect I don't need to lose weight, I need to gain confidence, but it's not always that simple, is it?

I just love the way it smells here, but I can't quite describe what it smells like. I feel as if, no matter where I am, even if I'm in one of the bars, it smells like outside, like a mixture of the ocean and the trees. I wish I could bottle it up and take it home with me, although I'll bet it would only give me the post-holiday blues every time I caught a whiff.

The sound of the phone ringing inside catches my attention – not my phone though, the suite phone. It's the first time I've heard it ring, so I hurry inside and answer it with caution.

'Hello?'

'*Buongiorno, signora,*' a man's voice says. 'This is Lorenzo, calling from the hotel. Just to say, you have a visitor here.'

My face tightens with confusion.

'A visitor?'

'*Sì*, a visitor.'

'Erm, okay, I'll be right there...'

How on earth do I have a visitor? I am in Italy... on an island!

I grab a black maxi dress and hurry it on over my bikini, before making my way down the hill to the hotel. Fuelled by curiosity, for the first time, I don't waste any time taking in the view as I usually would.

Could this be Daniel's weird way of getting to me, on my own, so that we can talk? Normally, I wouldn't think he would be so sneaky, but it turns out he has this sneaky side I've never been aware of.

There's no sign of Daniel inside the busy hotel lobby, but as I scan the room I do notice a familiar face, although, if I'm being completely honest, it isn't the face I notice first...

'*Hola,*' Ali screams at the top of her voice as soon as she claps eyes on me.

She's wearing a gold one-piece, although to call it a one-piece seems generous, it's maybe a third of a one-piece, thanks to the fact it has more cut-outs than a paper snowflake. Her bottom half is covered by a pair of black harem pants – I'd imagine (or at least really, really hope) that she had some kind of top on for the journey, which she whipped off the second she arrived.

As Ali hurries over to me, dragging her suitcase along behind her, she turns the head of every man in the room. A sixty-something man has an especially good gawp at her chest – the best fake boobs the Czech Republic has to offer she told me, after arriving home from holiday with them one day. Well, all she told me was that she was going on holiday – she neglected to mention that it was a cosmetic surgery holiday.

'All right, granddad, pick your jaw up off the floor,' she says to him as she struts past him.

'Ali,' I say, a combination of shocked, confused and delighted – the exact combination of feelings she gives her dates.

'Hola, Lila,' she says as she squeezes me.

'Ali, you're in Italy, not Spain,' I remind her. 'Oh, my God, you're in Italy – why are you in Italy?'

'I came to see you,' she says. 'Duh!'

'You pop to someone's house to see them, not their holiday.' I laugh. 'Not that I'm not over the moon to see you.'

'Well, when you said Daniel had shown up, I thought you might need some moral support. I cleared my diary, booked a flight and here I am.'

'Is that new?' I ask about her swimsuit.

'The twins need support too,' she says.

I don't think I've seen her sunglasses before either, now that I come to think of it.

'Did you really come all this way just because you were worried about me, with Daniel being around?'

'Of course,' she replies. 'And I blew off my date with the department-store heir – I should be twisted up like a pretzel, having my forty-fifth orgasm, and instead I'm here, looking out for you.'

I give her a look – a look deep into her soul.

'And, well, he was minging, and a holiday sounded nice. A holiday with my best friend!'

She hugs me again.

'Come on, let me show you the villa,' I say.

Ali dances on the spot excitedly. It's a miracle her breasts stay in her swimsuit – well, I think it's a miracle they stay in. The men in the lobby think it's a crying shame.

I'm excited to have my best friend here with me. Ali knows me inside and out, and she knows exactly what I've been through with Daniel, so she'll know what I'm thinking and feeling before I do. She's the shoulder I've needed to cry on for days, although I suppose I've stopped crying now.

I can't wait to show her the villa and the pool, and everything else the island has to offer. Now that she's here, I wish I'd just invited her from the start, although I'm sure she would've been gutted, to miss out on embarrassing Daniel on his wedding day.

'I'm not loving huffing and puffing up this hill,' Ali pants. 'This cozzie is going right up my arse.'

'It's a lovely walk,' I tell her. 'It's just easier in flats.'

'Never met a flat I liked,' she tells me, as if I don't already know. 'Oh, this is cute.'

She pauses to catch her breath and admire the archways.

'It must be nice, to be here with someone you love.'

'Are you saying you don't love me, bitch?' she jokes.

'I love you more than anyone,' I tell her.

'*Ciao,*' a male voice says, snapping us from our conversation.

I jump out of my skin. This is the first time I've crossed paths with anyone on this path.

'Oh, hello,' I say.

'*Ciao,*' he says again, but he's only looking at Ali. I'm used to this though – Ali commands the attention of men wherever she goes.

Ali smiles, but doesn't say anything. This is a strategic move that never fails her. Men want her anyway, but they want her even more if she acts as if she isn't interested.

The man is tall with olive skin – he's definitely Italian. His glossy jet-black hair is slicked back, and he's wearing a black shirt, which is a tell-tale sign that he works here. There is something undeniably attractive about the Italian accent. He could be saying anything and I'd be swooning – even just repeatedly saying '*ciao*' with his jaw on the floor as he gawps at my friend.

'Is everything okay?' I ask, to try and move things along.

'*Sì,*' he says. 'I deliver champagne to one of the other couples.'

Ergh, that will be Daniel and Eva – wait, does he think that Ali and I are a couple?

'Oh—' I start, but Ali doesn't let me finish.

'Lovely,' she says. 'We might have to do the same, right, babes?'

Is she talking to me?

'Erm, right,' I say.

The man, a bizarre combination of dejected and excited, heads back down the hill in his cart.

'Did you just make out like we were a couple?' I ask her.

'Yeah,' she replies casually. 'He works here. I'm not gonna shag someone who works here.'

'Newsflash, babe,' I start mockingly. 'This is Valentine Island. The clue is in the title: everyone is already in love. So when you're climbing the walls in a couple of days, you won't be so fussy.'

'I'll be fine, so long as you still have Barry.'

'Barry?' I ask.

'Yeah, you know, the stowaway in your suitcase...'

She wiggles her eyebrows.

'Oh, God, that thing? I threw it in the sea.'

'You threw it in the sea?'

'Well, no, I didn't throw it in the sea – I was worried a dolphin might choke on it.'

'Not if it knows what it's doing,' she jokes.

'Oi, come on,' I say, laughing as I take her by the hand and drag her the last bit of the way to the villa.

I watch as she looks back at the hotel employee – who is absolutely staring at her arse. She gives him a seductive little wave over her shoulder. Ali is truly a master. I could learn so much from her, were it not for my complete lack of confidence.

'Oh, wow,' she says as she claps eyes on the villa. 'This place is the shit.'

'It is,' I reply with a laugh. I can't believe how delighted I am to have her here. I feel like a scared little kid whose cool older sister has just shown up to show me how to do my eyeliner and to scare away the bullies. 'I should probably tell you, Daniel and Eva are staying in the suite next door.'

'Of course, they are,' she replies. 'I dare them to come out while I'm here. So, show me where I'm sleeping.'

I absolutely love that she's just turned up to stay with me. It speaks volumes about our relationship, that she feels as if she can – and that I'm delighted to have her here.

'There's a king bed upstairs and a really big, really comfortable sofa down here,' I reply.

'I'll take the sofa,' she says, eyeing it up. 'Just in case I pull, I don't have to wake you up.'

'Ahh, just like old times, when we swapped bedrooms in our flat so yours was nearer the front door and the bathroom.'

I say this with a real nostalgic tone, but at the time, it was a nightmare. I liked a wild night out as much as the best of them, but not like

Ali. Ali is always on it, 24/7. I liked an early night every now and then, and her entrances with her friends or her gentleman friends were very noisy and always in the a.m. The straw that broke the camel's back came when she only just made it through the front door before pouncing on her date in the hallway, right outside my bedroom door. The other bedroom was on the other side of the kitchen, so we swapped. At the very least, it lessened the sound effects.

'So, we need to go shopping,' she says. 'We need crisps, and lemon pop, and some alcohol and, oh, some Nutella. And we can just chill by the pool and chat, and I fucking dare Daniel and Eva to come outside.'

'That sounds wonderful,' I reply. 'There are plenty of shops so, if you want to put some pants on, we could take a stroll down?'

'Back down the hill?'

'Yes.'

'Only to come back up?' she whines.

'That's how hills work.'

'Okay, fine, but I'm fine like this, right? We're on holiday – I don't need pants.'

'You don't always think you need pants in London,' I tease.

There's a knock at the door.

'If that's the stare-y guy from before, tell him I'm not interested,' she says.

'Aren't you? He was handsome.'

'I'm low-key interested in a way that he doesn't need to know about yet,' she replies.

'Got it.'

I open the door, ready to give one of my speeches to one of Ali's rejected lovers – sometimes I'll take the kind route of 'it's not you, it's her', other times I'll get a little creative, saying that Ali has moved abroad to work for charity or they're sending her into space to see if she can communicate with aliens. If I'm feeling especially uncreative, but want something effective, I'll tell people she's at the gynaecologist's.

'Oh,' I say, when I open the door. It isn't one of Ali's admirers (although it probably will be, because it's a male), it's one of my fake ones.

'Well, that's not the reaction I expected.' Freddie laughs.

'Sorry, hello,' I say. 'I completely forgot we were meeting today.'

'Holy... fucking... shit,' I hear Ali say behind me.

'Good morning to you too,' Freddie says cheekily, waving at her.

'Ho-o-o-o-oly, fucking...'

'For future reference, this is how people usually react to meeting me,' Freddie leans in and tells me quietly. 'Not ask me to make them a drink.'

'Har-har,' I reply. 'Freddie, this is Ali. Ali, this is—'

'Edward Eden,' she says with a gasp.

'Only on the weekends,' he jokes as he offers Ali a hand to shake. Instead, Ali rushes over to him and hugs him, as if she knows him intimately.

'Do you know how many times I've touched myself to your movie?'

Oh, she does know him intimately.

'I understand why you're hiding on an island now,' I tell him.

He just laughs. I'm guessing he's used to this.

'What are you doing here?' she asks him. 'Why are you talking to her?'

I'm 'her' now, am I? I was 'babe' when we met the hotel employee.

'I'm here for my date with Lila. We're—'

'Oh, no, don't worry, this is my best friend, Ali,' I babble. 'You can tell her it's not a real date. Freddie has been helping me annoy Daniel, by pretending we're a thing. We're not a thing though.'

'We're not a thing,' Freddie echoes.

'Can I get in on this?' she asks. 'I love annoying Daniel.'

'Sorry, Fred, can we reschedule? I had no idea Ali was going to turn up but—'

'You are absolutely not rescheduling,' Ali insists. 'Go for your date. I'll just get acquainted with the pool.'

'Can you give me five minutes?' I ask Freddie.

'Sure,' he says. 'I'll wait outside. My manager has asked me to call him. Great to meet you, Ali.'

'Marry me,' she jokingly calls after him. She waits until we're alone before she says anything else. '"Fred"? You're on nickname terms with Freddie "fuck me" Bianchi?'

I don't know if that's a movie reference or just something my friend is hoping for.

I never call him Fred. I don't know why it came out so casually.

'Yeah, he's my neighbour. We've been hanging out. He pretended to be my... lover, I guess, to piss Daniel off when he turned up with Eva. It was so embarrassing, he really saved me.'

'Why didn't you tell me?' she asks.

'Because you just asked him to marry you,' I remind her. 'You interested?'

'Oh, I'm the most interested I've ever been,' she replies. 'But I'd never do that to you.'

'We're not a real couple,' I point out. 'There's no way he's interested in me. I'm not a movie star's type. You are.'

'Honey, I'm everyone's type,' she reminds me. 'But Girl Code is Girl Code. He's already yours.'

'He's pretending to be mine,' I tell her.

'Girl Code,' she says simply, with a shrug of her shoulders. 'Now go and shag him on the beach.'

'I think we're just going for a walk,' I tell her. 'Have dinner with me later?'

'Sure,' she replies. 'I'll go for a swim, catch some rays and then get ready.'

'Great,' I reply. 'I can't wait.'

Ali walks up to me and looks me straight in the eye.

'Are you honestly telling me you don't fancy him?'

'We're just friends,' I tell her.

'Hmm,' she replies suspiciously. 'OK, go and enjoy your day date.'

'Not a date,' I remind her. 'See you later.'

I feel embarrassed that every female apart from me recognises Freddie and falls at his feet. All I did was make him run around after me. Worse than feeling embarrassed, I feel weird. Telling Ali to chase him felt like the most natural thing in the world, but as soon as I said it, I wished I hadn't. Stupid really, because he's only doing me this favour because he's bored and lonely.

'Right,' I say, stepping outside, closing the door behind me.

Freddie is sitting on the veranda with his feet up, waiting for me. He's wearing shorts and a vest, showing off his arm muscles, and of course he has his sunglasses on now, now that we're heading out in public. I suppose Ali recognising him has shown him how much he needs them to remain as incognito as possible.

'Hey, friend,' he says. 'Ready for our not-date?'

Well, if ever I needed a reminder of where we stand, there it is. He's only saying it how it is though, and so am I. This relationship is just for show. And so we can ride the bikes built for two without killing ourselves.

18

'We need a safe word,' Freddie says.

I laugh so hard I choke on my cappuccino.

'Excuse me?' I say after regaining my composure. 'We need a safe word?'

'We do,' he replies. 'In case things get too messy.'

'Oh, wow, I feel like I'm in your mucky movie,' I say with a cackle.

Freddie smiles cheekily as he dips another biscotti in his coffee.

'We do actually have a safe word in the movie,' he admits.

'What was it?' I ask curiously.

'Caboose.'

'Get lost.' I laugh. 'There's no way that's your safe word.'

'Why not?'

'It's not sexy.'

'Safe words aren't supposed to be sexy,' he tells me. 'They're supposed to be safe. When things get too much, it's something you say to bring yourself out of the moment.'

I feel myself getting a little hot under the collar.

'Why do we need one?' I ask.

'Well, when we're pretending we're a couple, if we have a word we can say, to let the other one know to back off a little... I'm an actor, I don't want to get carried away...'

'Well, that's different, then. We're not going to be "in the moment",' I point out. 'So our safe word could be something sexy... Won't it sound weird, if I just blurt the word caboose?'

'Fair point,' he says. 'OK, well, perhaps our safe word can be "babe"? Like if one of us calls the other babe... That's natural?'

'OK, sure,' I reply. 'I don't think I've ever called anyone babe (except Ali earlier) in my life.'

'Neither have I,' he replies. 'It's perfect.'

We've been sitting in Coco's, a coffee bar, for half an hour now, drawing up boundaries. I know, it really does sound like something out of *Edge of Eden*, but our boundaries are less intimate – but no less physical.

A map of Valentine Island is laid out in front of us. Not only does it show how to navigate the island, but where all the activities are too.

Since we decided to buddy up, all activities are open to us... but we are not open to all ideas.

'Okay, back to our list of what we want to do,' I say.

'I'd love to try the couples' parasailing,' he says.

'Safe word,' I say quickly.

'You don't say safe word, you say the safe word,' he tells me.

'Babe, babe, babe, babe, babe.'

'Not your scene?' he asks.

'I'd be terrified, seriously.'

'It's just a little water,' he says. 'Water is nothing to be scared of.'

'It's a no from me,' I say firmly before draining the last of my coffee.

'Okay,' he says. 'I can't argue with that. What do you want to do?'

'I fancy the horseback riding,' I say. 'Riding the trail through the woods.'

'It's my turn to say no,' he says. 'Terrified of horses.'

'Are you making fun of me?' I ask.

Freddie shakes his head.

'Not at all,' he confesses. 'Genuinely scared of them.'

'It's just a little horse riding,' I say to him, mocking his earlier comment.

'Point taken,' he says. 'No parasailing, no horse riding. What else?'

I sigh.

'You know, I'm supposed to be working,' I confess. 'I came here with my laptop and the intention of finishing my book. But then I sat down with what I'd written so far, and I just couldn't bring myself to finish it.'

'How about I grab us another couple of coffees, and you tell me all about it?' he suggests.

'That would be great,' I say, although I'm not sure about talking to him about my books. I don't know why, I just feel embarrassed.

Don't get me wrong, I love writing novels, but talking to someone about them – especially out loud – just feels a little cringy. Even when I talk to my editor about my stories so I always pray she doesn't call me. I guess because, when you've made up a story, you feel a little silly talking about it out loud. You feel as if you're really putting yourself out there, talking about these characters that are a figment of your imagination, telling people what they're getting up to, as if you think they're real – and they do feel real, to the author. They exist in our heads.

At least, with Freddie being an actor, he'll have a firm grasp of the concept of fiction, which many don't seem to have. I'm not talking about your average reader, I'm talking about people like your auntie, who reads your books as if they're your diary, thinking every character is real and every scene is something you've done.

I explain this to Freddie before we get started.

'And I do like to take inspiration from real life,' I tell him. 'So, if I do include anything real, people use that as an anchor for the truth, and jump to conclusions to fill in the blanks.'

'I totally get it,' he says. 'People think I am Edward Eden, that I'm a miserable millionaire who wants to spank them. It's awful, when people interpret your work like that.'

'It is,' I say. 'If only it were so simple, like a no-frills cosmic ordering, where if I write something down, it makes it so. If that were true I'd be a millionaire, married to Henry Cavill, living in a mansion with at least five dogs – at the very least, my fiancé wouldn't have cheated on me with my least favourite friend.'

'Henry and I are friends,' Freddie tells me.

My jaw drops.

'He went up for the Edward Eden role too – couldn't believe my luck, when I beat him to it.'

I can't speak. I make jokes about marrying Henry Cavill all the time and now I'm sitting in front of someone who knows him.

'So, technically, I could facilitate all of the above,' he tells me.

At this stage, Ali would've asked for his number. I'm not Ali though, so a self- deprecating joke is where it's at.

'I don't think you can facilitate Henry Cavill finding me attractive,' I point out.

Hmm, maybe that isn't a joke, maybe that's just true.

Freddie just laughs.

'But if you have Tom Hardy's number, I'm sure Ali will take it,' I say.

'Ali seems great,' he tells me. 'Did she come all this way just to support you?'

'Yes,' I reply. 'She'll insist it's for the free holiday but... she's a tough lady, she's been through a lot. She gets what I'm going through. I'm going to write a book about her one day.'

'You should. That's a great way to honour a friend. What's your author name?' he asks.

'Lila Rose.'

'That's a great name, for a novelist. Is it a pen name?'

'It's my real name. I just got lucky.'

'So, Lila Rose, tell me about this next novel,' he says.

He eats a biscotti as he waits expectantly, as if he's in some sort of fancy movie theatre and I'm a one-woman show.

'Erm, well, I've scrapped it,' I remind him. 'But it was about a woman and her fiancé, and they're going through a tough time while they're planning their wedding, and then the big day comes along and it's hitch after hitch. It all works out in the end and they live happily ever after...'

'A bit too close to home, then,' he says.

'Exactly,' I reply. 'The scene I got to was where she thinks her fiancé is cheating on her. It turns out he's actually arranging for her dream wedding dress, but...'

'Oh, okay, I can see why you don't want to write this book any more.'

'The worst thing is that I do want to write it. I just want to change the genre, make it so he is cheating on her, because that's life. That happens.'

'Not, like, switching to horror, then?' he jokes.

'Have her murder him halfway through...'

'I'm worried you're a little too into this, so I'm going to quickly steer the conversation in a different direction,' he says. 'I have a profile to think about now. I can't be caught up in a murder.'

'I meant in the book,' I remind him with a smile.

'I know, I know,' he says. 'So, what are you going to do?'

'Start again,' I say. 'With something completely different. But what...?'

Abandoning my previous draft in favour of starting again means I absolutely am going to have to start writing while I'm on my not-quite honeymoon, or it really will be a stressful few weeks before my deadline. I really don't need this pressure right now, and it's not like having a regular day job where you can take holiday or be off sick. There's no such luxury in this gig. No matter what's going on in my personal life or how messed up my head is feeling, I have to write a book by a date.

For a moment, we pause.

I glance around the room for inspiration. The delicious smell of coffee, the delectable-looking cakes and pastries, the rustic wicker furniture all laid out with food and drinks... The only thing I'm feeling inspired to be is hungry.

I grab a biscotti and bite it meaningfully with frustration.

'This is such a unique brand of writer's block,' I tell him, 'because everything that's going on is making it impossible to write about anything else.'

Freddie leans forward in his chair, straightening his back.

'Okay, I have an idea for you,' he says. 'You ready?'

I nod. I get this a lot, people giving me their big ideas that they want credit for. They're almost always terrible though.

'So, to borrow a little from your idea, you've got this girl, right? And she's about to get married, and she suspects her fiancé is cheating on her, and he is. The girl finds out on the morning of her wedding, and decides to go on her honeymoon on her own.'

'I feel like this has been done before,' I joke.

'She arrives at the hotel where she meets a movie star, who she thinks is the barman... then her ex and his girlfriend turn up...'

'OK, so this is what's happening to me,' I point out, although I know he knows.

'Exactly,' he replies. 'You say you like to have a little bit of real life in your work. This is just a little bit more than usual. Think about it – it's a great story.'

'I suppose it does make a pretty good set-up for a novel,' I admit. 'It's not my autobiography – it's definitely going to be fiction. I'd probably change quite a lot of what has happened...'

'I'd definitely leave out all the stuff with the dildo.'

'You know, that's actually a really good idea,' I admit.

'Of course, it is,' he replies. 'Give it a go, see how it feels. When I'm struggling with a scene, I try and distract myself with something else, see if I can do better.'

Perhaps Freddie is right – maybe if I work on a different idea, I'll realise it's much better. It isn't dissimilar to what's going on in my real life either. Hanging out with Freddie has made me realise something about Daniel – he was never interested in my work, or helping me out.

It turns out I can do better, and not just with my work. I'm starting to realise that perhaps Daniel was never the right person for me at all.

19

I'm so far out of my comfort zone at the moment, a little extra discomfort barely gets a flinch out of me.

In some respects, I'm being pretty predictable. I'm at Sabatini restaurant again, eating arancini again, drinking a porn star martini – again. Sure, I like to try new things. But when something is this good, and accessible for a finite amount of time, why not go to town on it while I can, right?

This time I'm here with Ali and, unlike my date with Freddie, she didn't tell me I looked nice when I got ready. Instead, she talked me into borrowing a dress from her. A hot-pink, super-short dress with a mesh front, from the neck to the belly button. I've seen Ali wear this dress before and it definitely looks much better on her. Not just because she's in way better shape than me, but because her fake boobs need no assistance staying in place – my real ones don't hold their own, so I've been forced to wear my bra underneath. Still, it doesn't look so bad, I just don't feel like myself in it. It's way, way too sexy for me. Not quite as revealing as the blue boob tube Ali is trying to pass off as a dress though. She looks incredible, as she always does, but she's attracting a lot of male attention, and the thing you have to remember about this place is that everyone is taken.

Two new drinks are placed down on our table, but not by our waiter, by a barman – although I have been wrong before.

I quickly realise it is the man we passed earlier today, the one who couldn't take his eyes off Ali. He still can't.

'Oh, hello again,' I say.

'*Ciao,*' he says – I wonder if his English might be limited, but then he speaks again. 'Are you two together?'

'We certainly are,' Ali says. She reaches out and takes my hand in hers, not unlike the way Freddie did last night. I can't believe how much action I'm getting on my honeymoon – and none of it from my husband.

'You are a very lucky lady,' he tells me.

'Oh, I know,' I reply.

'Bye,' Ali says, encouraging him to leave.

'Well, at least he'll know you're not interested now,' I say as I dip a piece of bread in the bowl of yummy olive oil and balsamic vinegar on the table.

'Oh, I am interested,' she replies, letting go of my hand to grab her drink.

'You are?'

'Oh, yeah.'

'You know, he thinks we're a couple now,' I point out.

'Yeah, men lap that up,' she replies. 'He'll only want me more now.'

'Oh, Ali.' I laugh. 'I'll never understand you.'

'You'll never understand me? I'll never understand you.'

'How so?' I ask through a mouthful of bread.

'Well, for one, you're playing house with a movie star, and you're not going to try and have sex with him.'

'Right,' I reply. 'Because he's just taking pity on me.'

'Are you telling me you don't fancy him?'

'Well, yeah, but only in a movie-star, unattainable-crush kind of way. I hardly know him.'

'Who cares?' she replies. 'You might not know him, but you know he's your type.'

'He's nothing like Daniel,' I point out.

'Yeah, but Daniel wasn't your type,' she reminds me. 'Tall, dark hair, blue eyes, abs for days! And those dimples – I know you like those dimples.'

'Dimples are technically just a genetic defect, you know,' I tell her, changing the subject with a fact. 'Amazing, really, that we find them attractive.'

'Hmm,' is all she has to say about that. 'So do you and Dimples have a good holiday planned together?'

'Sort of,' I reply. 'Although now you're here, I want to spend time with you.'

'Lila, you spend so much time with me,' she points out. 'I'll be fine if you spend time with Freddie. I've got my eye on a few leads.'

'Promise me they're single leads,' I say.

I wiggle uncomfortably in my seat and I'm not sure if it's because I'm worried about Ali, or because of my dress.

'I'm sure you used to be more fun,' she replies through a pout.

Ali being here on Valentine Island is something that never should have happened. My man-loving, head-turning friend, here, where all the men are supposedly happy – and Ali says they're always happy, until they meet her – no, no, no. She's a going to be a real fly in the ointment, I can tell.

Normally I would tell her not to shag where she eats – literally, there are restaurants in London we can never go back to – but it's preferable to her flirting with the married men, even if she's only doing it for sport.

'Oh, he's on the hook already, the poor boy,' she says, glancing over at the bar.

'How old do you think he is?' I ask curiously.

'Hmm, maybe twenty-five?' she says.

'Just a baby.'

'Just the right age for me,' she says. 'The older ones don't have any stamina, not any more.'

'Age-appropriate men just aren't what they used to be,' I tease.

I look down at my drink, and think about Freddie. His porn star martinis really are something else; none of the ones made by the actual staff even come close. That's Freddie, though, multi-talented. Listen to me, talking about him as if I know him.

I decided to have pasta tonight, seeing as I had pizza last night, and I didn't want to seem too predictable – I am, after all, drinking the exact same drinks and eating the same starter.

After a deliciously creamy spaghetti carbonara – which by some miracle I didn't spill down my dress – I thought I might be too full for dessert, but Ali talked me into sharing cannoli with her. I've had cannoli back home, but nothing compares to having it in Italy; there's just something authentic about it. Sweet ricotta cheese in a crisp pastry shell – Ali suggested we eat an end each, like Lady and the Tramp, purely for theatrics, she reassured me. I told her that I was pretty sure the barman was firmly convinced we were a couple – purely because we're on holiday, in the most romantic place on earth, together.

After a few more cocktails we decide to make our way home, back up the hill, which Ali isn't happy about.

'This is cardio,' she moans. 'You're tricking me into doing cardio on holiday.'

'We need it,' I point out. 'After everything we just ate.'

'And drank,' Ali adds, hiccupping right on cue.

We stop to take a breath at the viewing point that looks out over the populated part of the island. All the buildings – the villas, restaurants and shops –sit at different levels, which looks impossibly cute. You can just about make out the beach, down at the bottom. I haven't been yet, but tonight it looks alive with lights and people and music. I can hear fun in the air and that's where it's coming from.

'We'll have to check that out tomorrow,' I suggest.

'You not seeing Freddie tomorrow?' she says flirtatiously.

'You're obsessed with him,' I reply. 'Why don't the three of us go? Then you can spend more time with him.'

'OK, sure,' she replies. 'We'll spend the day with him, so I can spend more time with him.'

I don't think my friend believes that I'm not interested in him, but I'm not. He's an incredible-looking man with a big heart, but we are apples and oranges. Freddie is like a Ferrari – a beautiful car, but could I drive in it to the Co-op for milk? Would I be happy leaving it parked, unattended, or would I constantly be worried someone was going to bump it or steal it? And then there's the fact that I couldn't afford a Ferrari...

'Right, get me to bed,' Ali insists.

Finally outside the villa, I can just about make out two people sitting on the leafy, green veranda. I watch as they clink their wine glasses together. They haven't noticed us, and Ali hasn't noticed them. If I could think of a way to get inside, without them seeing, or without Ali seeing them...

'Ali,' Eva squeaks excitedly. She hurries to her feet, to greet Ali with a hug.

'Save it, hoe-bag,' Ali replies. 'No girl who disrespects Girl Code is a friend of mine. Did you really think we could still be friends?'

Eva's bottom lip pokes out like a little kid whose parents just told her off.

Girl Code might sound like a dumb teenage-girl thing, and maybe it is, but I don't mind it. On the surface, it seems like a silly, childish term, but I'm all for anything that makes women be a little kinder to each other. Seriously, we're up against enough, we can't go turning on each other – especially not for a man. So, sure, I'll adhere to Girl Code, if it makes the world a better place. And anyway, who wants a friend who could steal their man? Freddie is only my pretend boyfriend, and Ali won't look twice at him. That's a friend – that's a woman.

'What's she doing here?' Daniel asks about Ali.

'What's she doing here?' she repeats, mocking his Yorkshire accent. 'What's *she* doing here?'

She nods towards Eva.

'Ali is here on holiday,' I tell him. 'She's staying in the hotel.'

It suddenly occurs to me that saying she's staying with me will blow the cover right off my Freddie story, exposing the lie I didn't tell in the first place. More than not wanting to look like a liar, the security of the Freddie tale gives me a confidence I wouldn't have, if I were just here by myself, with the two of them loved-up next door.

'I so want the three of us to be able to hang out again, like we used to,' Eva says. 'Now that things are all out in the open, can't we be mature and figure it all out?'

'We didn't want to hang out with you before,' Ali snaps.

Ali wouldn't normally be so mean, and it's absolutely not true that we didn't want to hang out with her, we just didn't see all that much of her because we weren't that close – oh, and because she was banging my fiancé, I'd imagine.

It's hard, seeing them both here together, seeming so in love, having a lovely holiday, all the while knowing what they've done and who they have hurt. If someone had done this to Ali I'd be furious too, and there's no way I'd stay friends with someone who could do that either. If someone is willing to steal a man from someone else, how do you know they won't do it again?

'Did you pull some stranger on the plane too, then?' he asks Ali angrily.

'Not this time,' she claps back.

'Ali is seeing one of the barmen here,' I say.

'Since before you arrived?' Eva asks. 'How did you meet him?'

'I stole him off my friend,' Ali says. I can see the anger consuming her, puffing up her chest beyond anything a Czech surgeon could achieve.

'She met him on Tinder,' I say. 'She likes to set her location to nice places, to see who she can meet.'

This is absolutely true, generally. It's just not true this time.

'I can't believe the nerve of you,' Ali tells Daniel, inching towards him. His body stiffens with fear. I feel as if he's just remembered who Ali is. 'Didn't I tell you at the wedding, to stay the hell away from my friend?'

'Oh, yeah, when you embarrassed me in front of everyone,' he reminds her.

'Yes,' she says, taking full ownership of the situation. 'Then. And yet here you are.'

'Ali, do you want to come in for a quick drink while Freddie is at the gym?' I ask her as casually as I can. I'm certainly no actress.

I would love to watch her lay into them, tear them apart, obliterate them with her acid tongue – if not her talon-like nails – but I don't want a scene. That's the one thing I keep reminding myself: that no matter how much I want to scream at them until I lose my voice and slap and swear and punch and kick, I can't, can I? I'd only regret embarrassing myself, or posting things online for everyone to see, giving them all the details. I always feel so sorry for people when they over-share online, because people just love other people's drama, don't they? These things are fascinating when they are happening to other people.

'I'd love to,' she says. 'So long as it doesn't hold up your shagathon with Freddie.'

'Oh, he'll go all night if I let him,' I tell her as I unlock the door. 'A quick drink won't make a difference.'

Once the door is closed behind us, we fall about laughing.

'It must feel so good, getting one over on him like this,' Ali says.

'It does and it doesn't. It's great to show him that I've moved on, and that I don't care... but I haven't moved on, and I do care.'

'I get it,' she says, hugging me tightly. 'Hey, you want to mess with that barman some more? We could get in bed together, order some drinks, see if he brings them?'

'I am not going to help you titillate the barman,' I tell her. 'You don't even need to.'

'Not now you've tangled me up in your web, saying I'm seeing him.'

'You're welcome,' I tell her. 'Now you have an excuse to pounce on him.'

'I wasn't planning on it before,' she lies. 'But now I'm doing you a favour...'

'You won't be moaning when he sweeps you off your feet.'

'Oh, I will,' she replies.

I smile. I'm so happy she's here.

'So, we're going to the beach with Freddie in the morning?'

'You want to?' I reply.

'Hmm, do I want to hang out with a movie star?' she ponders out loud as she falls back onto the sofa. 'Yep.'

'Okay, then, we'll do that.'

'So long as I'm not intruding on your date.'

'How many times do I have to say it?' I sigh. 'It's absolutely *not* a date.'

20

DAY 8

It's hard to say if the water is blue or green – it's both, depending on when and where you look. No matter what colour it appears, it glistens under the hot summer sunshine. It looks so inviting, like a warm, velvety blanket I want to wrap myself up in.

The beach on this side of the island is massive. At one end it is seemingly deserted and natural, with a stretch of near-white sand separating the sea from the forest. As you walk along the beach, it gradually transforms, eventually unveiling the more resort-looking side. There's a large building, built into the side of the rocks, which I believe is filled with more restaurants and shops. Just down from there, practically on the sand, there's a beach bar. Along with the large, well-stocked bar, there's a large stage and a dance floor, which I think is where all the buzz was coming from last night.

No matter which part of the beach you opt for, it's busy, with loved-up couples everywhere, sunbathing together looking as relaxed as they would in their own bed, or floating around in the sea holding hands, like a pair of sea otters.

All of the sunloungers are in pairs, but with me sitting with Freddie, and Ali being here alone, it means that we have a spare, entirely redundant seat, which we've covered in snacks and drinks.

It's great having Ali here, if only because I felt comfortable asking her to rub sun cream into the hard-to-reach places on my back. I don't think I would've dared to ask Freddie to do it, and I absolutely need it. Ali has talked me into wearing my bikini – I don't think I would've done it without her pep talk. I keep draping an arm self-consciously across my midriff, but then I realise that I'll tan with a big white arm mark across my stomach so I move it.

It's a great vibe here, with people of all ages, shapes, nationalities and sexual orientations. It really does feel like a utopia for couples. If the world ended, and I had someone who cared about me, I could happily hole up here. Plus, with all the big beds and aphrodisiacs, it wouldn't be long before everyone repopulated the world.

The three of us have been hanging out, enjoying the sunshine, eating and drinking as we listened to the live band playing in the beach bar. We've all been getting to know each other too, and by that I mean Ali has been asking Freddie a bunch of personal questions, and she's been offering up a bunch of unsolicited 'too much information' in return.

It feels so wonderful lying here, with the warm sun on my skin, and beautiful music in my ears. And the smells! The sea, the smell of my coconut-scented sun cream – even the smell of the crisps we're eating – they're all part of the summer-holiday experience.

Everything is wonderful, until something casts a dark shadow over the day. Literally, even with my eyes closed, I can tell that the sun has disappeared all of a sudden. I open my eyes and see Daniel standing over me.

'Hello,' he says.

'What?' I ask, making no time for pleasantries with the man who ruined my life.

'Can we ask a favour, please?' he starts as Eva steps out from behind him, a cocktail in each hand. 'Can we have that sunlounger? It's the only available one on the whole beach, and we've got our drinks now – even if we can just use the table...'

I want to tell him to get lost – to go and sit in the sea, for all I care. But they don't sound like the words of someone who isn't bothered, do they?

I'll sound very bothered if I say that – or petty at the least. I'm trying to be the bigger person here, or at least seem it.

I glance at Ali. She lifts her sunglasses and narrows her eyes at me, telepathically imploring me to say no. Freddie, on the other hand, gives me an encouraging smile.

'Sure,' I reply. 'Why not?'

'It's nice that we can all still hang out,' Eva says.

If I'm being honest, I think she's being more of a bimbo than a bitch. She's always been a bit dim, and a complete lack of understanding of this situation only goes to prove it. If I were her, I'd be mortified, and if I saw the look on Ali's face, I'd probably fear for my life. Perhaps she finds confidence in knowing me, knowing that I'd never physically hurt her – I'd definitely give Ali an alibi though.

'Hey, Lila,' Freddie says to snatch my attention.

I look over at him as he sits up on his sunlounger. He's wearing a rather small pair of shorts, which have ridden up his legs, over his massive thighs. As he sits forward his rippling torso muscles look even more defined than usual. I move my eyes from his body to meet his gaze.

'Sit with me,' he says, patting the space between his legs. 'Then Daniel and Eva can have a seat each.'

I stare at him for a moment. My God, he's smart. By suggesting I cuddle up with him, not only is it going to drive Daniel crazy, but with two seats up for grabs, it means I won't have to watch Daniel and Eva snuggle up together. So smart.

'Okay,' I say, trying to sound casual, rather than over the moon and slightly terrified.

I sit down on the edge of Freddie's sunlounger. As I scoot closer to him, he swipes me up with one of his strong arms, placing me lying on my side between his legs, with my upper body rested on his – cuddled up to his.

Ali is watching like a hawk over her sunglasses. For her, I imagine this is happening in slow motion, with wah-wah pedal-heavy music playing in the background.

Freddie's body is surprisingly comfortable, given how rock hard he appears to be from head to toe. His warm, smooth, coconut-scented skin feels glorious on my body. Between his tiny shorts and my itsy-bitsy bikini, almost every inch of our bodies is touching. He places one hand at the back of his head and plays with my hair with the other. If it weren't already so hot out here, I'd be roasting.

'Comfortable?' he asks me.

I imagine he's asking me if I'm comfortable with the show we're putting on, rather than if I'm in a good position.

'Very,' I reply, which is the answer to both questions. My first thought, when I lay on top of him, was that I probably look like a walrus slumped down on top of an iceberg, but I feel so at home with Freddie, which I suppose just goes to show what a good actor he is. He's almost got me convinced and I know it's an act.

As Daniel and Eva get comfortable on their separate sunloungers, they both stare daggers at me. I understand why Daniel is doing it, but not Eva. I think she's jealous because she obviously has a crush on Freddie. We might not be a real couple, but she doesn't know that, and if she tries to steal this one from me as well... I suppose I could let her try, distract her with Freddie while I steal Daniel back. I'm annoyed at myself for even considering it. I do not want Daniel back... It's just hard to shake off someone you've spent four years with.

Am I making him jealous to try and win him back, or just to annoy him? I'm not stupid... but, I don't know... it's hard, to throw away someone you've been with for so long. I'm angry now, and I don't even want to look at him, but when the anger calms down, am I going to want him back? It's easy to look at other people who take back cheating partners and say 'wow, what a mug, I would never do that' but when it happens to you...

'Are you having a good time?' Eva asks Freddie. Her entire body is pointing in our direction and you can tell she's just bursting to talk to him. I can't blame her. Still, I nuzzle into his chest, just to annoy her. I'm sorry, but dating, engaged, married or just plain faking it – she can't steal every man I encounter from under me.

'Amazing,' Freddie tells her. 'This one is just something else.'

As he squeezes me I feel emboldened.

'It's just a shame we're not doing any of the activities we fancied doing,' I say. 'We just seem to struggle to leave the villa.'

'Us too,' Daniel quickly adds. 'We had to make ourselves come here today. If you hadn't given up your seat, we would've gone back to bed.'

Ha! I find that hard to believe. Daniel Tyler isn't exactly Mr Boombastic in the bedroom.

I would never have said our sex life was up to much, but I thought that was just something that came with settling down. If you sleep with the same person for long enough, you're bound to get into a bit of a rut, right? But who cares? I'd rather be happy with someone I love than sexually satisfied by someone who is otherwise a terrible person, who I don't feel anything else for.

We just never had a spark in that respect – perhaps he does with Eva? Although I seriously doubt his lack of staying power and inability to light the fireworks is anything to do with me specifically... I don't think... I don't know if it's preferable, that the sex drove him elsewhere, otherwise it's a problem with me – how I look or, worse, my personality. I never professed to be a porn star, but I do like to think I'm a good person.

'Oi,' Ali says to me, yanking me from my thoughts – it's as if she knows! 'Fancy a double-date later?'

'Yes,' Eva squeaks.

'Not you two,' she replies. 'Freddie, Lila, me and my bloke. Double. What would a date with five people look like?'

'I'm sure you'd know,' I tease.

Ali wiggles her eyebrows.

'Ciao, bonjour, hola, hello,' a man says. He's a twenty-something guy, with olive skin and dark hair, the ends of which are frosted. It reminds me of when I was at school, and a bunch of the boys tried Sun-In spray, to give them that boy-band look all the girls were on the hunt for. He's wearing a bright red San Valentino T-shirt, as is the tall blonde woman next to him.

'Hey,' she addresses us, revealing an American accent. I feel Freddie squirm awkwardly, but she doesn't seem to recognise him – I don't mean recognise him because they went to the same school, I realise America is a big place, but she could be a fan. Her gaze does linger over him, for maybe a split second longer than it does with everyone else, but that could just be because he's so beautiful, so easy to admire. With his messy hair and his sunglasses, he still looks like someone... it's just not always easy to tell who.

'I'm Matteo, this is Zoey,' the man starts, enthusiasm surging through his veins, causing his limbs to flail around in all directions. 'And it's our job to make sure you guys have a good time.'

Eva shuffles excitedly in her seat but the rest of us are otherwise indifferent. We didn't come here expecting Disney World, with Mickey and Minnie entertaining us throughout our stay. Like most people, I imagine, we came here to relax.

'You guys have come at a very special time,' Zoey says. 'Tonight is the start of our Mr & Mrs Valentine.'

'Mr & Mrs Valentine?' Ali says, practically spitting the word back at her. Ali has absolutely zero time for corny stuff. 'Like the naff TV show?'

'Yes,' Matteo continues, his enthusiasm not waning, not even for a second. I'm not entirely convinced he's heard of the show from his reaction, but he seems excited. 'It's our job to find couples to take part. You guys want to play some games and maybe win some prizes?'

We don't all rush at once.

'Prizes?' Ali prompts.

'Yes,' he replies. 'Surprise prizes.'

'Hard pass,' Ali says, as she pours the remainder of a bag of crisps into her mouth. 'Surprise prizes are probably not worth it.'

Matteo and Zoey stare at us expectantly.

'What kind of games?' Eva asks.

'Fun games,' Matteo replies.

'Some rounds are about how well you work together as a couple, doing physical tasks. Others are based on how well you know each other – it really is a lot of fun. It's a big event – not everyone wants to take part, given that it takes place with an audience, but everyone loves to spectate these things.'

'Let's do it,' Eva urges Daniel, yanking on his hand like a little kid.

'Ha,' I can't help but blurt.

'What?' Daniel asks.

'Sorry, I just... I'd be interested to watch you two taking part in some-

thing that required knowledge of each other, given the, erm, under-
ground nature of your relationship.'

Zoey shrugs and smiles. She clearly has no idea what I'm getting at.

'So shall I put your names down?'

'Yeah, put us down,' Daniel says. 'We'd do better than you two ever
could. You're basically strangers.'

'Ooh, fighting talk,' Zoey says. 'Are you going to take that from them?'

I realise she's talking to me directly. I've taken much worse from them.

'Sign us up,' Freddie says.

'Really?' I squeak.

'Really,' he replies. 'I think we'll be good at it.'

Daniel wasn't wrong, Freddie and I are basically strangers... but, I
don't know, I suppose it could be fun?

'Yes, sign us up,' I say.

'All right! A friendly rivalry,' Zoey says. 'So, the first round is tonight...'

As Zoey explains how the competition works, and takes our details, I
almost feel sorry for her. With myself and Freddie, and Daniel and Eva
taking part, this rivalry is going to be anything but friendly.

21

It turns out that everyone is pretty excited for Mr & Mrs Valentine. Participating couples will be taking part in a series of events over the course of this week. It seems as if there's always some kind of event going on here, to keep guests entertained. I'm not sure if there was a better or worse time to be here, but it doesn't sound too bad. Only a certain number of couples progress to the next round, which means that by the time you get to the final event, only the best of the best are left. I can't imagine Freddie and me, or Daniel and Eva being crowned the best, not when we're competing against conventional/real couples, but if we can just get further than our rivals...

Freddie seems excited. He says he's been so bored and lonely, after being holed up in his apartment so long, before coming here to be even lonelier. I suppose, at least when you're feeling lonely in your own home, you're surrounded by your own things. Not that things can keep you company, but familiarity can, to an extent. Here, though, surrounded by no one he knows and nothing he recognises, Freddie must feel it even more. I think that's why he's clung onto me as tightly as I have him. I'm like a project for him, someone he can take care of. And now we've got this competition.

'I just want to win this one round,' I tell him. 'And then we'll bow out, because we're ill or shy or something. So long as we kick their butts once.'

'Kick their butts once and then don't give them a chance to equalise?' Freddie asks.

'Exactly,' I reply. 'All is fair in love and war.'

Freddie just laughs.

The beach bar is a wide, circular open space. There is a large stage at one side, with an open space for a dance floor in front of it. Tables and chairs are set up everywhere else, all facing the action.

Fairy lights hang around the edge of the space, creating the illusion of a sort of wall around us, and at the centre of each table is a clear glass wine bottle, with even more lights packed inside. I think my favourite thing about Valentine Island might be the recurring theme of twinkling lights and leafy green plants. I definitely feel as if I'm in some sort of dreamy utopia, a million miles from my usual life in the big, polluted city.

It still feels so warm, but without the sun beating down on us, it's a more pleasant heat. I'm wearing a strapless dress, but now, after a day sunbathing, my shoulders have white strap marks from my bikini, which just scream 'Brit abroad'. I think perhaps Freddie has been working on his tan for longer than I have, or perhaps because he's almost always shirtless he's just colouring more evenly than I am. Tonight he's wearing a muscle-hugging, V-neck T-shirt and a rather tight pair of chinos. I don't know if his clothes are supposed to be tight, or if he's just up against it, muscle-wise. I tick myself off every time I catch myself staring at him, admiring him.

Ali decided not to come along and watch, because it 'sounded lame' and 'might make her sick' – she also told us that, if I was going to make out as if she was 'banging a barman' then she 'may as well be banging a barman' so she's gone off to find the one from the restaurant last night.

It's absolutely packed here, so I can't see Daniel and Eva – perhaps they've chickened out.

Matteo and Zoey take to the stage. They're both wearing radio mics that poke out in front of their faces, which makes me wonder what the hell we're going to be doing that they need both hands for. Zoey takes the lead, saying everything in English. Matteo is only a few moments behind her, repeating everything she says in Italian.

'It's time for the first round of Mr & Mrs Valentine Island,' she announces to an ocean of applause. 'So, let's get our couples up here and find out just how much they know about each other.'

'Crap,' I say quietly. 'We're not exactly going to smash this round, are we?'

'Let's give it a shot,' Freddie says. 'If we don't go first, and it sounds difficult, we can bail.'

We reluctantly make our way to the stage, with all the other couples. I finally notice Daniel and Eva. They might not know each other all that well, but it's bound to be more than Freddie and I know one another. Why couldn't it have been something I'm better than them at, like comma placement or not being an adulterer?

Matteo removes a large red velvet sheet to reveal a box. It's sort of like a wide telephone box, divided in two with a little window at the top. It's all red and sparkly, which makes me think it is made for purpose. In which case, they really do take this seriously.

'So, for the first round, we're going to find out just how well our couples know each other – the ultimate test in any relationship. For some rounds you need to be strong, but for this one, your relationship needs to be ironclad. Couples will sit in separate sections of the booth, with one person answering questions about the other. If the answers on the cards match, it's a point. It's time to see who is hopelessly in love, and who is just plain hopeless...'

Freddie and I watch the first few couples go through the questions and answers. It's incredible, just how many couples get the answers wrong for some of the most simple-sounding questions. And these are real couples, not fake ones who have only known each other a few days.

Next up, it's Daniel and Eva. The two of them take their seats in the booth, with Eva opting to answer questions about Daniel. That makes sense; Daniel is so self-involved, I doubt he's ever asked her a personal question.

'Question one,' Zoey starts. 'What colour is your partner's eyes?'

Well, that one is easy: his eyes are brown. You don't need to know

Daniel all that well to know that one – even Freddie could've answered that one about him.

'And your answer,' Zoe prompts Eva.

Eva holds up her dry-wipe board. She's written 'brown' on it, in impossibly swirly, girly handwriting. She bites her lip as she waits to hear if she's right.

'And your answer,' she says to Daniel.

Daniel flips his board around to reveal that she has the right answer.

The audience dutifully applauds, as they do to each question that is answered correctly. Oh, she knows what colour his eyes are, big whoop.

'Question two,' Zoey continues. 'What does your partner keep on their bedside table?'

'Obviously I know this one,' I tell Freddie, under my breath. 'Because it's my bedroom too. He has this moon that lights up.'

My side of the bed is messy. I always have a couple of books on the go, squashed on there with my light, my chargers, and whatever I've left on there like lip balm or a water bottle. Daniel's side is always tidy – the only thing on his bedside table is his moon lamp.

Eva lifts up her board, which says 'moon' on it, and I feel as if I've been punched in the face. Freddie wraps a supportive around me, which I appreciate more than he can imagine. I feel as if I'm going to pass out.

She's been in my bedroom. Eva has been in my bedroom. *My* bedroom. I don't know when, or where I was, but I know I've never taken her in there. I knew she'd been sleeping with my fiancé but, call me naïve, I never actually believed they'd done it in my house, in my bedroom, in my bed.

Daniel holds his board up, and their answer is a match.

I touch my cheek with the back of my hand. I don't know if it's just warm tonight, a touch of sunburn, or because I am fuming, but I feel as if my face is radiating heat.

'Question three,' Zoey says.

At this point, I don't even want to be here any more. Not just taking part in this competition, I don't even want to be on the same island as them.

'Where were you the first time you said you loved each other?'

Freddie squeezes me tighter.

I suppose this serves me right, for thinking I could get one up on them by playing some stupid game.

If I were answering this, my answer would be the park. When we were dating, as he started to open up a bit more, Daniel said he wanted us to go for a walk. We'd never been for a walk before, that wasn't really something we did for fun, but I was just so happy to be spending time with him, I didn't care where we were or what time it was. I was pleasantly surprised, during out first sunset walk together, when he just blurted out that he loved me. I immediately knew I loved him too.

Eva holds up her board, which reads 'park'.

Are you fucking kidding me? Is this what he does? He takes girls to the park, walks them around a bit and then tells them that he loves them? Oh, he must think he's so smooth, strolling woman after woman through the trees, before sitting them down on the grass, facing the sunset, tucking their hair behind their ear before whispering his phoney declaration of love into their ear. At the time, I thought he was wonderful. Now, I think he's a massive creep, and as for Eva... She isn't just intruding in my relationship and my bedroom, she's invading my memories now, tainting them, claiming them for her own, just as she's doing with everything else.

Of course, her answer is correct.

Zoey is pulling questions out of a box, so she has no idea what's coming. I wish I knew; this is torture. Each question seems to wind me up even more than the previous one.

'Question four... what was the first thing you argued about?'

Eva dances in her seat excitedly. She knows this one.

For some reason, it upsets me even more to know that they argue; it legitimises them as a couple. It's normal for couples to argue, and it bothers me that they do, even more than the idea of them exchanging 'I love you's'.

'Well, I can't imagine the two of them arguing about politics,' Freddie whispers to me.

'No. I can't even imagine them conversing,' I reply. 'All he talks about is football, and all she talks about is herself.'

Eva holds up her board, which says 'missed first Valentine's Day' along with a sad face. As Daniel reveals that his answer matches, the audience playfully boo him.

'Oh, no,' Zoey says. 'I hope you had a good excuse.'

'He spent it with his fiancée,' I whisper to Freddie. 'That's his excuse.'

'Well, Daniel and Eva are currently on four out of four, which is our joint highest score so far. If they can get this one right, they'll be our new leaders. So...'

So far, no one has answered their fifth and final question right. The final questions come from a separate box and are supposedly harder than the previous ones.

'What was Daniel scared of when he was younger?' Zoey asks.

Eva scratches her head theatrically before writing something down. She holds her board up to reveal the word 'clowns'.

'Ooh, clowns,' Zoey says. 'Shall we see what Daniel wrote?'

'It's dogs,' I tell Freddie.

When Daniel was seven years old, he and his cousin were playing on the street where Daniel lived, when a dog approached them and bit his cousin. Daniel remembers the dog biting him, but his mum insists it was his cousin who got bit. This left Daniel with a crippling fear of dogs, which I helped him overcome when we met, by introducing him to my parents' Pomeranians. Well, who could be scared of a Pomeranian? They're basically small clouds that bark if you don't give them enough attention.

'Oh, unlucky,' Zoey says. 'The answer was dogs. But, the good news is that you're still our joint leaders, so you're definitely through to the next round.'

'I've got an idea,' Freddie whispers to me. 'You answer questions about me. No one will be able to see what you're doing in that booth – you can only see faces. Just pretend you're writing your answer down, and quickly look it up online.'

'Look it up online?' I reply.

'It never ceases to amaze me, how much random but accurate information there is about me on the web,' he says with a bemused chuckle. 'So look it up online.'

Daniel and Eva exit their booths and hug each other victoriously. As Freddie and I make our way over, we pass them on the stage.

'Good luck,' Daniel whispers to me with a smarmy grin.

There's no way I could possibly know as much about Freddie as Eva knows about Daniel. No matter how long their affair has been going on, they've known each other for years. I've known Freddie for days, and our relationship is entirely fabricated.

'Our final couple of the evening is Freddie and Lila,' Zoey tells the audience, reading our names off a card.

Freddie is still wearing his sunglasses, which seem to be doing the trick, preserving his anonymity. He looks like a bit of a poser though, given that it's definitely dark now.

We are shown into our separate booths. I grab my board and take the lid off my pen, before sneakily removing my phone from the little handbag I'm wearing across my body.

I need to knock that smirk off Daniel's face. I can't let him win this one.

'Question one,' Zoey begins. 'How tall is your partner?'

I quickly type in 'Freddie Bianchi height' and within seconds, I've got it. I write '6′ 3″' on my board.

Zoey checks Freddie's answer with mine, and I am correct.

'Question two,' she continues. 'What is your partner's favourite movie?'

It only takes a few seconds for me to find an interview where Freddie mentions his favourite film is *Casablanca*.

And would you believe it? We have another match.

I manage to coast (read: search) my way through the next couple of questions, correctly figuring out Freddie's favourite colour and where he went to high school. I find it amazing that people who have never met him care about his favourite colour – I don't even care about my own favourite colour. Still, I think I got really lucky, being able to look up the correct answers. This means that we're neck and neck with Daniel and Eva, which is fine. I really wanted to win, but I'll settle for not losing.

The fifth and final question – the supposedly hard question – is up next. I don't suppose it matters how hard or easy it is, they're all hard for me, because Freddie is pretty much a stranger... a stranger I'm spending my holiday with, cuddling up to, and we've seen each other fleetingly naked. Seriously, what a bloody weird honeymoon.

'So far none of our couples have successfully answered the final question correctly – will Freddie and Lila be different? Here we go... Lila, if Freddie won the lottery, what's the first thing he'd do with the money?'

This is the type of question I was dreading, because I can't look it up, and there's no obvious answer. Some might splash out on a house or a car, others might go on holiday or throw a party. I don't know Freddie well enough and I can't get inside his head...

The thing is, though, I know the answer to this question. I know it because I asked him. You can count on one hand the number of proper conversations we've had, and I've already asked him this question, just in a slightly different way – what are the chances?

I write my answer down with the biggest grin on my face. I'll bet Daniel is out there, rubbing his little hands together, over the moon because he knows I haven't known Freddie long. He'll think there's no way I can know this.

I look for him, but the stage lights are too bright to make people out; everyone is in the shadows. I'll bet he can see me though, and I'll bet he thinks I'm bluffing.

'Okay, what have we got?' Zoey asks me.

I flip over my board to show my answer.

'Lila has written that, oh, okay, she thinks her significant other would pay off his parents' mortgage. I wasn't expecting that. Let's see what Freddie has...'

It feels as if it takes him forever to turn his board around. It's as if the music stops, everyone goes quiet, even the ocean stops lapping at the shore. You could hear a pin drop.

'It's a match!' Zoey screams, shortly followed by Matteo, who yells the same in Italian.

I feel as if my smile is going to rip my face right open, I'm so pleased with myself. Sure, it's a small, petty victory, which doesn't exactly level the playing field, but unless I'm willing to sleep with one of Daniel's friends for revenge (no effing way) then this is the best I can do.

Round one: Lila. Well, Lila and Freddie.

After we are set free from our separate boxes, I finally see Freddie's face and he looks just as pleased as I do. He picks me up off the ground and twirls me around. When he finally stops, I get to claim my reward. Daniel and Eva's miserable faces.

'They're looking over at us,' Freddie whispers to me. 'Grab my ass or something.'

'You grab my arse,' I reply, feeling a little too shy to do it.

'Okay,' he says as he grabs me.

I squeak with delight, mostly for the benefit of our audience. I can see a look of fury on Daniel's face and I take so much pleasure from it. Let's see how he likes it.

'This means that, at the top of our leader board, we have Freddie and Lila,' Zoey announces to a roar of cheers. 'Join us tomorrow, when our remaining couples will compete again, for a chance to win the surprise prize, which I can now reveal is... 5,000 Euros.'

I freeze on the spot, slowly cocking my head like a dog who has just heard a whistle. Excuse me, what?

Freddie looks puzzled too.

'Did she just say...?'

'She did,' he replies. 'Come on, let's get a drink to celebrate.'

22

It's a perfect night for a stroll. On the one side, you've got the island all lit up and alive, on the other, just the black moonlit sea, and starry sky. I love looking out, into the nothingness, focusing on the sound of the tide. It's like being pulled from the real world and dropped straight into relaxation.

As chilled-out as I feel right now, I'm also excited.

'I can't believe there's a 5,000 Euro prize,' I squeak. 'And we're winning.'

'We did cheat,' he reminds me.

'We did,' I reply. 'But that was before we knew it was for money. We just thought we were messing with my ex.'

'That's also true,' he replies.

'Imagine what a person could do with 5,000 Euro,' I say, twirling around on the sand. Then I remember that Freddie is probably a million-aire. Freddie winning 5,000 Euro is probably the equivalent of me finding a twenty-pound note in a handbag I haven't used for a while. 'Well, I could certainly do a lot with it. I could pay off what's left of my wedding, for a start, just cancel the whole mistake out. I could put some towards buying the house off Daniel, if that's even possible... I suppose I'll need to find somewhere of my own...'

I'm getting carried away.

'Let's win it, then,' Freddie says casually. 'Well, win it together, but you can have it.'

'What?'

'Let's play – properly, without cheating – and let's win. If we take this seriously, I think we have a good chance. We've done the part where we answer questions... We've got a real shot, Lila.'

'But... we're not even a real couple?'

'So what?' He laughs. 'What's the difference? There's two of us, we were going to spend the holiday hanging out together anyway. The only real difference between us and the others is that they share a bed.'

'So we're more like a married couple, is what you're saying,' I joke. 'Do you really think we could win?'

'I do,' he replies. 'And if we don't, we'll have fun trying. Wasn't tonight fun?'

'It certainly was. Seeing that look on Daniel and Eva's faces – my gosh.'

'So...'

'If we did win *together*, I couldn't just take the whole prize,' I say.

'Lila, I'm doing OK for money,' he responds. 'The movie industry pays quite well.'

I smile.

'Okay, sure, I'm in,' I say.

I can feel the excitement rushing through my veins, giving me life. To be on such a high, after feeling so down in the dumps... it almost makes it all seem worth it.

I hug myself as a cool breeze glides over the beach. I don't know if it's the sea air, the excitement of the day or a combination of both, but a wave of tiredness washes over me. I yawn.

'Shall we head back?' I suggest. 'I'm pretty tired and it's starting to get a bit cold, isn't it?'

'Sure,' he replies. 'I'd offer you my jacket if I had one.'

'What a gentleman,' I say with a smile.

'People never think I am,' he says. 'People think I'm going to be the arrogant, sex-mad deviant I play in the movie.'

Okay, I am going to have to watch this movie. I need to see this version of Freddie for myself. I just can't imagine the sweet, charming man standing in front of me being a raging pervert, even if he is just acting.

Freddie offers me his arm for the walk back to the villa, which makes me smile.

'Can you hear that?' Freddie asks, stopping in his tracks.

I listen carefully and hear those familiar little squeaks I heard a few days ago.

'Oh, my gosh, that's my buddies,' I tell him, hurrying over to the bushes.

'Your what?' Freddie asks me, following close behind.

I carefully move the branches to show him the kittens that live there.

'Oh, wow,' he says. 'I'm usually more of a dog person, but these guys are cute.'

Today their mum is with them. She rushes over to us, to see if we have any food.

'Hey, cutie,' Freddie says, reaching down to pet her. 'Wow, she's so tame for a stray.'

'She is,' I say. Then again, who wouldn't want to be all over Freddie, human or feline?

There's something so attractive about big sexy men either petting animals or holding babies, isn't there? Seeing Freddie give this cat attention just makes him seem all the more swoonsome.

As we continue back towards the villa, normally you'd expect the night air to grow quieter and quieter. But tonight, as we approach my suite door, I hear something. It's a familiar sound, coming from inside my suite. It's...

'Oh, God.'

'Is that...? Can I hear someone...?'

'Yep,' I reply.

I am uncomfortably familiar with the sound of my best friend's orgasm, after living with her for so long. Her rhythmic moaning always left me feeling worn out. I could never understand how she could make so much noise for so long. I don't know if it's an auditory illusion, because I'm focusing on it, or if the noise is getting louder.

'I'm guessing she really hit it off with that barman you told me she was pursuing,' Freddie says.

'God, I hope so,' I reply with a laugh. You never know with Ali – she could just be alone and bored. Oh, nope, there's a man making noise too. I can hear him. God, I can really hear him. Perhaps she's finally met her match. If she has, it's going to be like a game of tennis between two pros. It will go on, and on, and on.'

'Do you want to come in for a drink?' Freddie suggests.

'No, it's late, don't worry, you get to bed. If I know Ali, this is going to go on all night,' I tell him with a sigh.

'Okay, well, come and sleep with me,' he suggests. I notice him instantly regret his choice of words, before awkwardly trying to regain control of his offer. 'I mean, come and sleep in my bed tonight – I'll sleep on the couch.'

I don't know what kind of face I pull, but Freddie reacts.

'I know, it's a little awkward but...' Right on cue, Ali screeches like an owl in the night. I wouldn't be surprised if her head was turning all the way around too. 'It can't be more awkward than going in there.'

'Are you sure?'

'Of course,' he replies. 'I can't leave you out here, can I?'

I smile. I can't believe how good to me this man is, when I'm pretty much a stranger to him (and a ridiculous one at that).

'Thank you,' I say.

Inside Freddie's suite – which, it turns out, is bigger than mine – you can still hear Ali and her new friend going at it like rabbits, but the wall between us dampens their sound effects enough to try and pretend it isn't happening.

'You can take the bed,' he says. 'The maids changed it this morning. I'll sleep on the couch. I'll show you up – I need to grab a blanket anyway.'

It's a little awkward, heading up to Freddie's bedroom with him – made all the more uncomfortable by the sex noises coming from next door. For a moment, I feel my footsteps fall into a rhythm with the grunting, and it makes me feel weird, as if I'm participating.

'Your bedroom is so tidy,' I say, looking over his neatly made king-sized bed, his clear bedside tables and the tiled floor that isn't littered with a scattering of clothing as mine is.

'I knew the maids were coming to change the bed today, so I made sure all my things were tidied,' he says. 'I don't want them thinking I'm some asshole, leaving my stuff everywhere, expecting them to tidy up after me.'

Oh, why does he have to be so dreamy?

'Here's a clean T-shirt for you to sleep in,' he says, tossing me one over.

'Thanks for this,' I say again.

'You're welcome. Well, I'll leave you to get some sleep.'

'Yeah, hopefully Ali isn't too noisy to stop us,' I reply.

'If they get any louder, I'll bang on the wall.'

'That's probably what they're doing,' I joke. 'They'll just think we're joining in.'

My cheeks heat up with the fire of a thousand suns. Why did I say that?

Freddie laughs as he bids me goodnight, before heading downstairs. He's left me. And you know what I'm going to do now, don't you?

I slip off my dress, leaving it exactly where it lands. Freddie might be tidy, but I'm not – and anyway, I'll be putting it back on before anyone sees me.

I take my phone from my bag before climbing into bed and loading up a video. Before I press play, I listen carefully, waiting for Freddie to stop moving around. If I wait until he's settled and I keep my volume low, he'll have no idea what I'm doing – plus the cloak of Ali's multiple orgasms will provide an extra layer of privacy.

I place a finger on the volume-down button, ready to mash it as soon as the video starts playing. It doesn't take long on the Netflix home screen before I find it... *Edge of Eden*, Freddie's movie.

I've never been a fan of the so-called 'mummy porn' books that have been all the rage for the past few years, so I didn't bother with any of the big-screen adaptations either. It's a strange one, isn't it? Because for me, going to the cinema is such a social activity, and going to see a mucky movie with my mates – even if the sex scenes are acted – is something I can't imagine doing. And, anyway, why pay for it when my best friend tries to supply me with my fix for free?

I suppose anything is great that gets women talking about sex and being more open about their sexuality. We're weirdly conditioned to think that sex is for men and that women shouldn't talk about it – in the same way we're not supposed to talk about periods, and all we're supposed to want in life is to procreate. Hilarious, really, given how closely linked sex, periods, and having kids are.

Sometimes you just don't fancy a movie, not until you bump into and strike up a friendship with one of the leading actors, while you're on your honeymoon alone. You know, that old one.

Now that I know Freddie, and given what I know about the movie, I *have* to watch it. I have to.

Certain the coast is clear, I press play. I only need to watch a little bit of it, just to satisfy my curiosity. Then I'll get some sleep.

23

DAY 9

It's that weird kind of light, somewhere between the sun setting and the sun rising.

My senses feel heightened. I can smell the leaves on the trees, the dirt on the ground, the rain in the air... and then Freddie steps closer to me, and all I can smell is him. All I can think about is him – how much I want him.

'What?' I ask him nervously as he approaches me.

As he slowly moves his body towards mine, I lean back against the tree behind me.

'I want you,' he whispers into my ear. 'I need you.'

At first, he takes my earlobe in between his lips, nibbling it gently before kissing down my neck. My eyes roll back into my head as I moan, until I remember where we are.

'Wait, someone might see us,' I say. 'People walk through here all the time.'

'I don't care,' he says breathlessly. 'Do you?'

'I don't,' I reply. It surprises me, but I really don't. All I can think about is Freddie and how much I need him too.

Freddie takes both of my wrists in one of his big, strong hands and holds them together tightly before pinning them to the tree above my head. With his free hand he tugs the string of my bikini top and in one swift movement it's gone.

The breeze lightly brushes over my bare skin as I stand there, waiting, wondering what Freddie is going to do.

It feels like an eternity before he finally makes his move. Freddie lifts me up with one hand, pressing his body against mine, holding me in place against the tree. I lock my legs around him as he kisses me passionately.

It feels so naughty, being out here in the middle of the woods. Anyone could walk past at any point, but that's half of the thrill – a thrill I never knew I wanted.

The clouds open and rain showers down over us. It does nothing to dampen the mood though, as our open mouths fill with water and our bodies become slippery. I hold on extra tight.

'Mmm, you're a bad girl, Lila,' Freddie tells me between kisses. 'Lila, Lila, Lila...'

I open my eyes.

'Lila, are you OK?' Freddie asks me. 'You were making some really strange noises.'

I sit up in bed quickly. Oh, God, I was dreaming. That was all a dream? It felt so real.

'Yeah, I, erm, I'm fine,' I say, but it's hard to look him in the eye. I shield my eyes, making out the light is bothering me, but it isn't the sun that's got me all hot and sweaty. 'I was having a bad dream.'

'What happened?' he asks curiously. 'Were you running? You sounded out of breath.'

Oh, God, I was definitely breathless.

'What time is it?' I ask him, changing the subject. I unlock my phone, which opens on the Netflix screen for his movie. I quickly close it, which makes me seem like I'm in even more of a flap than I already was, when he caught me having a sexy dream about him.

It's all his bloody movie's fault; I watched it right before I fell asleep. That scene, in the woods, in the rain, was pulled straight from the *Edge of Eden* playbook. A lot of the scenes were your classic S&M-type stuff – exactly what I expected. This one scene in the woods... It was all about

Edward Eden trying to please Hannah, his love interest, instead of him using her, which is what 99 per cent of the movie is all about.

I don't know why that scene, of all the scenes, is the one that got under my skin and crept into my dreams, but it did. Today, I feel as if I'm seeing Freddie in a whole new light, one that is almost too bright to bear. I just can't look at him, not after the things I've seen him do (even if he was acting). Edward is nothing like Freddie, he's so powerful, egotistical, sexual... but it was Freddie, doing all those things, saying those words.

'Are you OK?' he asks me. 'You seem a little flustered...'

'I'm fine.'

'Okay, good,' he says. 'Well, I want to take you out for lunch, if you fancy it?'

'Lunch?'

'Didn't you see the time?' he says, nodding towards my phone.

I look again. It's nearly midday.

'Oh, my God, I have super slept in,' I say.

'Usually more of a sign of good dreams than bad ones,' he says with a cheeky smile. 'So, lunch?'

Freddie is already up and dressed. He looks good, in his shorts and T-shirt, and his hair looks a little more tamed than usual. I suppose he doesn't have to hide around me, so he's safe to brush his hair back.

'I'd love to,' I reply. 'I just need to pop next door and get changed... if it's safe.'

'They got tired eventually,' he reassures me.

'If I know Ali, they'll probably start up again,' I tell him.

'Well, you'd better hurry, so you don't miss your window.' He laughs. 'I'll wait here, but I'm ready when you are.'

'You don't want to come with me?' I say with a smile.

'Not a chance,' he replies. 'It sounds like you're used to it – I'm just an innocent boy.'

I watched a two-hour movie last night that begs to differ.

I put on my dress and wipe off some of the rogue make-up (that I should have removed before I went to sleep, and I'm usually so good at it but, in my defence, I didn't have my remover with me). I don't wipe too much off though, because I am blushing something fierce.

I slink out of Freddie's suite, making sure no one is around before dashing to my own. I feel as if I'm doing the walk of shame – not because of the dream, I'm not that deluded, but because if Daniel or Eva see me, I'll have some explaining to do – they think we're sharing a suite. The two of them thinking I'm here with Freddie is my safety blanket; it gives me something to hide under and staves off the cold feeling. I know it's not real, I promise you I know that, but it's all I have right now, while I wait for time to fix me up. Just because I'm not alone, doesn't mean I don't feel lonely right now. I have Freddie to spend time with, and Ali is here, but Daniel and I had something you can't get from a friendship – I was supposed to spend the rest of my life with him. The only thing that hurts more than him going behind my back with Eva is just how easily he has replaced me with her.

I think I'm safe the second I close my suite door behind me, but I think I was better off outside.

'Ciao,' the tall, naked Italian man standing in the kitchen in front of me says awkwardly.

'Hi,' is all I can get out in response.

More troubling than the fact he's naked is that he's covered in something... something I sincerely hope is Nutella.

He's surprisingly ripped, for a barman, so he must take good care of himself. Then again, I don't imagine you absorb too many calories from your food, when all you do is smear it across your abs.

Ali walks out of the bathroom, a white hotel towel wrapped around her. I really, really hope she keeps the towel away from the Nutella – it's my laundry the maids think they're doing.

'Lila,' she says, hurrying over to me. 'There you are – I was worried sick.'

'It shows,' I reply, hugging her back.

'This is Massimiliano,' she tells me, of the naked man standing in my suite. It's nice to be kept in the loop.

'Call me Max,' he says. As he approaches me to kiss my cheek, I raise my hands in front of my body.

'Oh, relax, it's just chocolate,' Ali says.

'I don't want to spoil my lunch,' I joke.

It's as if there's an elephant in the room, in many, many ways. In psychology, they say don't think about the pink elephant, in an attempt to show you how hard it is to take your mind off something as soon as you try. That's pretty much how I feel right now. Trying not to think about the fact that Max has little Max out, just hanging there, makes it harder and harder (not like that, although now that I mention it...) for me not to think about it. I feel as if it's following me around the room.

'I'm going to get dressed and head back out,' I tell them, heading for the stairs with my eyes as high as I can force them.

'Not so fast,' Ali says. 'Where were you last night?'

'Why don't you come with me while I get dressed and I'll tell you?' I suggest.

Ali looks over at Max, then back at me.

'Hmm, okay, he'll keep,' she says.

We head up the stairs, to talk more comfortably – without the prying eye in the room.

'So, spill,' Ali demands as I riffle through a pile of clothing on the floor, looking for my nice sundress. Freddie looked amazing, so I want to try and scrub up as well as possible too.

'Well, Freddie and I won the competition last night – the first round of it anyway – so we're going to keep playing, see if we can win.'

'That's amazing,' she says. 'So, you had a good night?'

'Until we got back here, and we could hear you two... So Freddie said I could sleep with him.' I instantly regret my choice of words. 'In his bed. Without him.'

'You spent the night with Fit Freddie?'

'I spent the night in his bed,' I correct her. 'He spent the night on his sofa.'

'We only spent the night on your sofa,' Ali says. 'Well, on and around.'

I'm terrified to think about what would happen if you shone a UV light in that room right now.

'You two hit it off, then,' I say, hurrying one dress off and another one on. I can't wait to get back to Freddie, to see what he has in store for us today.

'He's a bit of me, that Max,' Ali says, sounding so impossibly Essex. 'A proper sort.'

'You seem... well suited. You certainly sounded it.'

'Were we that loud?' she asks.

'They heard you back in London.'

'Oops,' she says, not sounding all that much as if she means it.

'I'm so lucky Freddie let me stay with him.'

'Do you think he'd let you stay with him again tonight?' she asks. 'After Max's shift is over, we were talking about hanging out again, and I'm not allowed in the staff quarters.'

I'm not at all surprised.

'Erm, I can ask,' I say. 'But you've got to promise not to use my food.'

'Deal,' Ali says, offering me her hand to shake.

'Too soon,' I tell her, looking at her hand as if I know exactly where it's been.

I feel bad, imposing on Freddie, and I'll feel so cheeky asking him if I can stay with him again... It's so unlike me, but I don't care. I want to stay with him again, even if it isn't quite as it is in my dreams.

24

As Freddie leads me into the woods, this time for real, I feel my face flush. I can't stop thinking about my dream and this absolutely isn't helping. And, of course, my stupid writer brain is running away with me, wondering what we're doing here.

Outside our villa you can either follow the driveway down towards the main part of the island or, I've just found out, there is a little pathway that leads around the side, into the woods.

'What are we doing here?' I ask him. I sound almost suspicious, but I'm not. I'm just low-key hoping it's my dream come true, and I'm nervous.

'We're nearly there,' he tells me as he leads the way. 'Just before we have lunch, I thought you might like to see this.'

I wonder what 'this' could be.

'I thought it might be something cool to put in your book,' he says. 'If you're writing about your story.'

Gosh, I wish I were writing something – anything. I do think it's a good idea, to plagiarise my own tragic tale, but I just can't bring myself to sit down and do it. I don't feel all that romantic or comedic right now, and that's pretty much all my books are made of.

'This is the villa's secret path, down to the beach,' he explains. 'No one really knows it's here. What's also here is... this.'

I realise where the sound of rushing water is coming from as we approach a waterfall. It's big, but it isn't a sheer drop. The water thunders down over the rocks below, which go on for further than I can see.

'That leads all the way down to the beach,' he tells me. 'You can walk alongside it.'

'It's stunning,' I admit, gazing at the crystal-clear water. There's something so hypnotic about watching it. It's the cold shower I need to cure me of my thoughts about Freddie giving me the Edward Eden treatment against a tree.

'Okay, lunchtime,' he says. 'It's just a little further.'

'Further into the woods?' I reply.

'Yeah... you look worried. What do you think I'm going to do?' he asks with a chuckle.

God, if only he knew.

'Nothing, nothing,' I quickly insist. 'But I don't imagine there are many restaurants in the woods.'

'There's an exclusive restaurant inside a cave on the other side of the island,' he tells me. 'We'll have to go – I didn't fancy going solo. It only has five tables.'

'Wow, that sounds amazing,' I tell him. 'Like something out of a...'

As we approach a clearing in the woods, my voice fails me. The trees have been decorated with flowers and lanterns, and on the floor there's a blanket, laid out with an impossible amount of delicious-looking food and drink.

'A fairy tale,' I say, eventually finishing my sentence.

'What do you think?' he asks.

'Freddie... it's amazing... how did you...?'

'I organised it with the hotel,' he says. 'I thought it would make a great scene for the book and, you know, if you write a character like me into it, I want to look good.'

He flashes me that cheeky smile of his, showing off his dimples.

Okay, so he's only doing this as a mate, to give me ideas for my book, it's not a romantic lunch, but it's amazing.

'Come, sit down, let's dive in,' he says.

I don't need telling twice. My bum only just touches the blanket before I'm biting down into a Parma ham, mozzarella and sundried tomato sandwich, served in fresh focaccia bread.

'Oh, my God, this might be the best sandwich I've ever had,' I say through a mouthful.

I don't know if it's the authentic Italian ingredients, the stunning location or the fantastic company – perhaps it's all of the above.

'I'm glad you like it,' he replies, before popping an olive into his mouth.

'This is definitely like something out of a romance novel,' I tell him, trying to take it all in. 'It's just... unbelievable. I didn't think it happened in real life.'

Freddie removes a bottle of champagne from an ice bucket and pops the cork before pouring us each a glass.

I take a sip and it's so cold and crisp. I feel as if I'm in heaven.

'Tell me more about your books,' he says.

'Erm...' God, I hate talking about my books. I always feel so silly, as if I'm telling someone about a weird dream I had. Having said that, I'd rather talk about my books than my dream last night. 'They're romantic comedies. I get the feeling they're about to get more com than rom, given how laughable my love life is now.'

'What did you say your name was?' he asks, taking his phone from his pocket.

'Lila Rose,' I say. 'Wait, don't look me up me in front of me!'

'I just want to see what you've written,' he says. He waits for the go-ahead before he moves another muscle.

'Argh, okay, sure, go for it,' I say.

If I wasn't being shifty around Freddie before, I definitely am now. Sometimes it feels like giving someone a glimpse into my writing is like letting them peer into my soul.

'Oh, wow,' he says. 'Are you the Lila Rose who wrote *Spanked*?'

'What?' I reply. 'No!'

'It says so right here on Google, the first result...'

'What? I definitely didn't write that. Spanking is more your scene, Mr Eden.'

I don't know why I'm getting so defensive. It's as if I think that, if he can tap into my sexual side at all, he'll see straight through me. He'll know I'm interested in that side of him, that I had an X-rated dream about him...

'A-ha,' he says, gotcha-style. 'I thought you said you hadn't seen the movie or read the books.'

He raises his eyebrows and purses his lips knowingly.

'I haven't,' I say, quickly correcting myself. 'Well, hadn't. I was curious, so I watched... how did you know?'

'Because you can hardly look me in the eye today.' He laughs. 'My poor mom was exactly the same – I did warn her not to watch, but she was so proud of me for landing such a huge role... for about fifteen minutes of the movie.'

My eyes widen, as I recall the scene he's talking about. I can't imagine my mum watching me acting in a sex scene – I won't even let her read the naughty bits in my books.

'Also,' he starts, 'I saw it open on your phone this morning. Did you watch it last night?'

'I did,' I confess. 'I just wanted to see what you did.'

'I don't mind,' he replies. 'Of course, I am going to have to read one of your books, to level the playing field.'

'You can read the new one if it ever gets written.'

'I feel like I'm the only person trying to write it at the moment,' he teases. 'Anyway, you're not getting out of it that easy. What do you think?'

'Of the sandwiches? I'm on my third.'

'Of the movie.' He laughs. 'Of my movie... what did you think?'

He isn't giving me an inch to wriggle out of this one.

'It's a strange one because it's not something I would usually watch. I wouldn't have watched it if you weren't in it,' I insist, but then I soften a little. 'I actually rather appreciated it.'

'Oh yeah?'

'Yeah,' I reply. 'It made a nice change. You're weirdly doing your bit for feminism, even if you are beating a woman.'

'A consenting woman,' he points out.

'Well, that's exactly my point,' I continue. 'The male gaze is absolutely a thing... It was... refreshing, to watch a movie that was completely different. It was all for a female audience. It was nice to see a man being objectified for a change.'

Freddie laughs.

'I wasn't expecting such a deep analysis,' he says. 'But you're right. I think that's part of the reason women like it so much.'

That's partly the reason, but I'd imagine it has a lot to do with how absolutely delicious Freddie is. His character is so masterful and domineering, and it turns out I'm here for it. The only way Daniel was domineering in the bedroom was when he'd hog the duvet at night.

'We can't have too many movies that show a woman's attitude towards sexy accurately,' I say, dragging my mind from the gutter.

'Well, I'm glad you approve,' he says, raising his glass. 'Cheers.'

'Cheers,' I reply, gently clinking my glass on his.

I can't believe how unbelievably perfect this moment is. It's a shame he's wasted it on me.

'Seriously, Freddie, this is absolutely incredible,' I say.

'Incredible?' he replies. 'Already incredible and I haven't even mentioned that there are cakes in this box.'

He lightly taps a pink box next to him that is just begging me to open it.

'Oi, I'm being serious,' I say, but I will absolutely be tucking into the contents of that box in a moment. This is exactly what I wanted my honeymoon to be like – well, obviously this plus being married. There's no way Daniel would've organised anything like this though, and if I had he would've thought it was 'daft' and then I would've felt silly. I almost feel like a fraud, writing romance when it is severely lacking in my life. I just don't suppose I noticed until I took a step back and looked at the bigger picture.

'If this were a scene in one of your books, what would happen next?' he asks curiously.

'Erm...' I bite my lip. 'If this were a scene, and not a fake relationship to win a competition...'

It feels so forced, reminding him of that fact. Of course, he knows that's what this is – I suppose I want him to know that I know, just in case he thinks I'm reading anything into his efforts. I'm just a solution to his loneliness and his boredom, and he's just a way to make my ex jealous and hopefully win me 5k Euros.

'This is the kind of scene where someone makes a move,' I tell him. 'Usually the person who set it up – that's what it's all for. To woo the other person. Doing something like this – a big, romantic gesture, but a slow-burn one – gives you the chance to assess the situation. Is the other person interested or do they seem uncomfortable? Most importantly, are they going to kiss me back? It's a good way to test the water.'

Freddie is just staring at me, smiling, listening attentively.

'So, it always goes that way?' he asks. 'It's always the person who sets these things up who makes the first move?'

'Well, yes,' I reply. 'If someone does all this for you, maybe they have a whole thing planned out? Let them do it. And you don't want to just throw yourself at someone because they did a nice thing for you – it might seem like it's just out of gratitude. And if you get into territory where you have sex with people out of gratitude...'

'You're in one of my stories,' he says with an awkward chuckle. 'It's okay, I know.'

'Our genres are just apples and oranges,' I insist. 'People who read my books want a happy ever after. People who read the *Edge of Eden* books want—'

'A happy ending,' he jokes.

'Exactly,' I reply.

Freddie shuffles closer to me.

'Okay, so a character is going to make a move, what would he do? Would he move close to you like this?' Freddie places his face next to my ear. 'Maybe find a reason to whisper to you, just to get closer?'

I feel the hairs on the back of my neck stand to attention. Every inch of me is waiting with bated breath, to see what Freddie does next. I feel the tip of his nose brush against my cheek and it sends such a strong shockwave through my body, I jump to my feet.

'Oh, okay, wow,' I babble. 'That's, erm, really good thinking. Good idea for a scene. You know what, I'm going to go write it right now, while it's fresh in my head.'

'Oh, right now?'

'Right now.'

'Are you sure you don't want some dessert?'

'Sweet enough,' I reply, inwardly cringing. I hate it when people say things like that.

'Okay, if you need to write then don't let me stop you. I'll see you for more Mr & Mrs Valentine Island later?'

'Not if I see you first,' I reply. Another cringe. 'Yes, you will see me later – I'll see you later.'

I just need to stop talking.

'Okay, bye,' I say with a wave. An actual bloody wave, to say goodbye to someone a few feet away from me.

I hurry back towards the villa, jet-propelled by embarrassment.

That felt uncomfortably close to the dream I had about him last night. I know he's just trying to inspire me but I don't need to write, I need to take a cold shower. And learn how to look him in the eye again, before it's time for the next round of the competition.

25

Physical education was not my strongest subject at school. In fact, the only record I set during PE was for the most periods in one year, because I had an awful lot of notes to excuse me from taking part, all citing my menstrual cycle as the reason. If my PE teacher had cared at all about her job, she probably would've noticed that I almost always had my period or some kind of muscle strain – although muscle strain from what, I have no idea, because I avoided exercise at all costs.

Regrettably my passion for physical fitness (or lack thereof) has followed me into adulthood, and other than the occasional half-hearted trip to the gym whenever I start developing writer's butt (a fatter arse than usual) I've done well to avoid almost all types of physical activity. This has left me low-key unfit, in a way that would only hold me back if I wanted to play a sport or lift something heavy, but it's never really mattered... until tonight, because tonight apparently things are going to get physical.

We're all hanging around at the beach bar, waiting for the competition to begin. I don't know what it is yet, only that it's a physical thing. I'm really hoping Freddie can carry me, because I'm going to be useless.

Eva is on top form tonight. She's so sickly and full-on, which is probably why we weren't that close. She's kind of like a cross between a hippy and a toddler, with this blank whimsy about her that I'm almost certain she puts on because she thinks it makes her seem cute. She'll dance around on the spot, like a zombified, flossing eight-year-old boy who has spent too much time on Fortnite, but even when she's standing still she's got this sort of sway to her. It's as if her limbs are so weightless they just float off in all directions. She has a similar manner with her lips – if the competition tonight involved talking as much as you could, they would take one look at her and hand her a cheque.

'Oh, my God, can you imagine if Freddie Bianchi bought me a drink?' she says, by way of a hint. 'It would be the weirdest thing.'

Hmm. Would it be weirder than being on another man's honeymoon with him? I'm not so sure.

Freddie picks up the hint she's dropped.

'Lila, shall I dash to the bar and grab the four of us a drink? There's time, right?'

'Sure,' I reply, reassuring him with a smile.

I'm sure that most of the questions he asks me are not as they appear at face value. I don't think he's asking my permission to go to the bar, I think he's asking if I mind if he buys Daniel and Eva a drink. I don't actually mind – or, at least, acting as if I don't mind makes it seem as if I don't mind, which makes me look better than if I did mind... What a ridiculous mess of a thought.

'Oh, my gosh, I'll come with you,' she says, bouncing on the spot, almost popping out of the sides of her halter-neck top.

'Okay, sure.' Freddie laughs, averting his eyes.

Eva quickly fiddles with her straps before following him to the bar. For every one of Freddie's steps, Eva takes about four to keep up with him.

'Try not to shag him,' I say quietly, solely for Daniel's benefit. I turn to face him. 'I'm sure it's like muscle memory for that girl.'

'Christ, leave her alone, Lila,' Daniel snaps at me. 'In fact, leave us both alone.'

It makes me feel sick to my stomach, having to play nice with them. If it weren't for the prize money, I would be doing my best to keep as far away from them as possible.

'Are you kidding me? I didn't invite you here. I didn't ask to hang around with you. Eva is the one following me around like a pigeon, eyeing up my chips. She's all over Freddie and you're an idiot if you can't see that.'

Am I an idiot, for not realising something was going on with Daniel and Eva? I honestly didn't even think they liked each other all that much. I suppose that was a marked effort, to throw me off.

'You're paranoid,' he tells me.

'Is it any wonder?' I ask. 'After what you did to me? And if Eva thinks you're not going to do the same to her, well, she's an idiot too.'

'You're just as bad as I am,' Daniel snaps.

'Oh, this ought to be good,' I utter. I can feel a surge of the sassiness that accompanies my temper surging through my veins. My fight or flight reflex always tends to favour 'fight' although my weapon of choice is always my wit. Well, I call it wit, but my zingy one-liners can quickly turn into the kind of chat you'd expect from an angry teenager in a park who has had one too many alcopops. 'How am I as bad as either of you?'

'You moved on – on the day of our wedding.'

I roll my eyes theatrically. The hypocrisy is overwhelming.

'You moved on before our wedding day,' I remind him. 'You were cheating on me in the run-up to our wedding – and on our wedding day – and then you've got the gall to show up here with her, on our honeymoon! When you realised I was here, why not just go home, instead of continuing your weird little fling right under my nose, rubbing it in my face?'

'And you're not rubbing Freddie in my face?' he replies.

'Careful, Daniel, you sound jealous,' I reply. 'Freddie and I were already together before you got here.'

'You're clearly only with him because he's famous, because you think it will upset me,' he says.

'For your information, I had no idea who he was when I met him.'

'You had no idea who he was? Everyone knows who Freddie Bianchi is.'

'No, they don't,' I reply. 'You certainly don't. You know nothing about celebrity culture. You thought Armie Hammer was a toothpaste.'

'So you would have just moved on with any old person as fast, then?' he asks.

'I moved on when it was appropriate to move on.'

I know that I didn't technically move on, on our wedding day – and I still haven't. I'm still so angry and so obsessed with the two of them, wondering how they're spending their days here together and feeling angry that Eva has just assumed my life, and that Daniel hasn't only let her, he's facilitated the whole thing with intent.

'You could still be respectful of the fact that I'm next door,' he fumes. 'I heard the two of you at it last night – all night long, obviously for my benefit.'

It takes me a couple of seconds to figure out what the hell he's talking about. It makes sense though – if I could hear Ali and Max from one side of the wall, he and Eva will have been able to hear from the other.

So Daniel thinks it was me screaming, howling and banging on the walls... well, I'm not about to correct him.

'I wasn't doing anything for your benefit last night,' I insist – not technically a lie, I'm just letting him wander down the wrong path.

'That's rubbish,' he replies. 'I've never heard you make noises like that.'

'Well, then, I guess perhaps Freddie just knows what he's doing more than you did,' I say. 'Did you ever think of that?'

Before we have chance to continue, Freddie and Eva arrive back. Freddie is carrying a tray of drinks. He gestures towards my usual porn star martini.

'Did they let you make it?' I ask him.

'No such luck, sorry,' he replies. 'The staff here are so funny about the customers trying to do their jobs for them.'

I giggle, which makes Daniel seethe. His face is almost as red as Eva's bottle-dye job.

'Gosh, so warm tonight,' Eva says, changing the subject.

I think one of the reasons she's making me so angry is because she isn't acting as if she's stolen my man, she's acting as if we're on a double date. As far as Eva is concerned, she's just on a lovely holiday with her boyfriend, her friend and her friend's new boyfriend. Nobody likes an atmosphere, and I wouldn't accept her apology if she offered me one, but she's acting as if everything is fine.

I wonder if I would feel better if she apologised. I suppose, in a way, even if I didn't want to accept her apology, the fact that she offered one up would at least show that she knew she had done something wrong and that she felt guilty about it. If Ali had done this to me – my best friend of, oh, I don't know, however many years doesn't make us sound old – would I be so willing to throw my friendship away? Probably not, but, then again, a true friend like Ali would never do this.

I don't think I can forgive Daniel either. Four years are a lot to throw away, but he didn't just have some drunken one-nighter that he regrets. Even if they did and it lasted, what, seven minutes if we're going on Daniel's average endurance, then that's seven minutes to realise you're making a mistake. Set yourself a timer for seven minutes, and spend that time imagining doing something awful to someone you love. Seven minutes is actually quite a significant amount of time to think about the same thing. It seems to me though that Daniel and Eva have been at it for a long time, which means multiple bursts of seven minutes and everything that happened in between. All time that could be spent rethinking or regretting. He can't have given either of those things a second thought or he would have stopped – or at the very least, finished with me to be with her.

I've thought about it a lot – it's almost all I can think about – and, no matter which angle I come at it from, I just cannot wrap my head around the magnitude of what they have done – and continue to do. Why bring her on our honeymoon? Why stay, when they realised I was here? They really, really don't care about anyone but themselves. Why would I want to forgive and forget with people like that? He's a shitty boyfriend and she's a shitty friend.

Matteo and Zoey burst onto the stage to the tune of Olivia Newton-John's 'Physical'. They're wearing San Valentino vests with matching shorts, as well as sweatbands on every part of their bodies that can accommodate sweatbands. They're doing some kind of choreographed, exaggerated version of a jog, perfectly in time with the beat of the music.

I'm not sure this is completely necessary but, even if it were, it goes on for about two minutes longer than it ought to.

'Good evening and welcome to Mr & Mrs Valentine Island,' Zoey bellows into her microphone. 'All of our wonderful couples are back and ready for tonight's round of the competition and tonight we are getting physical!'

It's amazing, how big a crowd Mr & Mrs Valentine Island pulls. Every seat is taken and every person is cheering excitedly. If I were here on my honeymoon, I'm not sure how into this I would be, watching other couples potentially making fools of themselves. Freddie and I don't exactly have anything to lose – it's not as if our relationship will take a knock if he doesn't know when my birthday is. If I were doing all of this with my actual significant other, though, I'd be terrified. Daniel and I couldn't even put together Ikea furniture without falling out, and we weren't competing against anyone. As a keen gamer Daniel is very competitive and, even though this isn't FIFA, I'm worried we're going to see that competitive side of him tonight.

It's warm tonight. I know, we're in southern Italy, but this is the warmest night we've had yet. It's muggy – a word that sounds so awful it accurately represents how it feels. The air feels thick and hard to take in, which only adds to that warm, suffocating, begging-for-a-breeze, just-want-to-jump-in-the-sea feeling. Of course, it had to be this sweltering on the night when we're 'getting physical'.

'Tonight will test our couples' staying power,' Zoey says, the suggestion in her voice inciting 'woos' from the crowd. I hear one especially loud man shout out 'oioi' – he sounds as if he's from my neck of the woods. It's comforting, to hear a little bit of home.

A couple of hotel staff members lead us all out onto the dance floor in front of the stage, which is clear tonight in preparation for whatever the hell is going to happen. It worries me that we're all out here on the floor at the same time. I worry about what they're going to get us to do. God, I hope it doesn't involve dancing. I'm definitely more can't can't than cancan. In fact, the last time I tried to dance in public a man thought I was choking and tried to perform the Heimlich manoeuvre on me.

Zoey announces that this round will test our physical strength (I don't have any), our strength as a couple (we're not one, I hardly know the guy), and our stubbornness – yes, finally, a quality (not sure it's a quality) I have. It's amazing how stubborn and petty I can be when I'm annoyed. Daniel is also the kind of person who likes to have the last word, so our arguments would be fun. To be fair, we never really had that many arguments and I always thought that was testament to how strong we were as a couple, which I guess we weren't. Looking at it from the outside, perhaps he never cared about me enough to fight for anything.

'So, our lovely couples will decide who is going to be the strength in their relationship, and who is going to be the moral support,' Zoey continues. 'We're all about equal opportunities here at Valentine Island, so it's up to you who does what, but the aim of the game is for the strongest person to pick their partner up and hold them for as long as they can. Ladies, you can lift your fellas if you'd prefer – although we've got some nice, strong-looking boys out there tonight.'

I notice her eyes linger on Freddie for a moment. It makes me just the tiniest bit jealous, for some reason. Silly really because – you know what I'm going to say, so all together now – he isn't my real boyfriend.

'Now, you can hold your partner in any way you like,' Zoey explains. 'Anyone who lets go of their partner, whether it be by accident or on purpose, will be eliminated. First place will get the most points, followed by second, third – et cetera. So, are you ready?'

It doesn't seem as if we're getting any time to discuss strategy; we're just expected to go on her whistle. It's been a little awkward with Freddie since earlier. When he knocked on my door to walk me here, Ali walked with us on her way to linger around the bar where Max works. Then, when we got here, Eva and Daniel were straight over to us.

And now, without so much as an air-clearing chat (I was so awkward earlier, he must've noticed) Freddie is going to be literally holding me.

'Okay, I'll just pick you up in front of me, wrap your legs around my waist and your arms around my neck, got it?'

'Are you sure that's the best way?' I ask, but as the whistle blows and it's time to go, I do exactly as Freddie says.

In a split second, I'm in his arms, clinging onto his neck, my legs locked around his waist. It all happens in a heartbeat; as I move into position I feel my dress roll up my thighs and sit pretty around my waist. I know, without looking, that my arse is exposed – thank God I put knickers on!

'Is that okay?' I ask Freddie. 'Shit, I think everyone can see my knickers.'

'Well, I can't see, so not everyone can,' he jokingly reassures me. 'At least you have knickers on.'

I do... but they're massive. I'm sure that should be better, because bigger knickers equal more coverage, but they're so unsexy that it might even be more embarrassing than if I didn't have any on at all.

'We've got this in the bag. I can hold this position all night,' Freddie tells me.

'That'll be your *Edge of Eden* training,' I reply.

'You mean from the gym, to get the physique Edward is supposed to have, or from filming sex scenes for hours and hours at a time?'

'All right, show-off.' I laugh. 'Does it matter which?'

'I suppose not,' he replies.

I glance over at Daniel and Eva. Daniel might not be all that strong, but Eva is basically weightless. I, on the other hand, wish I hadn't eaten so much while I've been here. I'm already much taller than her, with a bigger frame, so I'm bound to be heavier, even without the carb-binge I've been on recently. Everyone indulges on holiday though, right? It's not usually a consideration, that you'll need to be light for a competition.

'Hold on tight,' he says. 'I'll pull your dress down.'

'Can you do that?' I ask. 'Without dropping me?'

I look around at the other couples. Some of them are really struggling already.

'Are you worried about me dropping you or us losing the competition?' he replies with a knowing smile.

'Is it okay if it's both?'

When Freddie smiles his dimples deepen and his eyes twinkle. Wrapped around his body like this, with him holding me so tightly, we couldn't be closer if we tried. There's an awkwardness that comes with being so in someone's face. We're not usually forced to look each other in the eye – with near-constant eye contact – from nothing more than a couple of inches away. This discomfort doesn't just come from being in such intimate proximity though – the sweltering evening heat isn't helping. Where my arms are touching each other they are slick with sweat, which is making it harder for me to hold out. Thankfully Freddie has this covered and with one swift arm movement my modesty (as if I even have any at this point) is restored.

As other couples' arms grow tired and patience wears thin, the competition begins to slowly fall away.

'How long do you think it's been?' I ask Freddie.

I feel obliged to keep talking to him, as if it might make this a bit less awkward if we behave like civil colleagues who share an office.

'Why don't you check your watch?' Daniel asks Freddie.

Daniel and Eva are still in, but Daniel can't even begin to hide the strain in his voice. Eva has slid down his back, turning their piggyback hold into something that looks desperately uncomfortable. She's so low down that her bottom is pointing towards the floor, and her arms are bolt straight, her elbows hard as she clings onto his neck. I think Daniel's strange, almost robotic voice is a product of trying to support Eva's weight when most of the pressure will be from her hands around his neck. It's funny, she almost looks as if she's attacking him from behind, trying to strangle him. He certainly looks as if he's being attacked; he looks as if he's going to drop her any second.

'Nice try,' Freddie replies, before whispering to me, 'Does he really think I'm that stupid?'

'He thinks everyone is stupid,' I tell him.

Freddie is definitely finding this much easier than everybody else is. I'd say he wasn't breaking a sweat, but everyone is sweating tonight, even without the physical activity.

It isn't unpleasant, being this close to him, though. I can smell his aftershave, masculine yet sweet, the shampoo he has used, which I recognise from the suite bathrooms, and then just something else, something I can't explain – something undeniably attractive.

There is something about Freddie that is just so inviting, that makes you want to get up close and personal with him, bury your face in his neck, wrap your limbs around him. As awkward as this situation is, I've never felt more at ease. I feel so safe and secure. Freddie isn't just holding me up in the competition, he's holding my head up high for me when I don't know how to do it myself. He's carrying me in more ways than he realises – and for absolutely nothing in return.

'Just lift yourself up,' Daniel snaps at Eva.

I am a little taken aback. Daniel might be a bit grumpy sometimes, but this snappy side of him is something new. I wonder if it's because he feels bad, but he seems to want to win this even more than I do.

'I can't,' she replies. 'I've only got little arms.'

Her cuteness is like eating a spoonful of sherbet. Somehow both sickly sweet and intolerably sour. She makes my eyes water and my teeth hurt.

'It's just us and them left,' Freddie whispers into my ear. 'Shall we try and psych him out a little?'

'Yes,' I say, my eyes widening with excitement.

Freddie readjusts his grip on my body, holding me securely before dancing with me, grooving to whatever Italian pop music is playing in the bar. The audience, finding it impossible not to be charmed, cheer and coo.

'It's working,' Freddie whispers to me.

I look over at Daniel, who is staggering to one side as if he's trying to walk home after a few too many. Eva has sagged, practically down to behind his knees.

'Just hang on,' he groans. He's panting like a pregnant lady on a labour ward, and the tiny woman partially hanging between his legs isn't helping to dissuade this comparison.

'I can't,' Eva says, breathy but casually. She doesn't seem to care all that much about winning the round. I suppose she knows that they'll go through to the next round regardless of whether they win.

Daniel and I are trapped in this unspoken standoff, both so desperate to win, to get one over on each other. Lucky for me I picked a stronger person to compete with.

Having had enough, consequences be damned, Eva simply lets go of Daniel's neck. Of course, Daniel is still holding onto her legs for dear life, so as Eva goes down, landing on her back on the dance floor with a thump that makes me wince, it's only a split second before Daniel falls backwards, landing on top of her. I wince again.

There is a beat of silence before every single holidaymaker in the audience erupts into laughter. Well, this is their entertainment, this lowbrow version of the Colosseum. And it's such infectious laughter, with Freddie quickly coming down with a case of it too. It isn't long before I catch it, unable to keep a straight face as they hurry to their feet, Daniel yelling at Eva for showing him up.

As Zoey announces us the winners, Freddie lifts me up like a trophy before gently placing me down next to him. An unimpressed Daniel marches over to us.

'What are you laughing at, eh?' he asks. He sounds so northern when he's angry. I think it takes Freddie a second to realise what's happening. 'I said, what are you laughing at, mate?'

As my angry little ex squares up to my mountain of a fake boyfriend, in front of all these people, I take it upon myself to step between them.

'It's just a bit of fun, Dan, calm down,' Freddie insists as his amusement fizzles out.

'My name isn't Dan,' Daniel says angrily.

'And I'm not your mate,' Freddie replies. 'So let's call it even.'

I am momentarily distracted as a light catches my eye. Eva's necklace has come out from under her top and is reflecting one of the spotlights into my eye. I am about to look away when I realise the necklace looks familiar.

'Is that my necklace?' I ask.

'What?' she replies. 'No. Of course not.'

She quickly tucks it back behind her neckline, but it's too late, I've already seen it.

A neat pink stone set inside a halo of diamonds on a rose-gold chain. Daniel bought me it as a pre-wedding present. It wasn't my style at all, but after I happened upon it by accident, when he was planning on surprising me with it, I felt bad.

'Oh, my God...' I blurt.

I look at Daniel. He looks petrified. He knows that I know.

'I found this necklace in your sock drawer when I was putting your washing away... you said it was an early wedding present, that you were saving it for the day before the wedding. It was for her, wasn't it? So you gave it to me, and you bought her another one. I thought it was weird, you'd buy me something so tacky. Now it makes sense. It was for that tacky little Barbie.'

'It's not my fault he likes to buy me things,' Eva protests.

I think she might actually be an idiot.

Freddie wraps an arm around me.

'Forget that bastard,' Freddie tells me.

Daniel sees red.

As Daniel tries to push past me to get to Freddie – although Lord knows what he would do if he did – he accidentally elbows me in the ribs.

'Ow,' I involuntarily blurt.

The next thing I know, Freddie has Daniel on the floor.

'You need to calm down,' Freddie tells him firmly. 'You just hurt Lila. Did you even realise or were you too busy lunging at me?'

'Get off me, you silly bastard,' Daniel mumbles from the floor.

I hear sobbing and turn around to see Eva.

'Why is everyone trying to ruin my holiday?' she cries out.

'Your holiday?' I say angrily.

Matteo, along with two burly security guards, steps into our personal space.

'You need to come with us now,' Matteo instructs.

As the four of us are frogmarched away from the bar, I notice the silent audience, their jaws on the floor as they take in our little performance. I bet they can't believe their luck, getting more of a show than they bargained for.

As we're led towards the hotel building, Freddie takes hold of my hand. Why do I feel as if we're in big trouble?

26

DAY 10

'Spent the night at Freddie's again, I see,' Ali teases as we head for the cafe where she's arranged for us to have lunch. 'You dirty mare.'

'Are you kidding me?' I ask. I'm so flabbergasted my voice goes higher than I knew possible. 'I had to stay with Freddie again because when I got back last night, you and Max were at it again!'

Ali scrunched up her face.

'We waited for ages before we got going, but when you never came back I figured you were just on the *Edge of Eden*.'

Ali wiggles her eyebrows and jiggles the assets she paid good money for.

'I suppose we were back quite late, but you won't believe what happened,' I tell her.

I watch as nothing more than a hint of something juicy powers Ali's engine, lighting up her eyes. Gossip is her lifeblood.

'Wait, don't tell me,' she insists. 'Wait until we sit down, when I've got a drink in my hand. I want to enjoy this.'

As promised, I wait until we are seated in the Rosso coffee bar.

'Shall we order first?' I ask before I get going.

'It's all arranged,' Ali tells me. 'I thought we deserved something special.'

'Oh, okay,' I reply. 'That's lovely.'

'I know,' Ali says with a dismissive bat of her hand. 'Now, spill the tea.'

'Okay, well.' I wiggle my bum down into the cushion-covered seat, ensuring I am in prime storytelling position. 'It was round two of Mr & Mrs Valentine Island last night.'

I pause, so that Ali can remind me of how lame this is, but she doesn't. She has her chin resting on the back of her hand and her eyes are glued to me.

'So, the aim of the game last night was for the men to lift their women up and see who could hold them for the longest,' I explain.

'Freddie will have crushed that, surely?' Ali replies.

'Of course,' I reply, weirdly proud of my man (who isn't my man).

'How did Eva and Daniel do?' she asks.

'They came second.'

'Ergh. I suppose the little snake just wrapped herself around his neck,' Ali suggests.

She isn't a million miles off.

'It was weirdly fun, and I was delighted that Freddie and I won! But Daniel wasn't – he got really upset. He started on Freddie. He accidentally shoved me!'

'That puny little moron,' Ali replies just as a waiter approaches us. She turns to him. 'Not you, babe.'

The optionally oblivious Italian man places a series of items down in front of us, along with a bottle of champagne. He fills our glasses before wishing us '*buon appetito*' and leaving us, just the two of us, surrounded by candles and rose petals.

'Ali, are you coming on to me?' I joke. 'This is pretty romantic.'

'It's their romantic chocolate lunch,' she tells me. 'But, sadly, you're already in the friendzone.'

A romantic chocolate lunch involves a chocolate fountain, rhythmically pumping rich-smelling, silky-looking chocolate, accompanied by a variety of things to dip into it – marshmallows, biscotti, little bombolini donuts that, upon closer inspection (ate one the second they hit the table) are filled with a delicious vividly yellow Italian custard. Everything you've ever dreamed of smothering with chocolate (except maybe Freddie, although that might just be me – well, me and the 7.2 million followers I found out he has on Instagram last night) is right here on this table.

'So, go on, what happened?' Ali asks as she places an entire chocolate-covered strawberry into her mouth.

'So, it all kicked off – all in front of an audience – and I think Freddie thinks he has everyone fooled with his sunglasses, but, other than me, I'm pretty sure everyone knows who he is, so we've got this massive crowd watching. The security blokes come over, march us off, take us to some little office room in the hotel. It felt like school, waiting to find out what our punishment was.'

'If Edward started spanking you, this is definitely just a sexy dream you had last night,' she says. 'Weird you included your ex in it.'

'Erm, you mean Freddie, not Edward,' I remind her. 'I am terrified that, since I watched the movie, I'm going to accidentally call him Edward... but no, that was not our punishment. There is a punishment though.'

'No!' Ali's champagne glass hovers in front of her mouth as she waits for a taste of something juicier. 'What's your punishment?'

'Get this,' I start, hoping to psych her up as much as possible. 'It turns out that Valentine Island isn't just for those who are wildly in love, it's for couples who are struggling too. They have multiple therapy programmes for couples... and they want Freddie and I to attend a couple of sessions.'

'But you're not even a real couple,' Ali reminds me, her glass still held firmly in place.

'I know,' I reply. 'There's a group session tomorrow – which Daniel and Eva will be at – and then we have to have a one-on-one session – well, technically I think they're two-on-two sessions.'

'How kinky,' Ali says.

'Two therapists,' I point out. 'One male, one female. So no gender feels ganged up on.'

Ali finally allows herself to fall about laughing. She roars, bangs the table, throws her head back. It's quite the scene, for everyone else here – real couples – trying to have a romantic lunch.

'Can they make you do it, though?' she asks. 'They can't, right?'

'I don't suppose they can, no,' I reply. 'But they've told us that, if we want to continue to take part in the competition, then we have to resolve our issues. So...'

'So, if you want to wipe the smile off Daniel and Eva's faces...'

'And win enough money to pay off my wedding debts,' I add. 'Then yes, I have to go to therapy.'

'Oh, my God, this is honestly the best date I've ever been on,' she jokes. 'This is hilarious.'

'It's definitely better than the last date we went on together,' I point out.

'Oh, God, yes – I don't know if I ever truly thanked you for that.'

'You definitely owe me one,' I remind her. 'Worst date of my life.'

Years ago, before I met Daniel, I ended up going on a double date with Ali – my first and only double date.

Ali had met this guy called Gareth – I think he was some kind of surgeon, which is probably why Ali was so interested in him. Ali going out with a surgeon would be like me going out with someone who sold chocolate... just with opposite consequences. She was about to 'seal the deal' with Gareth, as she phrased it at the time, until his brother came into town and he said he would have to cancel. Ali was so sure that, if she didn't bed him that night, she never would, so she told Gareth that he should bring his brother along on the date, because she knew someone who would be perfect for him... me.

Gareth's brother Howard was certainly an interesting character, but I was in no way perfect for him, and he could not have been more wrong for me. At first I figured we just didn't have all that much in common, but that didn't matter too much; I was just here for my friend. Howard was talking about the PhD he was writing at the moment – something about animals. That's the thing with PhDs, though, they're always so deep into a particular topic that, to a layman, the theses are impossible to wrap your head around. Had he been writing about something closer to my area of expertise – say, an analysis of hegemonic social constructs in *Gossip Girl* – then we could've been talking, but the way things were, I was just politely listening.

Howard finally committed a blatant date sin, when we were walking outside afterwards. It was a chilly evening but, when Ali pointed out how

freezing she was (a ploy to get Gareth to touch her) and I quickly pointed
out how I wasn't cold at all (so that Howard didn't feel obliged to wrap an
arm around me) Howard began to explain to me how the excess fat on my
tummy (the little plumpness we all have, if we don't live in the gym)
worked like whale blubber, keeping me warm. He even suggested I put
my hand up my top and feel my stomach, telling me that if my skin felt
cold, my blubber was working... By the time Gareth chimed in about
liposuction (I absolutely did not need liposuction) Ali gave them both a
slap and we parted ways. A very weird night and, true to her promise, Ali
has never asked me to go on a date with one of her lovers' friends or rela-
tives since.

'I'll pay you back one day,' Ali says.

'Want to go to this group therapy session for me?' I suggest.

'I don't think the recast would go unnoticed,' she points out. 'Are you
really going to go?'

I examine the donut in my hand for a second, before popping it in my
mouth.

'Yep,' I eventually say. 'If I want to win the competition and I want to
kick Daniel and Eva's butts...'

'And if you want to keep hanging out with Freddie,' she points out.
'There's that too.'

I purse my lips and shrug my shoulders. She's got me there. Couples
therapy sounds like an absolute nightmare but, with Freddie... I don't
know, I think it's going to be fun.

27

Freddie and I are one of several very different couples gathered in one of the large therapy rooms.

It's a very calming space, with light colours, soft lighting and ambient sounds drifting from the speakers.

We're all sitting on chairs in a circle – me, Freddie, Daniel, Eva, a therapist leading the session and a bunch of other couples.

I thought for a second that perhaps Daniel and Eva wouldn't show up, but I guess they're in it to win it as much as I am.

Each couple is taking it in turns to speak a little about their lives together and why they have ended up giving talking therapy a go. We're in one of the English sessions, so everyone here is from the UK or the US. I suppose it makes things easier, if everyone is speaking the same language. Victoria, our therapist today, doesn't have an overly strong accent but I can hear the subtle Yorkshire undertones. Here in this room I could almost think I were at home in England, were it not so, so warm. Luckily the air con is keeping us cool in here; it isn't doing much for the tempers though.

'I'm Jen and this is my husband, Kevin,' a woman who appears to be in her late thirties says. I instantly like her because, although she sounds quite shy, she has the same accent as I do and she's tall. I see a lot of myself in her.

'And what brought you two to Valentine Island?' Victoria asks.

'Lies upon lies,' Kevin scoffs.

'Oh?' Victoria prompts. I've noticed she does a lot of prompting. Another thing she does is wait for ages before she speaks, letting people talk and talk and then, when she remains silent, they talk a little more. I feel as if she's trying to bleed us dry of information. People talk the amount it makes sense to talk, but then she therapists them into saying more than they ought to. Well, she isn't going to trick me into sharing my feelings.

'My darling wife – of seven years – told me that she was taking me somewhere special on holiday,' he explains. 'She arranged for her mum to look after the kids, drove us to the airport and then brought me here!'

'You don't think here is special?' Victoria asks.

'Look, Jen knows there's only one place I want to go. Hobbiton in New Zealand. When she told me she was taking me somewhere special, she knew what she was implying.'

Victoria can't wait for a second to ask this question.

'Hobbiton?'

'It's from *The Lord of the Rings*,' he tells her, very matter-of-factly. 'You can do these pilgrimages through Middle-earth.'

'You're a big fan of *The Lord of the Rings*?' Victoria asks.

Kevin's wife, Jen, blushes with embarrassment.

'Is Bilbo Baggins a hobbit?' he replies – I imagine rhetorically.

'Did you mislead him?' Victoria asks Jen.

'I knew he'd never agree to a therapy holiday so, it's true, I didn't tell him where we were going – but I didn't think he'd be disappointed.'

'You know all I want is to go to New Zealand,' he replies, leaning forward. 'It's all I talk about. It's ridiculous, saying you didn't think I'd assume that's where we were going.'

'What's ridiculous is a grown man, crying on a beautiful beach, wearing a pair of hobbit feet.'

'Oh, yeah, I'm the nutcase,' he snaps back. 'You're the one who took me into a therapy session with two therapists who I thought were guests here too. I was like, "Oh, these two nosey buggers ask a lot of personal questions.'"

'Okay,' Victoria interrupts hurriedly, stopping things before they get going. 'We all understand a lot more about why you two are here. Who do we have next?'

'We're Eva and Daniel,' Eva says, all smiles, her head bouncing up and down like a nodding dog. She has his hand tightly between both of hers. 'We recently celebrated our first anniversary.'

My ears ring and my vision blurs. I feel so overwhelmed with shock and anger, I feel as if I'm going to pass out. I feel an arm wrap around me; it's Freddie, pulling me back from the other side. He rubs my shoulder reassuringly, which makes me feel a bit calmer, but I'm still so furious and upset.

'Congratulations,' Victoria says. 'And what brought you to Valentine Island?'

'We recently went through a little bit of turbulence,' Eva explains as Daniel nods emphatically. Victoria nods as she listens. They're all bouncing their heads up and down as if they're at an indie gig. 'But we continue on our journey, and we're stronger than ever.'

Listening to Daniel and Eva talking about their relationship is a real out-of-body experience. Daniel was with me. They were going behind my back. And yet I feel so detached from it all, as if I'm a fly on the wall, watching a reality TV show. They're both characters I recognise and I can't believe what shocking thing they're doing now... but, as upset as I am, I feel removed from it. I feel as if my day-to-day life was taken from me and, with no idea what's going to happen next, all I know now is this. Valentine Island is my new normal. I know that it's just a holiday, and I'm not saying I want to live in a perpetual state of post-break-up, with the two of them living next door, messing around with Freddie to try and show them how over it I am... but here, things are easier. I don't have to go back to my day-to-day routine, working, shopping, paying the bills, sharing a house with Daniel. Here really is a holiday – and Freddie is a fantastic distraction – but back home I'm going to have to face up to everything. At least while I'm here, it isn't just a holiday. It's a break from reality. A reality that I'm terrified to go back to.

'How lovely,' Victoria says.

Victoria will know why the four of us are here, which does make me wonder why she thought it might be a good idea to sit us next to each other. One wrong word and this circle of chairs could form the barrier for a fighting pit.

'And finally,' Victoria says, turning to me and Freddie.

I'm about to speak when Freddie takes the lead. He removes his sunglasses before he speaks.

'Holy crap,' Jen blurts.

'What?' Kevin asks her.

'F... F... F...'

'You sound like a steam train,' he tells her. 'Spit it out.'

'Freddie Bianchi... from *Edge of Eden*...'

'The mucky movies for women?' Kevin asks, looking Freddie up and down. 'Fair play to you, mate. I think my wife has sex with you more than she does with me.'

I wince. I feel as if I'm watching my parents argue, caught in the middle trying to eat my fish fingers and not get scarred for life.

'I'm Freddie,' he continues, quickly pulling attention back from Jen and Kevin's bickering. 'This is Lila. We're still in that honeymoon phase where we can't get enough of each other.'

'That's lovely,' Victoria replies. 'Any issues so far?'

'Only in the bedroom,' Freddie replies.

I am taken aback by his response. He's going rogue and the fact I have no idea what he's going to say makes me feel vulnerable.

'Would you like to elaborate?' Victoria prompts. I swear I just saw her bite her lip. It seems as if all women really are mad about Edward Eden – even the therapists.

'Well, we're here on this wonderful holiday... but we really struggle to get out of bed. We want to make the most of it and see the sights, but... you know.'

'Well, there are worse problems to have,' Victoria replies. 'I understand you had an altercation with Daniel last night during Mr & Mrs Valentine Island.'

'Daniel is my ex,' I explain. It's on the tip of my tongue to dish every devastating detail of what has happened but will it make me feel better? Probably not. I'm sure I'll just feel embarrassed, and it might delegitimise my showmance with Freddie. If I do start having it out with Daniel, I really will need a therapist.

'Oh,' Victoria replies. 'Daniel, do you think perhaps you were jealous that Freddie is with Lila now?'

'No,' he quickly snaps back, his shifty little eyes bouncing from side to side. 'Of course not.'

'Perhaps you feel emasculated by Edward?'

'Freddie,' Freddie corrects her. He laughs awkwardly. It seems as if this happens a lot.

'Sorry, Freddie,' she replies, her cheeks flushing.

'Of course, I'm not emasculated... by him,' Daniel insists unconvincingly.

'No shame in it, mate,' Kevin chimes in. 'Wait until you've been together seven years – you'll be happy your wife has someone else she's interested in. Bloody hell, you can't win with women. You either want too much sex from them, or you're not giving them enough...'

'I'm not threatened by him,' Daniel snaps.

'Hmm, that's interesting,' Victoria says. 'No one said "threatened" – do you think you feel threatened?'

'What?' he replies. 'No. I just said that I didn't feel threatened by him. He's just the muscle who got hired to be in some rubbish film. He isn't better than me.'

'Daniel, shut up,' I snap.

'It's okay,' Freddie reassures me. 'Let him talk, it's funny.'

'You think this is funny?' Daniel asks, jumping to his feet.

'I do,' our resident hobbit says, before his wife jabs him in the arm with her elbow.

'Okay, okay, okay,' Victoria says. 'Everyone in their seats now. I need to regain control of this session. No more judgement, let's try some positivity.'

Daniel, scowling at Freddie, angered by his calm smile, reluctantly sits back down.

'Can you stop acting like you're bothered,' I just about make out Eva whisper to him.

'I want everyone to take a turn at telling the group something positive about their partner, okay?' Victoria suggests. 'Claire and Simon, you go first.'

Claire and Simon, other than introducing themselves, have been otherwise pretty silent throughout everyone else's mess. They both utter perfectly reasonable but otherwise unremarkable traits they like in each other.

'Jen is a good mum,' Kevin offers up, after a few seconds thinking about it.

'The nicest thing you can say about me is that I'm a good mum?' she repeats angrily. 'I may as well be the nanny.'

'I don't know why I bloody bother,' he replies.

Watching them argue, it is crystal clear why they are both here... but they're still together and they're trying. That's what you do when you're unhappy with your partner, right? You try and you work on things, even if they're driving you mad. You don't shag one of their friends.

'Skip me,' Jen insists.

'Eva,' Victoria prompts.

'Hmm, well... he's very generous. He buys me lots of things,' she replies, sounding a little bit like a kid, talking about why they like their birthday.

'Okay,' Victoria replies.

I'm not about to claim that I can psychoanalyse a person who psycho-analyses people for a living, but it's plain for everyone to see that Victoria can detect the cracks in Daniel and Eva's relationship. Well, it serves them right. That's what happens when you try and forge a relationship out of parts of someone else's. It would be like trying to build yourself a house with whatever is in your shed along with half a stolen caravan. It's just a messy nightmare that isn't going to hold up.

'I like that Eva isn't a nightmare like some women I've dated,' Daniel says. 'She isn't messy, she doesn't nag me, she isn't dramatic.'

Eva gasps theatrically.

'Oh, Daniel, I love you so much,' she says, closing her eyes as she hugs his arm tightly.

Nope, she isn't dramatic at all.

'Okay,' Victoria says. 'But try to keep your comments completely positive. Lila?'

'I love that Freddie does whatever it takes to make me smile,' I say. 'It's like nothing is too much for him.'

We might be here pretending to be a couple, but every word I just said is completely true. I mean, look at him, he's a movie star on holiday, and yet he's sitting here in this warm room with me, having counselling, pretending to be my boyfriend, being insulted by Daniel... I can't believe he's still sitting here.

'Lovely,' Victoria replies. 'Finally, Freddie... what do you like the most about Lila?'

Freddie looks at me for a moment. As his dimples deepen, I smile back at him. With our eyes we exchange a look that acknowledges how ridiculous this is. I try to apologise to him simply by adjusting my smile, turning my grin into a sort of awkward, constipated-looking gurn, to let him know how sorry I am that he's been put on the spot like this. I hope he realises.

'What do I love about Lila?' he starts. 'I love that she never gives up on love. After everything she's been through and how everyone has treated her, you could forgive anyone in her position for losing hope... but not Lila. She's a brilliant, romantic, wonderful person, and I am so lucky that she didn't give up on love before she met me.'

'God, you're good,' Kevin says. 'You guys should get drinks with us.'

'Oh, yes,' Jen quickly adds.

'We'd love to,' says Freddie. 'Right, gorgeous?'

'We would,' I add, but that's about all I can say. I'm stunned by Freddie's amazing reply. I suppose he's right, I haven't given up on love, as much as I probably should have. I just wish that everything he said were true because, now that I think about it, I don't think it's just love I want... I think it's Freddie.

28

I'm not sure our counselling session went all that well, not by anyone's standards. I don't feel any better for attention, Daniel only seems to be angrier, the poor couple who wound up sitting next to Jen and Kevin are probably scarred for life, and I wouldn't be surprised if our therapist was currently updating her CV, looking for work in a less stressful environment like a prison or a bomb-disposal unit.

For a moment I was worried that they wouldn't allow us to carry on competing in Mr & Mrs Valentine Island, but it turns out that, after last night's display, the crowd are loving watching Freddie, and I think the staff have realised that they would be stupid to kick him out of the competition. By association, this means that I get to carry on competing with him and, to avoid Daniel and Eva kicking off about the special treatment, they have been allowed to continue in the competition too.

I might mind, had we not just kicked their butts again, in round three of the competition. I suppose tonight it was easy. We were all blindfolded and shown to the dance floor, where we were told that the aim of the game was to find our partner simply by using our hands. My eyes were already covered, but I heard the audience 'woo' when this was announced – I think this is the resort's attempt at doing something semi-saucy, but I suppose it's only as saucy as you make it, and we were categorically told behind the scenes that, whatever happened during this round, we were not to 'touch anyone where they wouldn't want to be touched' – words that, before I knew what the aim of the game was going to be, absolutely terrified me.

It wasn't so bad though. I didn't have to encounter too many random wandering hands (nor did I accidentally grab onto anything I would rather not), and of course we won, because Freddie is so much larger than everyone else, I didn't struggle to get my hands on his body straight away. Of course, that is a concept I can't get out of my mind at the moment, so I suppose I was bound to find it a piece of cake.

Daniel and Eva came second but I don't mind, because not only is second place the first loser, but finding Daniel was almost as easy as finding Freddie – perhaps even easier, given that Daniel is the only man here with a long hipster beard.

I used to like Daniel's beard. Well, I liked what it stood for. I loved that he has his own sense of style and that he likes to look good. Beards generally never really did much for me, but I got on board with Daniel's. Now, looking at it from the outside, I'm not really sure what I saw in it. I suppose beauty really is skin deep and if you like someone you wind up liking everything about them. Now I've been spending time with Freddie, I appreciate his designer stubble way more than any beard.

After claiming our victory we grabbed a couple of cocktails and sat down at one of the free tables, waiting for Ali and her hunky barman Max to join us. Ali seems to really like Max, but she really likes everyone in the early stages of lust. Still, if she wants us to meet him then we're happy to...

I catch myself talking about Freddie as if we're a real couple and remind myself that we're not – and thank God we're not, because if we were then this would be a double date, and we know how I feel about those, don't we?

There weren't many free tables when we sat down. Not long after we took our seats, Daniel and Eva sat down at the table next to us. It was still busy when Ali and Max arrived so the six of us are in uncomfortably close proximity. I doubt Ali has told Max what's going on with my and Freddie's showmance, so it's not as if we'd be chatting about it anyway.

Now that it's getting late, and the bar has nearly emptied, I'm itching to find an excuse to move, or hoping Daniel and Eva go to bed soon – words I never thought I'd say.

'See, sometimes we do things outside,' Ali says, a reference to earlier, when I said that she and Max only had things in common when they were horizontal – well, the Ali equivalent of horizontal, because that girl's legs know the *Kama Sutra* like the back of her head.

'I see that now,' I joke, and then I remember that Daniel can hear us. 'Us too.'

Freddie leans over to whisper in my ear, covering his mouth with his hand so no one can tell what he's saying.

'Don't look, but Daniel is staring at you,' he tells me. 'So I'm pretending to whisper something funny or sexy into your ear.'

'Oh, my gosh, Freddie,' I squeak, giving him a playful shove.

I can't resist glancing over at Daniel to see how he reacts. He looks sick with anger. I can see the beads of sweat rolling down his face from here.

'Ooh, Max, tell them about that thing tonight,' Ali says, running a finger seductively up and down his arm. They may be outside, but they're clearly in the midst of foreplay right now.

'What's tonight?' I ask through a yawn. I don't want to sound old but tonight is over; we're heading towards morning territory now.

'Every year, when we do Mr & Mrs Valentine Island, we do our own version after everyone has gone,' Max explains.

'What do you mean?' Freddie asks him.

'What he means is that when your lame version is over, Max throws his own after-hours version,' Ali explains, a glimmer of something in her eyes.

'He throws his own version of Mr & Mrs Valentine Island?' I ask, laughing as I try to make sense of why.

'Yeah, like a fun, spicy version... for the older boys and girls,' she explains. 'You two fancy it?'

I look at Freddie. I'm not exactly sure what we're being invited to but I'm a little bit worried it's going to involve putting our keys in a bowl on the table.

'I'm up for it if you are,' he says.

'Erm... Okay, sure,' I reply.

How bad can it be?

'*Fantastico*,' Max says. 'Gunnar, the island photographer, is going to play. I tell him to bring a woman.'

'Oh, I cannot wait,' Ali squeaks. 'Max says it's what Mr & Mrs Valentine Island should really be like, but most couples are not brave enough.'

'Can we play?' Eva asks.

'What?' I hear Daniel say behind me. 'No.'

'I'm not sure it's your thing,' Ali tells her tactfully. 'Max says it's only for adventurous couples.'

'It's a sexy game,' Max says. God knows what that means.

'We're adventurous and sexy,' Eva insists.

'No, we're not,' Daniel replies under his breath.

'Yes, we are,' she says through gritted teeth.

'It's okay with me,' Max says.

'Yeah,' Ali adds. 'The more the merrier.'

I'm not sure she means that.

'Ali, let's get some drinks in, before the bar closes,' I say, gesturing for her to follow me.

'Okay, sure.'

As we walk towards the bar I hook my arm through hers.

'Do we really have to let them play?' I ask. 'I can't seem to get a break from them.'

'Is it making it hard for you to crack on with Freddie?'

'What? No! I mean, that's not why. I'm just sick of the sight of them. I dislike them both intensely.'

'Okay, calm down.' Ali chuckles. 'No need to get defensive.'

'I'm not being defensive,' I say, probably defensively.

I love Ali's optimism and I admire her confidence, but I'm not her. Men instantly fall at her feet, and if they don't she lays out something for them to fall over, making sure they do. But I'm not Ali, I'm not charming or confident, I'm awkward and I disguise my shyness with rubbish jokes. Plus, even without the big boobs and the lip fillers and the Botox, Ali is an absolute babe. I'm a little squashy, with these chubby little cherub cheeks when I smile, and I imagine the way I carry myself reflects my insecurities. Ali could pull a movie star, but I can't.

'Anyway, don't worry,' she says as we carry our drinks back over. 'Max has told me all about these adult Mr & Mrs Valentine Island. I'm going to help him host. It's pretty raunchy, Eva is going to lose her shit.'

'How raunchy?' I ask from a place of self-preservation.

'Don't worry,' she insists. 'But me, Max, you, Freddie and this photographer guy... we're all single. None of it will faze us. Daniel and Eva are a couple though, and a bloody dull one at that. They're going to bow out and then we can all have fun without them.'

'What if they don't bow out?' I ask, because they do seem hell-bent on proving a point at the moment.

'Well, we'll see how strong they really are, won't we?'

'What time do we start?' I hear Eva asking Max as we arrive back.

'We start here in thirty minutes,' Max says. 'Now the bar is emptying, I'll set everything up.'

'Okay,' Eva says excitedly. 'I'll just pop back to the villa to get a cardigan. It's chilly now.'

'It is,' Max replies. 'They say there's going to be a storm tonight.'

Given everything I've learned about these after-hour Mr & Mrs Valentine Island games, and who is going to be competing, I don't doubt it.

29

There's something in the air tonight. A thickness, making it hard to breathe.

I keep hearing about this storm that is coming, but I don't think it's that. It's the atmosphere here, at the after-hours Mr & Mrs Valentine Island that has been, so far, so X-rated.

It's a funny feeling, down to a combination of things. There's a tension here, amongst us all. The regular Mr & Mrs Valentine Island is just competitive but what we're doing now... it's a combination of terrifying and exciting. I feel so nervous, in that awful, stomach-churning way when you know something bad could happen, as well as that buzzing, excited feeling when it feels as if something amazing is on the horizon.

There are ten of us here, coupled up in the deserted beach bar in the small hours of the morning. Max and Ali are our gracious hosts, competing together where possible, and of course there are me and Freddie, and Daniel and Eva.

Then we have the two couples I don't know: Gunnar and Rosa and Phillip and Annie. Gunnar and Annie both work here. Gunnar is the island photographer, a tall, blond Icelandic chap, who circulates snapping pictures at island events as well as working in the photo studio where couples can go to have corny portraits taken. Rosa is one of the new girls in the hotel. Her English is so good you could be forgiven for thinking she'd spoken it all her life. It seems as though, as some kind of grim welcoming tradition, Gunnar is trying to sleep with her.

And then we have Phillip and Annie, a very lovely couple in their late thirties who I am absolutely certain agreed to play these games with us by mistake, and now they're just too polite to leave. They're really nice, with clean Oxfordshire accents and sensible clothing. They definitely don't belong here, playing with the likes of us.

I first had my suspicions about Phillip and Annie when we were all given team names – a combination of our first names, to give us our couples' names. Max and Ali became Mali, Freddie and I because Frila, Daniel and Eva became Deva, Rosa and Gunnar became Runnar, and Phillip and Annie... were named Phannie. And everyone found this absolutely hilarious apart from them. Sure, it's juvenile, but it's been the tip of the iceberg for far.

The first round was a sort of sexy version of charades. It soon became apparent that it wasn't your regular game of charades when we realised that all the titles involved had room for sexy interpretation, as far as physically describing them went. So we'd work in our teams, guessing movies, TV shows, songs and books with titles like *Moby Dick*, *Kiss Kiss Bang Bang*, *Blow* and *Commando*. Not only did we have Phillip and Annie cringing their way through some of the more sexual gestures, but Daniel had a proper go at Eva in front of everyone, because she kept guessing *Free Willy* when the answer was actually *Moby Dick*. I think the kicker for him was when, straight after, when Freddie and I were up, the card we chose had *Free Willy* written on it, so we managed to get it in record time.

Round two, which we're currently trying to finish, involves everyone having the name of a famous person stuck to their heads. We then have to ask questions with yes/no answers to try and work out who we are. Ali and Max dished out the names, ensuring that people would only have names on their heads of celebrities they have actually heard of, depending on where they are from. It didn't take Freddie long to guess that he had Leonardo DiCaprio stuck on his head (it took Ali even less time to ask him if he has Leo's number – he does, it turns out, but he's reluctant to hand it out), and I wasn't far behind him guessing that my forehead was graced with Beyoncé. Annie and Phillip had Britney Spears and Elton John, and Gunnar had George Clooney while Rosa had an Italian pop star I had never heard of. Everyone has guessed the names on their heads, apart from Daniel and Eva.

I look over at Ali and smile. She's been a little cheeky with her choices for these two.

'So I'm an American woman with brown hair,' Eva reminds herself. 'Not a singer or an actress. A real person... Am I an entertainer at all?'

'No,' Ali answers.

'Hmm.' She carries on thinking.

We're all sitting around the table, waiting for Daniel and Eva to guess so that we can get on with the next game. They're undoubtedly in last place, but too stubborn to give up. I'd say it was getting boring, were I not excited for them finding out what names are on their heads.

'I'm an American, male actor, in my thirties,' Daniel says. 'I'm not in action movies, I'm not in any TV shows. I'm single... am I a sex symbol?'

'Gosh, yes,' Eva says.

'You are indeed,' Ali confirms.

'Am I in the news?' Eva asks.

'You have been,' Ali replies. 'You were caught up in a big scandal.'

'Oh, no, is this a politics thing?' she asks.

'Yes,' Ali replies.

'Right, well, I'll never get it, then,' Eva says, taking the sticker from her head and examining it. 'Monica Lewinsky? Never heard of her.'

I laugh quietly to myself at the fact that Ali stuck the name of probably the world's most famous side chick on Eva's head. The reference isn't lost on Freddie either, who gives me a covert nudge of acknowledgement.

'You might be happy to give up, but I'm not,' Daniel insists. He frantically itches away at his beard as he wracks his brain for answers. 'American, thirties, actor, movies, sex symbol... Blond hair?'

'No,' Ali replies.

'Brown hair?' Daniel continues.

'Yup,' Freddie confirms.

A slow wave of realisation washes over Daniel, cycling him through

the emotions. Confusion, disbelief, shock and finally anger, as he comes
to the obvious conclusion.

'Am I him?' he asks, nodding towards Freddie.

'Yey, you got it, congratulations,' Ali says, as if she's talking to a three-
year-old who just managed to eat beans without getting any in their hair.
'Zero points, unfortunately.'

It's an informal competition with no prizes, but couples in first,
second and third place receive thirty, twenty and ten points respectively.
In this competition, no one cares about a prize, because there is no prize
greater than wiping the smile off the faces of people you don't like. I am
determined to win this competition – and the real Mr & Mrs Valentine
Island – and show Daniel once and for all that I don't need him, that I'm a
better version of myself without him (and if that could be true, that would
be great).

'Okay, next we have round three,' Max announces. 'In this game the
men need to take off their shirts.'

'What?' Daniel says. 'No way.'

Freddie takes his off without thinking twice, which angers Daniel
further.

'We don't all take our clothes off for a living,' Daniel points out in a
blatant swipe at Freddie.

'He's an actor, not a stripper,' I remind him, amazed at how quickly I
jump to Freddie's defence without thinking.

'So, the boys take off their tops and the women put on lipstick and
they have to kiss the man all over the torso. To win, you need the most
kisses when the time is up.'

'It's a shame Max and I can't compete properly,' Ali says. The pair of
them have to sit out of any rounds that need a judge, a timer, a quiz
master, etc. 'I've been training my whole life for this.'

Phillip approaches Ali and speaks under his breath.

'Annie isn't feeling very well,' he says. 'I'm going to take her home.'

'No worries,' Ali replies. 'It was nice to meet you both.'

From the look on Annie's face, I don't think she feels the same.

'Okay, so, just the three couples competing in this one,' Ali says,
handing a lipstick to me, Eva and Rosa.

'Black,' Eva announces, by way of a complaint about the colour of lipstick she's been given.

'To match her heart,' Ali tells me quietly, handing me a sexy shade of rouge.

'This is debasing,' Daniel says.

'You don't have to join in,' Ali reminds him. 'We did tell you, adventurous couples only.'

'Fine,' Daniel says, taking his shirt off. 'But I'm not happy about it.'

Daniel is a skinny, slightly toned kind of fit. He's so white, apart from where he's bright red with sunburn. Gunnar is your typical large, Viking-esque Icelandic build with the kind of tan you'd expect from someone who works here all year round. Freddie has a movie-star body, with sun-kissed skin and perfectly defined muscles – the kind you don't actually think exists in real life. All three men have completely different bodies, and I wonder which one will be an advantage in this competition.

Eva, Rosa and I load up on lipstick. I keep mine in my hand, so that I can top it up if this coat starts wearing off.

'God, I am so jealous right now,' Ali says. 'Okay, on your marks... get set... kiss.'

I can't really think of a technique for this one, other than to go for it, kissing Freddie all over his abs, his pecs, his bulging biceps... Oh, wow, I can feel myself blushing. It's okay though, I'll just try and pass it off as red lipstick smeared all over my cheeks.

I quickly glance at my competition. Eva is struggling to reach Daniel so he lies on the floor. A dumb idea, if you ask me, because it means she can only kiss his front. Rosa seems to be doing okay with Gunnar, but she appears to be holding back a little. I suppose they hardly know each other – not like me and Freddie, who have over a week under our belts now.

I can win this, if I try. I just need to forget that it's Freddie standing there, smiling back at me, smelling absolutely delicious, like cocoa butter and aftershave. If I just ignore that it's him – and with his body being quite firm – it should be easy to plant kiss after kiss after kiss. I just need to focus.

I'm so in the zone I can just about make out Ali counting us down from five.

'Five... four... three...'

I move to his neck, to plant a final couple of kisses where there's plenty of space, just as the time is about to run out.

'Two... one... Okay, stop.'

As Ali announces that the time is up I don't know what comes over me, but I plant a firm and final kiss on Freddie's lips. It's just a peck, but I can't help myself. As soon as I realise what I've done, I panic inwardly. I look Freddie straight in the eye, my face blank of any emotion. He looks almost as shocked as I do.

'I saw that,' Ali whispers to me as she comes over to count our kiss prints.

I try to laugh it off. God, what was I thinking? I can't believe I did that; I don't do stuff like that. I've never done anything like that. Not even with a regular man who was in my league, let alone a film star. Shit, why did I do that? What will I say to him, if he mentions it? I'll tell him it was for Daniel's benefit, to make him jealous. He's bound to believe that, right?

'Lila and Freddie are our winners,' Ali announces.

'Of course, they are,' Daniel moans. 'Aren't they always?'

'We won?' I squeak.

'There is one round left,' Max says. 'For this round, ladies, we need to blindfold you.'

'Oh, my God, now I really am gutted I'm not taking part.' Ali groans before biting her lip.

'What's going to happen?' Rosa asks curiously. I feel as if we might have hit her limit.

'It's better as a surprise,' he says.

'I keep telling you all, only the bravest couples can take part,' Ali says.

I do think it's funny that Daniel and Eva are the only real couple here. The stakes are so low for everyone else.

'Okay, I think I am going to bed too,' Rosa says.

'Babe, stay,' Gunnar pleads.

'No, no, it's my bedtime,' she insists, laughing it off.

'I'm going to walk her home,' Gunnar says, looking just a little disappointed. 'Goodnight, guys.'

'Goodnight,' we all call after him.

And then there were six. Three couples. Only two left in the competition.

'Lila, Eva, are you down for a blindfold?' Ali asks.

'Sure, why not?' I reply with faux confidence.

'Yeah, sure, why not?' Eva chirps after me, sounding even less convincing.

Ali stretches out the elastic on an eye mask, holds it over Eva's head and carelessly lets go. She places mine on with a little more care.

'You're going to like this,' she whispers into my ear.

'What's going on?'

'Don't worry,' she replies under her breath as she hugs me. 'This is all for you.'

With my eyes covered all my other senses become heightened. The air smells warm and salty, the breeze tickles my bare arms. As an unexpected rip of thunder tears through the air I jump out of my skin.

'We'd better wrap this up,' Ali says. 'It must be that storm that's coming.'

'What are we doing?' Eva asks.

'Okay, so,' I hear Ali start. I can't see her, but I can imagine the hand gestures that are accompanying her words. If actions speak louder than words, the wild hand movements that always accompany Ali's words are probably what give her so much volume. 'Our ladies are blindfolded. Men, you have to kiss both ladies, and then the lady chooses the best one and if it's your partner, you get fifty bonus points.'

'We're kissing?' I say in disbelief. 'All of us.'

'You don't have to kiss Eva,' I hear Ali say. 'I imagine she would though.'

'Erm, I don't kiss my friends,' I hear Eva snap back.

'Nope, just their fiancés,' Ali replies. 'So, men, don't say a word. When I tap you, kiss one girl, then the other. If you think perhaps a girl might not want to kiss you, don't.'

I do wonder if this after-hours Mr & Mrs Valentine Island is something that happens every year, or if this is something Ali has orchestrated. It seems very her, and she appears to be running the show. This whole thing feels like Ali's unnecessarily convoluted way to get me and Freddie to kiss. I appreciate what she's trying to do, but she's barking up the wrong tree. This is a sham relationship to win money. I keep telling her and telling her, but she just won't listen.

'Okay, first man, you're up,' she says.

With my eyes closed I can hear much more clearly. I hear kissing coming from Eva's direction. I scrunch my eyes tightly shut under my blindfold, as though it might make my hearing better, to try and work out what's going on. The thought of Freddie kissing Eva makes me feel sick with jealousy. I suppose she's already kissed my real man, I don't want her getting her claws into my fake one too.

'Okay, onto the next girl,' Ali instructs.

I don't have long to feel nervous before I feel a pair of hands take hold of my shoulders and pull me close. As his lips meet mine a sense of familiarity washes over me. I'd know Daniel's moves anywhere. As his beard brushes against my face and his hands firmly squeeze my shoulders, it feels like home. Like my favourite pair of snuggly pyjamas and my own, lovely bed... and yet it feels so wrong. It's like something pretending to be something of mine – it might seem familiar, but it's a copy of something I used to have. It only takes me a few seconds to adjust my body language to something unwelcoming, shrugging him off.

There's one thing that's bothering me more than how wrong the kiss felt, and that's why he kissed me – he really kissed me. He kissed me like every single passionate kiss he's ever given me over the four years we've been together. Why would he do that to me now, with his new girlfriend standing right next to us?

'And the second boy,' Ali prompts.

I know that was Daniel, so this has to be Freddie. I listen carefully for his kiss with Eva.

I hear a loud, overly exaggerated 'mwah' sound. Freddie is doling out pecks, which is a huge relief. Not only because I don't want him to kiss Eva, but because, after I pecked him earlier, it kind of levels the playing field. I already know how the peck goes.

'And the second girl,' Ali says.

A few seconds go by, but nothing happens. I can hear every shallow breath I take, roaring in my ears, louder than the ocean lapping against the shore.

I feel someone... not physically, but I sense them moving into my personal space. It's a bizarre feeling, being able to tell someone is so close to me, without actually touching them.

First his hands rest lightly on my cheeks. Then they slide slowly over my neck where his palms rest, his fingers lightly creeping up my head, getting lost in my hair. As his body moves towards mine, pressing softly against mine, it feels like an age before our lips finally meet. The peck I was expecting never comes. Instead, Freddie takes my bottom lip and sucks it lightly for a split second. As his mouth pulls away from mine, my lips find a mind of their own and follow his, as if they're under some sort of spell. Our lips find each other again and we kiss – I mean, really kiss, and the fact that my eyes are covered makes it all the more intense. I run my hands up Freddie's sides and across his bare back, which is still uncovered from the previous competition.

All of a sudden our kiss comes to a halt, as buckets of water cascade down over us. I can't help but think about what a shame it is because I was really starting to get into this game.

30

I take off my blindfold but there's no sign of my summer holiday anywhere.

As the rain lashes down on us it's safe to say the storm everyone has been threatening has finally arrived.

'I'm calling time, Freddie and Lila win,' Ali shouts. 'Night, all.'

Everyone runs off in the same direction, but Freddie stops me.

'Let's take the shortcut,' he shouts over the hiss of the rain. 'Through the trees, by the waterfall.'

I swallow hard before I can reply.

'Okay,' I blurt.

We hurry through the beach bar, towards the secret path that leads up to the villa. Hidden behind a wall of leaves is a secret gate, which Freddie ushers me through before leading the way.

It's a particularly tricky balancing act, hurrying up this path, battling the rain, weaving in and out of trees in heels, and all the while being unable to think about anything but how Freddie just kissed me.

The kiss from Daniel was just awkward and confusing – can you imagine what Eva would say, if she knew? She'd be horrified. But the kiss from Freddie... did I just escalate the showmance, by giving him that peck on the lips? I wasn't even doing it for the benefit of our audience (I don't really know what I was thinking), but perhaps that made him think that I wanted to put on more of a show? But my God! What a show he put on! I know he's an actor but... my God! The hands, the way he uses his lips, the flick of his tongue. However much they pay him to star in *Edge of Eden*, he's worth it. Worth every penny.

I make conversation to distract myself.

'Is this a safe shortcut?' I ask. 'In this weather?'

'Of course,' he replies. 'I was here nearly two weeks before you arrived. I know this path like the back of my hand.'

'Wow, two weeks?'

'Yeah. Don't worry, the lightning is still far away and at least the bigger trees shield us from the rain.'

I'm surprised how long Freddie is here for, given that he's here solo. I was hoping he'd say more...

At the exact moment I hear a loud ripping sound I feel my body jolt to a stop. I fall forwards onto the ground, which is thankfully quite a soft landing.

'Shit!' I blurt, in that foul-mouthed way I often do when I slip up.

'Lila!' Freddie gets down on the floor to help me up. 'Are you okay?'

'I'm fine,' I reply. 'Just a little embarrassed.'

As Freddie helps me to my feet I hear that tearing sound again. By the time I'm on my feet I realise I'm standing there in my underwear. My strapless dress, having firmly snagged itself on a particularly sharp branch, has got stuck, torn, and as I've stood up, thanks to a lack of straps, it's fallen to my ankles.

'Make that a lot embarrassed,' I correct myself. I don't know what else to say, standing here, drenched in rain, in my mismatched pink bra and black knickers.

'I turn my back on you for a minute and you're naked.' He laughs. 'Why is it you're always naked or flashing?'

I try to playfully shrug it off but the fact he has a point makes me feel even more embarrassed.

Freddie ushers me under the protective branches of one of the large trees.

'I'll get your dress for you,' he insists.

'Thank you,' I reply. 'I'd be mortified if anyone else saw me like this. I'd have a lot of explaining to do.'

I watch as Freddie tries to untangle my dress from the branch. He's hunched over it, so soaking wet his hair is dripping down over his eyes. Eventually he hurries over with it.

'I don't think you can wear this,' he says, holding it up to reveal a significant tear.

'Oh no,' I squeak. 'That was my favourite sundress.'

Freddie looks at me for a moment. I notice a glimmer of something in his eye a split second before his dimples become more pronounced. Then he rips open his shirt, pinging off buttons in all directions.

'That was my favourite shirt,' he tells me with a playful shrug.

Then he takes off his trousers.

'What are you doing?' I laugh.

'You said you'd be mortified if anyone saw you. Consider this... solidarity,' he replies.

'I feel like both of us in our underwear would take even more explaining.'

'Well, at the very least I can create a distraction,' he says. 'Misdirection, while you run for cover.'

'My hero,' I joke.

The smell of the wet trees hits me like a train. I find myself distracted, watching droplets of water rolling over Freddie's muscles as I back into the tree behind me.

'Ouch,' I say.

'Be careful,' Freddie insists, quickly stepping towards me to save me, lest I fall again. 'Are you okay?'

And just like that we are in position, just like in the movie and just like in my dream. The perfect set pieces for a perfect play.

'I'm...' I start, but I don't finish. There's this tension between us, so thick we can hardly move in it. Neither of us moves away from the other. In fact, we grow closer by the second. It's only a millimetre or two at a time, but it's happening.

'That kiss before,' I start. I can't help myself. All I can think about is kissing him again. 'Was... was that because Daniel was watching? Was it just for show?'

'Do you think it was for show?' he asks me.

'I, erm... well, yes.'

'You don't sound convinced,' he says. 'How about I kiss you now, with no one watching, and then you can make your own mind up about what's real and what's for show?'

I open my mouth to speak but nothing comes out. No witty remark, no self-deprecating joke. I'm speechless.

We snap together like north and south magnet poles; from head to toe every inch of our bodies touch. I don't know how I'll ever let go.

We kiss, just like before but with a difference. This time we kiss as if no one is watching. There's a real urgency to it, as if the hunger I've had growing inside me is reciprocated. I feel Freddie has to have me just as much as I have to have him and that only turns me on more. He can have any girl he wants, genuinely. There are women (and probably even a few men) on the island who would leave their significant other in a heartbeat for him (I've known people hurt their partners over much less) – what the hell is he doing with me?

Reading my mind, Freddie stops.

'Sorry,' I apologise. I don't know why or what for.

Freddie scoops me up in his arms and kisses me again for a few seconds to show me that it's okay.

'Let me take you back to the villa,' he says.

'I'd like that,' I reply.

Freddie carries me up the path, safe in his arms. I'd say I'm in no danger of falling but that couldn't be further from the truth. I think I am falling. I'm falling for Freddie.

31
DAY 11

I wake with a jolt and puff air from my cheeks. I've been dreaming again and they're getting raunchier and raunchier.

I wipe my eyes with the backs of my hands before running my fingers through my hair. In some places it's still damp, in others the rainwater has caused it to triple in size. As soon as I remember the rain I remember the kiss – both of them.

Freddie is lying next to me in bed, completely naked. I look under the covers at my own body. Also naked. I didn't dream it; we did get together last night.

I bite my lip as I relive every incredible moment of it. I've never been with anyone so attentive, so strong, so powerful yet so sensual. Never mind the thunder and lightning, the fireworks drowned it all out.

After watching that stupid movie, I don't know why, but all my Freddie fantasies involved recreating scenes – I suppose that was all I had to go on. But he didn't shag me against a tree or spank me or make me wear a leash and bark like a dog. He brought me back to his bed and somehow it was still like something out of a movie. I never knew great sex existed. I thought it was a myth being peddled to try to ensure the continuation of the human race.

When I lie back down on my pillow, Freddie wakes up.

As his eyes adjust to the light, his brain remembers what we did last night. I am so relieved when his eyes light up.

'Good morning,' he says.

'Good morning,' I reply. 'Sleep well?'

'Eventually,' he replies with a smile. 'You?'

'Best night's sleep I've had in ages,' I admit.

'We should retrace our steps,' he suggests. 'Work out what it might've been, that made you sleep so well.'

'I think I have a good idea,' I reply, running my hand from his chest slowly down his abdomen.

I feel emboldened by his interest in me. I'm not usually an instigator, unless I'm with a boyfriend and I know it's a sure thing. But with Freddie I feel full of confidence – because he makes me feel as if I ought to be – but also intoxicated by the risk I'm taking.

'Again?' he jokes.

'Again,' I insist.

Freddie finds a surge of energy to jump on top of me. We've barely started kissing when we're interrupted by a knock at the door.

'Could it be Ali?' Freddie asks.

'I doubt it – she'd call,' I reply.

Whoever it is knocks again.

'I'll go get rid of them,' he insists, jumping out of bed, throwing on a dressing gown and heading downstairs.

'Hurry back,' I insist with my best attempt at 'come to bed' eyes.

I roll around in bed with joy. I can't believe Freddie and I slept together. Even more surprising than that, suddenly I feel an overwhelming urge to write my book, just, y'know, after we do it again.

My phone vibrates on my bedside table. I open a text from Ali saying she'll be round in ten minutes – we're definitely going to need more than ten minutes. I'm just about to type a reply, buying us some more time, when I hear raised voices downstairs.

'Freddie Bianchi,' I hear an east coast American accent boom through the suite.

'Marty,' I hear him reply. 'What are you doing here?'

Freddie's voice is much harder to hear that Marty's – and I never did learn my lesson when it comes to listening in on other people's conversations – so I creep across the bedroom to grab a dressing gown, my feet touching the floor as lightly as possible.

'I'm here to take you home,' Marty says.

'I'm on vacation,' Freddie points out. 'I'm allowed to go on vacation.'

'Sure you are,' Marty replies. 'But they have to come to an end. You can't just go off, not tell me when you're coming back, not answer my calls or my messages. So I've come to drag you back to reality, kicking and screaming if I have to. You've got to get back to real life now – I mean, come on, you don't have to get back to *real* real life. *Real* real life is shit, working all day, going home to your wife and screaming kids who don't appreciate you. You're a movie star. You're Freddie fucking Bianchi.'

This is honestly the worst pep talk I've ever heard, and Ali prepped me for my first bikini wax by telling me I'd die alone if I let things 'grow over' down there. I want to get a look at this guy, this loud, obnoxious person telling Freddie he has to leave.

I tiptoe down the stairs and peep into the living-room area. Marty is a middle-aged man with a middle-aged man's belly trying to hide under a designer suit. He has thick salt-and-pepper hair with a pair of eyebrows to match that jump up and down as he makes his case.

He must feel my eyes burning into him. His turns his head and spots me lingering by the bottom of the stairs. He stops what he's talking about and approaches me.

'*Ciao,*' he says, his American accent as strong as ever.

'Hi,' I reply.

'Great, you speak English, that makes this easier,' he says as he removes his wallet from his jacket. He removes a wad of dollars, which he hands me in two halves. 'Okay, thank you for your time. This is for the night and this is for your discretion. You are free to go.'

I look down at the money in my hands and then I realise what's happening. He thinks I'm a prostitute.

'Marty, Marty, no,' Freddie says as he hurries over, putting himself between us. 'Come on, man, not again. This is Lila, we're friends.'

I'm not going to worry about him referring to us as friends because it's certainly a big step up from prostitute, but I am concerned about something.

'Not again?' I ask.

'He's done this before, marching into my apartment, trying to pay off the first woman he saw – it was my auntie who had come to visit.'

'She found it funny,' Marty says, holding his hands up, a big dumb grin on his face.

'Right,' I reply. 'We just go nought to prostitute, then.'

'He said he was taking a vacation. He wanted to figure out who he was or some shit – actors, you know? – so I figured, yeah, prostitutes.'

'Well, that explains everything,' I reply sarcastically, tightening my robe.

'Sorry, Lila, this is my manager, Marty Caruso. Marty, this is Lila.'

'Well, I know I can shake your hand now,' he jokes, offering me his to shake. I do so reluctantly.

Freddie disappears for five seconds, ducking into the bathroom to put on a pair of shorts.

'Can you come back later?' Freddie asks Marty.

'So you can give me the slip again? No chance.'

'I went on vacation, I told you,' Freddie stresses.

'And now it's time for the vacation to end and you to come back to LA and do your job. I got products I need you on Instagram with – got a couple of dates lined up for you to be spotted out with. Now is the time, Bianchi. Some other beefcake is going to come along and steal your money and your game and your girls.'

God, I hate this guy's pep talks.

Thankfully, Freddie just laughs.

'I can't go home yet. We're in the middle of a competition,' Freddie tells him.

Marty looks back and forth between us.

'Freddie, you know there's that clause in your contract,' Marty says cryptically. 'You can't be doing anything to... mess you up.'

Freddie's eyes widen before he laughs uncomfortably.

'I don't know what you think we're doing –in fact, I really, really don't want to know – but it's nothing like what you're thinking. It's a competition for couples staying on the island. It's just fun stuff like answering questions and seeing who can hold their partner for the longest.'

'That's even worse!' Marty insists. 'Buddy, you can't do this shit without me around to manage you. People have cameras and they'll have their own interpretation of what you're doing. We need to control the narrative.'

'There's no narrative. It's just a bit of fun,' Freddie replies.

Marty massages his temples for a moment, recomposing himself.

'I hate to sound like your mom, but I gotta... You've had your fun, now it's time to go home.'

There's a knock on the door.

'It's probably Ali,' I tell Freddie. 'I'll go.'

'Do I need to pay this one off too?' Marty calls after me.

'Probably, if you want to live,' I say to myself under my breath.

As I open the door the sunny warmth outside pushes its way in. With the air con on, it's easy to forget just how hot it gets outside. Ali isn't far behind it.

'What's the plan today, sweet cheeks?' she asks me as she pushes past me.

She's wearing that ridiculously obscene swimsuit with all the cut-outs again, the kind you usually only see Victoria's Secret models wearing on Instagram, and you're always certain they don't spend much time in them. If I went swimming in that thing I would emerge from the water with a boob poking out of each armhole. I suppose Ali's are made of stronger stuff – she doesn't have to compete with nature giving them a mind of their own.

'You and that sort, Freddie, wanna grab some lunch?'

Ali realises that Freddie and Marty are also in the room.

'Oh, hi,' she says.

'Hi,' Marty blurts in a real slow, breathy voice. His jaw is hanging heavy as he stares at my friend.

'This your dad?' she asks Freddie.

Freddie cracks up.

'No, this is my manager, Marty,' he tells her.

'Nice.' She turns back to me. 'So, lunch? Max asked me if I wanted to grab something with him before work but... I think that's run its course now, don't you?'

'Judging from the timescale I'd say, yes, you are usually bored of them by now, but you two seemed great together,' I reply.

'Nah,' she corrects me. 'Anyway, we're going home in a few days, aren't we?'

'Yeah. Well, I can do lunch, but I'm not sure about—'

'Lila,' I hear Marty call from behind me.

'Yeah?'

'You got a minute?' Marty asks with stiff movements of his head, beckoning me over.

I feel my face scrunch with bafflement at what they would possibly want from me.

'Give me a minute,' I tell Ali.

'What?' I ask them in the hushed tone it feels as if the situation requires.

'Who's your friend?' Marty asks me.

'Ali,' I reply simply. I'm not sure what else he wants to know.

'I want to go on a date with her,' he tells me.

'Erm, aren't you married?' Freddie reminds him.

'Separated,' he insists, showing us his blank ring finger – except it isn't, he's still got his wedding ring on. He quickly removes it. 'Force of habit. Freddie, tell her I'm separated. Just trying to get a divorce deal that doesn't involve handing over my testicles.'

'That is true to the best of my knowledge,' Freddie says, choosing his words carefully.

'Ali is grown enough and terrifying enough to take care of herself and make her own decisions,' I say, also choosing my words carefully – she'd kill me, if she heard me say 'old'. 'Ask her if you like.'

'Yeah?'

'Yeah,' I reply.

'Okay,' he says excitedly, taking a deep breath before heading over to talk to her. He approaches her as she's checking out her reflection in the back of a spoon. I almost feel sorry for him.

'Hey, princess,' he says – take it from me, that's a terrible start.

'No,' she replies right off the bat. 'Not in a million years.'

'What?' he asks with an embarrassed laugh. 'What do you mean?'

'Me and you,' she replies, tapping him on the nose with the spoon before putting it back down on the worktop. 'Never going to happen.'

'Why not?'

'You're not my type,' she tells him firmly. 'Your son is,' she continues, pointing at Freddie.

Ouch.

'Ay, come on,' Marty insists. 'What do you want from me? I'm a successful businessman, I got money, I can be charming, I'm Italian – we're the most romantic people on the planet.'

Ali purses her lips, as though she's thinking things over. She isn't though – I can see the cogs turning in her head and the little glimmer you can always find in her eyes before she's about to get creative with her rejections.

I latch onto one of Freddie's arms, pre-emptively cringing.

'This isn't going to be nice for anyone,' I tell him. 'Nothing makes her angrier than someone who can't take "no" for an answer.'

'Let's unpack those one at a time, shall we?' she starts. 'First up, your money is no good here, chief. You might be charming sometimes, but you're not doing it right now. And finally, that "Ay, I'm Italian" line might work in the States, but you're in Italy now. *Mi fai impazzire.*'

'What does that mean?' he asks her.

'See what I mean?' She ignores his question. 'You're just plain old American here, darling. So that old Mickey Blue Eyes routine isn't going to work on me.'

'I can make you famous,' Marty says in a last-ditch attempt to turn this around. I imagine that line works for him sometimes – I suspect only in LA though, where everybody wants to be a star.

'No way,' Ali replies firmly. 'Not falling for that one again. Not after all the time and money it took me to get the video taken down from that German website.'

Freddie stares at me, his eyes wide with curiosity.

'Oh, God, don't ask,' I whisper to him. 'Don't ask and absolutely don't ask to see it.'

Marty stares at Ali for a second. Stunned into silence, he just blinks for a moment. Finally, he retreats back over to where Freddie and I are standing.

'I'm in love,' he tells us.

'What?' I squeak in disbelief. 'She just spoke to you like you were crap.'

'I know, and I am into it,' he says excitedly. 'I want to make her my third wife. Could you have a word?' he asks me. 'Convince her it's a good idea.'

I don't want to be rude to a person I have only just met – even if he's done nothing but offend me and those around me – but I can't convince Ali it's a good idea, because all I have is evidence to the contrary.

'Sorry, it sounds like her mind is made up.'

'I'd leave it, man,' Freddie advises. It sounds as if he's got the measure of Ali already. He knows she'll chew this guy up and spit him back out again and again and again.

Marty itches the back of his head for a moment.

'You want to stay here, finish playing your weird little game,' Marty says. 'Convince that girl to go on a date with me, I'll let you finish your vacation in peace.'

Freddie and I look at each other. He doesn't want to go home yet. I don't want to bow out of the competition (I'm saying that because I am not prepared to even consider whether I am feeling as if I don't want Freddie to go home either) ...

'Give me a minute,' I tell him.

'He-e-e-ey,' I say, in my nicest 'I need a favour' voice.

'Oh no, what?' Ali replies. I'm sure her brow would be furrowed, if she could move it.

'First of all, what was that thing you said in Italian earlier?' I ask her, buttering her up. 'Very impressive.'

'Oh, I don't know, it's something dirty Max taught me,' she replies. 'Now, come on, out with it.'

'You remember when we went out for lunch the other day, and you said you owed me one, after I went on that horrible double date with you?'

'Yes,' she replies. 'Wait, no... you want me to go on a double date with him?'

Ali makes no effort to lower her voice to spare anyone's feelings.

'No, of course not. I want you to go on a solo date with him.'

'I mean, I get that I owe you one, but obviously I'm not going to do that...' She thinks for a moment. 'Is there a reason you would want me to do that?'

'He's Freddie's manager,' I tell her quietly, hoping my calming tone will rub off on her and she'll lower her voice too. 'And he's trying to make Freddie leave and go back to work, but we've got two more rounds of Mr & Mrs Valentine Island and I'll be quids in if I win. I can use the money for the expensive hotel suite I paid for but haven't actually been sleeping in...'

'Because I've commandeered it,' she says. She thinks for a moment. 'Are you sure this isn't you trying to hang onto Freddie for a few days longer? Because, if you like him, a few days isn't going to make this any easier, when he goes...'

'It's for the money,' I insist.

Honestly, I can't even entertain the alternative right now. My head is all over the place...

'And I wouldn't even ask if Marty wasn't your type,' I add. 'Older, good-looking, successful.'

'Would you throw a future double date into the deal?' she asks. 'Just in case I ever need one.'

'Okay, sure,' I reply. It could never be as bad as the last one.

'Ergh, OK, fine, I'll take one for the team,' she says loud enough for Marty to hear.

'Yes,' he says, clapping his hands together. 'Shall we go get some lunch?'

'Okay, sure,' she says. 'You're paying, Mr successful, rich, sometimes charming Italian man.'

'Seriously, I mean it... I'm in love,' Marty tells me as he passes me. 'I'll take good care of her.'

He takes Ali by the arm – standing a couple of inches shorter than she is in her heels, which I know will be really upsetting her – and leads her outside.

I can't help but laugh at Marty telling me he'll take care of Ali – he's the one that's going to need to watch his back.

'Love's young dream,' Freddie says with a faux sigh. 'Speaking of which… didn't we say we were going back to bed?'

I smile.

'We did.'

'Well, we'd better get a move on, because we have another round of Mr & Mrs Valentine Island to win this afternoon,' he says. 'You know, I worked it out, and we could come last in this round and still make the final.'

'Amazing,' I reply. 'We make a pretty good team, don't we?'

'We do,' he replies.

He pulls me close and kisses me. I feel myself melting into his arms and it feels so good, but so terrifying at the same time. Ali is right: if I am falling for him, what does it matter if he goes home today, tomorrow or the day after that? Whichever day it is, he's going to go back to his life and I'm going to go back to mine.

I just need to put it out of my mind for now and make the most of it – and make sure I keep my head in the game, and win this competition!

32

What a difference a week makes.

It doesn't seem like yesterday (because it wasn't actually much more than that) since I was heartbroken, cheated on, crying my eyes out, panicking about being by myself.

Today, in a bizarre and shocking plot twist, Freddie and I are cooking together.

Not in the kitchen – we haven't just decided to go full-couple and spend the rest of our time playing house. We're at a pop-up kitchen at the beach bar, competing in the Mr & Mrs Valentine Island semi-finals.

Freddie and I already have such a lead at the top of the leaderboard that we have already qualified for the grand final. Still, it's good to try your best so that's what we're doing, up against four other couples.

Daniel and Eva are still in the competition, hot on our heels. I glanced over at them earlier and noticed them having some kind of argument, so I'm not sure how much of a threat they'll be today.

Today we are making pasta and the dishes we are making are to be judged by one of the hotel's top chefs. Everything I've eaten on Valentine Island has been insanely delicious so naturally I'm feeling the pressure.

Freddie, on the other hand, is cool as a cucumber, because Freddie has the confidence of knowing what an awesome chef he is.

Back home, cooking was usually down to me, what with Daniel misinterpreting my 'work from home' status as 'housewife' status. I can cook, but I'm no expert. Freddie, though, he seems as if he knows his stuff.

'I can't believe how amazing you are,' I marvel as I watch him washing basil leaves.

'Cooking?' he replies.

'Well, right now it's the cooking, but it's everything,' I admit. 'You just never cease to amaze me.'

'Try it first,' he says. 'Then we'll discuss how amazing I am.'

I love his cheeky little smile when he cracks a joke.

'Anyway, it's just pasta,' he says. 'Most people can make pasta, right?'

'I'd probably just buy it ready-made,' I point out.

He smiles.

'You know what this needs – some cream in the tomato sauce,' he says. 'Can you check the supply area for some? Maybe ask behind the bar if not.'

'Yeah, sure,' I reply, happy to be helpful. I take note of what kind and how much we need, which Freddie finds funny. I just want to show as much care and attention to this as he is showing.

I hurry over to the table where all the cooking supplies are. Earlier, Freddie, the resident chef in this faux relationship, gathered up everything we needed, so I haven't even taken stock of what there is.

With no sign of any cream I pinch one of the scrumptious-looking mozzarella pearls. It's the perfect size for popping into my mouth without anyone noticing. By the time I reach the bar, the evidence is gone.

Thankfully a very obliging barman agrees to fetch me a small amount of cream. I feel very pleased with myself for this. Our pasta is going to have something extra, that nobody else's has. Not just the cream, but Freddie's expertise.

'Lila, we need to talk,' Daniel says, taking a seat on the barstool next to me.

'I'm sure we do,' I reply. 'About our house, our car, the bills we need to pay, how we'll divide our Blu-ray collection... but not today, buddy.'

'I'm not your buddy, I'm your fiancé,' he replies.

I glare at him.

'No, you're not. Being engaged is a purely verbal thing. We were engaged because we said we were, because we were getting married. We're not getting married now, so we're not engaged, so you're not my fiancé.'

Incredible, really, that I'm having to point this out to him.

'This isn't what I wanted to talk to you about,' he continues. 'It's about Freddie.'

'Don't you dare talk to me about Freddie,' I snap. 'My love life is nothing to do with you any more.'

'Okay, but—'

'No, stop it,' I insist. 'Just leave me alone. I'm happy, I'm having a nice time – why are you trying to ruin it? Why did you give me that creepy kiss last night?'

'I was just playing the game.'

'No, you weren't,' I reply. 'You really went for it.'

'I just wanted to show you... to remind you... what we had,' he says.

'Why?' I ask. 'Actually, don't answer that. I don't care. I don't need reminding of what we had – I think about it every time I see you.'

'Well, that's good?' he says.

'No, it isn't,' I correct him. 'I see you, and Eva, and it reminds me what you did, and what you were willing to risk for... for what?'

'I don't know,' he admits. He places a hand on the small of my back. 'I don't think—'

'Daniel,' I snap. 'Get your hand off my back and leave me alone. Go back to Eva.'

'But Freddie—'

I don't let him finish, I just thank the barman for my cream and head back to Freddie, to help him finish the cooking.

'There you are,' he says, leaning forward to kiss me on the cheek. 'I thought you'd gone across to Naples for it.'

'Nope, just the bar,' I reply. 'My God, this smells amazing.'

'Thanks,' he replies as he pours the cream in, taking the sauce from a bright red to a creamy orange colour. 'Matteo was walking from table to table, seeing how people were doing. He told me after the judges taste our food we can eat it.'

'Yes!'

Freddie laughs.

'I knew you'd like that,' he says.

I help out where I can, but Freddie is doing pretty much everything, so my jobs are mostly small things, which keep me out of the thick of the cooking action.

Freddie plates up our dish. I'm not really sure what it is, but it looks amazing. I don't think I've ever met a pasta dish I didn't like. Creamy-looking sauce (our secret weapon for winning this), fresh basil leaves, mozzarella pearls. It looks like something they would serve here; I couldn't be prouder.

The chef doing the judging doesn't speak English, so Matteo translates as he judges each dish.

When the chef arrives at our table – last but certainly not least – he looks us up and down. You can just tell by the look on his face that he doesn't think we'll be up to much and, while he might be right about me, I know he's wrong about Freddie. The proof is in the pudding – well, the pasta, anyway.

'He asks where you learned to cook,' Matteo translates.

'From my mom, I guess,' Freddie replies.

'Chef wants to know if your mother is Italian,' Matteo continues.

'Nope,' Freddie replies. 'American.'

The chef mutters something else in Italian. His expression is blank, bordering on angry, but it gives nothing away.

'He says this pasta is best,' Matteo tells us. 'He says he would cook this pasta.'

'Are you sure?' I laugh.

'He says this pasta is the winner,' Matteo tells us before announcing it to everyone else.

The chef gives us both a congratulatory handshake – he must be impressed. After, Freddie picks me up and spins me around. He's done this a few times and I always thought it was for show – I suppose it still is, but still, it makes me dizzyingly happy.

'I was too scared to taste it before,' he tells me. 'Shall we try it?'

'I thought you'd never ask,' I reply.

'Mmm, it is really good,' Freddie says. 'If I do say so myself.'

Freddie stabs a couple of pieces of pasta – fusilli, he says it's called. It looks like cute little corkscrews, making it the perfect shape for scooping up lots of sauce with.

I lean over and open my mouth, waiting for Freddie to feed me.

'Hope you like it, babe,' he says.

Babe – our safe word, the one we said we'd use if things got too much and we wanted to cool off. Am I being too much for him? Is it all too much for him since we slept together? I'm almost annoyed at him, for springing this on me all at once.

As he holds out the pasta for me to taste, I don't know what else to do but try it, although I feel too upset to eat now, which is not at all like me. Before the pasta touches my lips, something knocks me to the ground.

I look up to see Daniel on top of me, pinning me down to the floor.

'What the hell are you doing?' I ask.

Before he has chance to explain, Freddie picks him up by his T-shirt, like a magician pulling a rabbit out of a hat. He holds him there for a moment, for everyone to see, holding him away from me.

'Put him down,' Eva screams.

'What's happening?' Zoey asks as she rushes over. 'Do we need to get Security again?'

I wonder to myself, during these events, how often they actually wind up needing to call Security. I wouldn't have thought it was ever – if so, we're about to set a new record for twice in one tournament. Perhaps just because this is such a nice place, they don't want anyone lowering the tone or killing the romance with drama. Nothing like a rowing couple (or couples) to kill your buzz.

'He just lunged at her,' Freddie says angrily.

'No, wait, I can explain,' Daniel says, squirming around in Freddie's grasp, struggling to speak. 'The pasta... it's got shellfish in it.'

I place my hands over my mouth.

'So?' Freddie replies.

'So, she's allergic, you moron,' Daniel tells him.

Freddie puts him down.

'Lila, I'm sorry, I had no idea.'

'Of course you didn't, you don't even know her,' Daniel shouts at him. 'You could've killed her.'

'Freddie, you weren't to know I was allergic,' I tell him. 'Daniel... thank you. Thank God you realised.'

'Yes, thank God,' he replies. 'He could've killed you.'

'Okay, can you stop saying that?' Freddie says. 'I feel bad enough.'

Freddie helps me to my feet and hugs me tightly.

'I'm so sorry,' he whispers into my ear. 'I'm so sorry. I... I just had no idea. It didn't even cross my mind that you might be allergic to anything.'

'It's not your fault. I should have been paying attention when you were cooking,' I reply.

'Well, it looks like Daniel has saved the day,' Zoey announces.

The crowd we've gathered around us all cheer and applaud.

My heart is in my mouth, I feel as if I just dodged a bullet. Shellfish is one of those foods that everyone raves about, but I have no idea what it tastes like. I've known about my allergy for as long as I can remember. I don't remember finding out that I had it, but I've known what to steer clear of ever since. I can't believe I nearly ate shellfish – I daren't even think about what could've happened.

'Daniel, seriously, thank you,' I tell him.

'You're welcome,' he replies. 'I'll always have your back. Not like this guy, this stranger, trying to poison you.'

'Okay, seriously, enough,' Freddie tells him. 'It was an honest mistake.'

'Or what?' Daniel asks him, squaring up to him, getting in his face. 'You'll try to kill me too?'

At this, Freddie shoves Daniel away from him. I don't think he means to do it hard, I think he's just trying to move him away, but his strength gets the better of him and Daniel is far lighter than he looks.

'Freddie,' I squeak as I instinctively crouch down on the floor next to Daniel.

'He was trying to provoke me,' Freddie protests. He looks awfully embarrassed.

'He succeeded,' I reply angrily, before turning to Daniel. 'Are you okay?' I ask him.

'I was just trying to help you,' Daniel insists.

'I know,' I start.

'What?' Freddie interrupts me. 'He was trying to come between us.'

'I didn't put shellfish in the pasta,' Daniel shouts. 'You did. I know my fiancée, you don't.'

'I know what you're doing,' Freddie says, real anger bubbling up inside him. 'I can see what you're doing and Lila can too. You're just using this to score points. Why not tell me she was allergic when you saw me with the prawns?'

'I saw you put it in when Lila went to the bar,' Daniel replies. 'And I didn't know she'd be eating it.'

It sounds as if Daniel is playing some sort of angle here, trying to be the hero. I'm about to get annoyed when Freddie does it for me.

'And she's not your fiancée any more, is she?' he adds.

'No, she isn't,' Eva interjects angrily.

'Okay, we all know I'm not,' I say, before suddenly becoming aware of our audience. I lower my voice. 'Let's just break this up, shall we?'

I help Daniel to his feet before trying to defuse the situation.

'Look, thank you for letting me know,' I tell him again.

'I care about you,' Daniel says, pulling me in for an unexpected hug. Out of the corner of my eye I notice Eva storm off.

'You've got to be kidding me,' Freddie says.

'Freddie, why don't you give us a minute?' I suggest tactfully. 'We've got that meeting in half an hour. I can see you there.'

I don't want to say 'couples' counselling' in front of all these people, not that I think they would be surprised. We've got our two-on-two session, the second condition of us being allowed to remain in Mr & Mrs Valentine Island after our performance the other day. I was hoping we could get out of it but after our reprise just now I think it's best we make sure we attend.

'Really?' he asks in disbelief. 'Okay, fine.'

'I'll see you there?' I suggest.

'Maybe,' he replies, before walking off.

33

I count myself lucky that Freddie has turned up for our two-on-two counselling at all, although I suspect it might have been better if he hadn't shown up, as at least then I could've made something up (because what's one more lie, in the grander scheme of things?) and said he was ill or had to take a work call or he'd fallen in the sea. Anything would've been better than this.

We're sitting side by side on a sofa but there's enough space between us to give the elephant in the room a seat.

Sitting in separate armchairs opposite us are our therapists: Victoria, who conducted the group session, and an American man called Arnold, who we are meeting for the first time. I suppose that makes sense and, with Victoria being English and Arnold being American, it really does feel as if we're on opposite teams. It's Team GB vs Team USA.

'Have you been having a nice time since we last spoke?' Victoria asks us. 'How is the competition going?'

'Well, we're winning,' I point out.

'You don't seem happy about that,' Arnold points out. 'Freddie?'

Freddie is in a bit of a sulk. I get that he feels bad about what happened, and I know that Daniel is a little shit – I'm hardly his biggest fan at the moment – but he did save me. So I'm in a sulk because he's in a sulk. We're like two naughty kids called into the head teacher's office for a chewing out, neither of us willing to admit an ounce of guilt.

Freddie shrugs.

'Is your ex still causing problems?' Victoria asks me.

'Ha,' Freddie says.

'Freddie, is there something you'd like to say?' Victoria asks him.

Up to now, Freddie's body language has been saying more than he has. Arms folded, legs crossed, body tipped away from me, pointing away from me too.

He sits forward and begins playing with a little tray of sand on the table, drawing patterns in it with the miniature rake that sits alongside it.

'Her ex is always around,' Freddie says. 'And sometimes I think she still thinks about him. He tried to make a fool of me today, over a silly mistake, and she didn't really speak up about it.'

'That's not fair,' I insist. 'I know you don't like it, but he did save me. And I know what you did was an accident, but the consequences still would have been bad.'

'What happened?' Arnold asks.

'I tried to kill her,' Freddie says.

In perfect synchronicity, both Victoria's and Arnold's jaws drop.

'Usual couple stuff,' I say, deadpan, before quickly clearing things up, so they don't call the Carabinieri. 'He accidentally nearly fed me something I'm allergic to.'

The second these words leave my lips, I realise just how daft they sound.

'I can't believe you think I still think about Daniel,' I say to Freddie.

'We're literally taking part in a competition against him, just so we can win,' he reminds me.

'Which you have been more than happy to take part in,' I point out.

'And then today... "Oh, Daniel. Oh, Daniel. Daniel, you're my hero."'

'Is that supposed to be my voice?' I ask him. 'You sound like Dick Van Dyke.'

'So do you,' he replies.

'That's a mean thing to say out of jealousy,' I point out, although I'm not sure I mean it. The idea of me being able to do anything to make Freddie jealous is laughable.

'Okay, let's slow things down a little, shall we?' Victoria suggests. 'Freddie, you think that Lila might not be over her ex and that she's spending too much time thinking about him/around him.'

'Yep,' he replies.

'Lila,' she continues. 'You think Freddie is exaggerating these issues because perhaps his ego is bruised, or maybe he's jealous?'

'I think you've got it in one,' I reply.

'How long would you say you've been having these relationship problems?' Arnold asks us.

'I'd say about an hour and a half,' I reply.

Arnold begins to write this down in an almost robotic way, but halfway through he realises this is an incredibly short amount of time.

'So you've had a falling out?' Arnold confirms. 'Today?'

'Yes,' I reply, feeling a bit daft.

'Any other issues in your relationship?' he asks.

Freddie and I look at each other.

'No,' he tells Arnold, while still looking at me.

'Okay, I'm going to tell you a story,' Arnold begins.

Arnold is a gentleman who I'd guess is in his late fifties. He wears these tiny glasses on the end of his nose that he only looks through when he's writing. While much younger Victoria seems like a progressive therapist, Arnold looks like your textbook psychiatrist – like the visual representation you see in a movie so that you instantly know what you are looking at. I imagine Valentine Island is the last stop on his journey before he retires. There are certainly worse places to work, even if you are dealing with the ridiculous problems of couples all day.

'One of the other couples we're working with... I must point out, anonymity is key in this game, so I can't tell you their names or any specifics about them. I can tell you their issues though. They met when they were in high school, fell madly in love, and, in that way that life goes, they put their personal dreams aside to focus on building a life together. They got married, had kids, they live in a nice house... but now that they've got it all, they take each other for granted, and they do so because they resent each other. He could've been a professional soccer player, she could've travelled the world. Instead he's working a job he hates to put food on the table and she's picking up his dirty pants while all he does is watch movies when he gets home. They are at a point in their lives where they wish they had done more, and they're angry at each other because they feel like the other has held them back.'

'Was this guy obsessed with *The Lord of the Rings*?' I ask.

Arnold's face contorts into something shocked and annoyed. He looks at me as if I've just opened up his head and climbed into his brain. Apparently therapists don't like it when you turn the tables on them. Of course, I'm not reading his mind, this just sounds as if it could be about Jen and Kevin who we met at the last session.

'That's not important,' Arnold says quickly. 'What's important is that they haven't held each other back at all. When it came down to it, when they were younger and they could have done whatever they wanted – and listen to my words carefully: they could have whatever they wanted – what they wanted more than anything was to be together, get married, and start a family. So they did that.'

'So, what now?' Freddie asks.

'Now they need to remember why they decided to do that,' Victoria tells us, quickly adding a disclaimer of, 'This completely fictional couple we're using as an example.'

'And why are you telling us this?' I ask.

'Because,' Arnold starts, 'you both need to ask yourselves one question: is anything more important than the other person? Is an ex more important? Is pride more important? If the answer is no, you have nothing to worry about. Spend the rest of your lives together – or until you feel yourselves growing apart, and even if you think you are, ask yourself one more question: would I have had a happier life if I'd spent it with anyone else?'

'I know you weren't trying to poison me,' I tell Freddie. 'And I know you couldn't have known I can't eat shellfish. I was just in shock, I think. It was really scary, having such a close shave. I didn't know what else to do apart from thank Daniel...'

'I know,' Freddie replies. He scoots up to me on the sofa and wraps an

arm around me. 'I was just embarrassed and upset that I could've hurt –
even accidentally – someone that I really, really care about.'

His words send a tingle down my spine, although I'm not sure what's
part of the act and what's real any more. I mean, we were pretending to be
a couple, then we slept together. Twice. And no one was watching (I
hope) so it's not as if we were pretending then... And now we're in
couples' therapy, talking as if we're an old married couple, airing problems that are barely hours old, and not actually real problems.

'I really care about you too,' I tell him, just in case he meant it. 'I think
I was more upset about you using our safe word, than you trying to
kill me.'

'I didn't use our safe word,' he insists.

'You have a safe word?' Victoria asks.

'We do,' I tell her. 'It's "babe" and he said it to me earlier.'

I don't waste time explaining.

Freddie laughs awkwardly.

'I, erm, I wasn't using our safe word,' he says. 'I... I guess I was just
calling you babe.'

'Oh,' I reply.

'This all sounds very complex... but your relationship can be as easy
as you want it to be,' Victoria points out.

I suppose that's a very good way of looking at it. If you just love and
respect each other, then what can possibly go wrong? But if you lie and
cheat then you're going to break someone's heart, give them lifelong trust
issues, and completely wreck the infrastructure of your relationship –
and without that it will just fall apart.

'What will happen to the other couple?' I ask, referring to Jen and
Kevin. 'The, erm, the made-up one you used in your example.'

'That is up to them,' Arnold says. 'Perhaps they'll realise just how
much they mean to each other, stop getting upset over the little things,
stop focusing on the road less travelled... or perhaps they are too far gone
now. No one can fix a relationship they are not a part of, and no one part
of the relationship can fix it alone. Relationships are work. Are you two
prepared to put in the hard work?'

'Our relationship this week has been a series of challenges,' Freddie says. 'Quite literally too, taking part in Mr & Mrs Valentine Island. But it all seems worth it. It's seemed worth it since day one.'

'When was day one?' Victoria asks out of interest.

'Last week,' Freddie and I reply at the exact same moment.

Finally discharged from therapy, and with a clean bill of mental health to take part in the final round of Mr & Mrs Valentine Island, I actually feel as if I've learned something.

Freddie and I might not be a real couple, but all the advice Victoria and Arnold gave us is solid advice. They're right, about making relationships work, and how it takes effort from both sides. I'm not sure it was the spirit of the conversation, but it does make me wonder whether I was giving Daniel enough – surely that's a preferable notion, that he cheated on me because I wasn't giving him enough attention, rather than because he thought Eva was better than I was or because he simply loved her more.

Most importantly though, everything they said has got me thinking about how important it is to be with someone who makes you happy, and if there's one thing I know for certain (confirmed by the fact that this is the most depressing period of my life to date) it's that I have never felt happier with a man than I do when I am around Freddie.

Now I just need to work out how to tell him...

34

'Do you ever feel like an extra in a porno?' I ask Freddie with a smile.

I'm referring to the fact that a large portion of our days is accompanied by the audible backdrop of Ali having multiple orgasms.

'It's like you don't know what my day job is,' Freddie replies with a laugh, swigging beer from his bottle.

'I mean, I really didn't know when we met,' I reply in my defence.

Freddie and I are currently curled up on the outdoor sofa that sits outside the back door of his suite. It's so dark up here it feels as if you can see every star in the sky. It's a cooler night, but I have Freddie to keep me warm, as well as a mug of thick Italian hot chocolate (so thick I have to eat it with a spoon rather than drink it) and a lovely warm blanket.

'I guess Ali found her way back to Max. I'm surprised he isn't tired, after his long working days,' I point out. 'Ali says she thinks he'd sleep with anyone, to have a few nights out of the staff quarters. She told me the other day that, before the first time they hooked up, he took her back there – to have sex in his bunk bed, with his roommate on the bed below. That's how I lost my suite and ended up in yours.'

'And they say romance is dead,' Freddie laughs. 'I wonder what she did with Marty...'

'You mean his body?' I reply. 'Probably at the bottom of the ocean.'

'At least it means I can stay on vacation a little longer,' he jokes. 'At least until they find him.'

'I'm sure he's fine,' I say. 'Even if she has chewed him up and spat him out.'

'Oh, Marty always lands on his back,' Freddie tells me. 'He'll be disappointing some other poor woman.'

I snuggle deeper into Freddie's embrace. I've never felt so safe... and yet still so fragile. I feel as if nothing bad can happen to me when Freddie is around. It feels impossible for anyone to hurt me... except him, of course. He could crush my heart in his hands.

'Please don't take any offence from this,' I start with caution, even though this is a phrase usually adopted by someone who is about to cause a great deal of offence. 'I can't imagine you living a movie-star life.'

'Would that be offensive?' he asks curiously.

'Well, look at Marty, for example,' I start. 'I'm sure he's a great guy.'

'He's my manager, not my brother – or my dad, as Ali wonderfully joked. You can say it how it is about him.'

'Well, he acts more like I would've expected you to act. Thinks he can have any girl he wants, treats them like prostitutes...'

'I can treat you like a hooker if you want,' Freddie jokes.

'If that means you're going to pay me, go for it,' I reply.

Jokes aside, Freddie is so unbelievably handsome and charming and funny, I do actually feel as if he should be invoicing me. For the acting work he's doing for me, not the sex. Although I'd certainly command a much higher wage for that performance if I were him. The Freddie you see on the big screen – the Edward Eden character – is almost too sexy. Unrealistically, unattainably sexy. But the real Freddie, the one I slept with... there's something far sexier about him.

Freddie sweeps my hair from my face before taking my chin in between his thumb and his index finger and kissing me on the lips. He is somehow even more delicious than my hot chocolate.

Sitting here, wrapped up in him, gazing at the stars and talking, pausing only to eat, drink or kiss, I can't believe my luck. Somehow the worst thing that has ever happened to me has turned into the best thing that has ever happened to me. Well, sort of. Living in the moment, everything is amazing, but my heart has taken this little burst of joy and run away with it. I know that it's one of the scariest things you can do, but I'm falling for Freddie. I need to know what he thinks the future holds.

'I know what I'm supposed to be doing,' Freddie says, resuming our conversation after yet another kissing break. 'I should be driving expensive cars, full of drugs and Victoria's Secret models, to my massive house in the hills.'

I laugh to myself, because my life is more a case of driving the Ford Fiesta I share with Daniel, full of shopping and the grandma I just drove for it, to her retirement home in South Croydon. My, how the other half lives.

'What's stopping you?' I ask.

'I became an actor because I wanted to act. *Edge of Eden* might not be my first choice of role, but I'm so lucky to have landed it, and we've all got to start somewhere. I know that, if I do this, I'll have my pick of whatever roles I want after.'

'You don't have that yet?' I ask curiously.

'Contracts,' he tells me. 'I've agreed to do the *Eden* trilogy, so I'll have to wait until after that.'

'I can't believe you're Edward Eden,' I say, laughing to myself. 'You're every woman's fantasy.'

'It's not all it's cracked up to be,' he says. 'It's a bit full-on for me. I'm not used to it. I was still serving people drinks the day before I got the call to say the role was mine. Pretty much from the moment they announced my name, I knew that my life wouldn't be the same. I just didn't realise how different it would be.'

Freddie pauses to sip his drink. He kisses me on the head before he continues.

'I'm so thankful for the role, and to be financially comfortable, for myself and my family, but I never realised quite how lonely I would feel.'

'You are on holiday on your own,' I remind him.

'Being alone and being lonely are two very different things,' he tells me. 'My life isn't my own any more. I can't grab a coffee without getting mobbed; people talk to me in the shower at the gym. Women are 100 per cent not interested in me at all – they think they're flirting with Edward. I think that's why we hit it off so quickly. At first I thought you didn't care who I was... but then, when I realised you didn't know, for the first time it felt like I could be myself, and that whether you loved me or hated me, it would be for me, not my job.'

'And I was awful to you at first,' I point out. 'Well, from the day after anyway. I'm so sorry.'

'You weren't yourself,' he reminds me. 'You were hurt. You were also naked.'

'Yeah, I was just so embarrassed,' I admit. 'But I'm still sorry.'

'That's okay,' he replies. 'All is well that ends well.'

As I finish the last of my hot chocolate his words bounce around in my head. All is well that ends well – is this the end? The end of the beginning, perhaps. But what happens now?

'You know how Arnold was blatantly talking about Jen and Kevin today – the *Lord of the Rings* couple,' I remind him.

'As though I could forget those two.' He laughs. 'But, yes, go on.'

'What do you want to do? How do you see your future playing out? The version that doesn't end with you being angry at your wife for not taking you on holiday to Mordor.'

'One does not simply go on holiday to Mordor,' Freddie jokes, in a northern accent far more convincing than his cockney. 'What was it Arnold said? They were obsessing over the road less travelled? The road most often travelled is the one that appeals to me. Wife, kids, dog, house, soccer mom car.'

'Can movie stars have that?' I ask. 'Won't you be travelling the world?'

'Well, I've been having trouble meeting girls who don't march up to me and ask me to choke them,' he jokes, although I suspect there is quite a lot of truth in it. 'I don't know. That's how I ended up here. I panicked and ran away. Told Marty I needed a vacation – he said two weeks, which I guess is why he's here now, trying to drag me back. I don't know, when you turned up... I just didn't want to leave. You make me feel normal.'

'Wow, thanks.' I laugh.

'Not by comparison,' he insists, but I already knew that. In a weird way, as surreal as all this is, he makes me feel normal too.

'What do you want?' he asks. 'What road are you taking?'

'I thought I was taking the well-travelled road,' I say. 'The safe route that everyone takes. But then Eva slashed my tyres and Daniel set the car on fire.'

'A real writer's metaphors,' Freddie says. 'Beautiful.'

'Thanks,' I reply. 'I wanted to get married. Daniel and I had already bought a house, we'd talked about filling it with kids. I saw myself spending my days writing books, looking after my house and my kids, cooking fantastic-looking family meals on an evening – of course, I'd have to learn how to cook before I could get to that stage, but it feels like the least of my worries now. Just pure domestic bliss – but the kind where I am also a strong independent woman with my own income.'

'That sounds good,' Freddie says.

'Too good to be true,' I reply.

'It sounds like we want similar things, doesn't it?' he points out.

'Yeah, it's a shame we live on different continents,' I reply. I don't know why I'm making a joke of it, when all I want to do is tell him that I think I'm falling for him, that I don't want to go back to my miserable life without him. I just can't muster up the guts to tell him. So much for being a strong woman.

'Well, we're on the same continent now,' Freddie says, lightly brushing my bare arm with the back of his hand.

'We are,' I reply.

With the inexplicable confidence Freddie fills me with, I find myself running my hand down his body.

In one swift movement, Freddie lies back on the sofa, pulls me down on top of him, and whips the cover over us. Movie-worthy choreography.

This moment, here under the stars, with this incredible man who I'm sure I don't deserve the attention of, might just be the most perfect moment of my life... at least were it not for the sound of Ali and her plus one grunting.

35

DAY 12

'Have you ever noticed how time passes much quicker when you're having a good time?' Freddie asks.

'Oh, definitely, I've definitely noticed the opposite too – how slowly it moves when you're bored at work or feeling under the weather.'

'Yeah, sometimes when I'm on set, there's lots of waiting involved and it can drag on forever,' he continues. 'Or when I'm supposed to be learning lines. I've got the script for the *Eden* sequel hidden away in my case. I'm supposed to be reading it – I told Marty that's what I needed this break to do – but I just never seem to get anywhere.'

I shuffle up to Freddie on the sofa. He places an arm around me and pulls me closer, even if it is already roasting hot this morning.

'I totally get it though,' I reassure him. 'It's like me, with this book I'm trying to write. I never wanted to be working on my honeymoon. At first I convinced myself that it would be a good distraction, something to keep me busy, and then I realised that I needed to start again, which only tightened the noose. Everyone thinks I must have it so great with my job. No boss watching me work, no office to drag myself out of bed to every day... I wish it were that simple. No one stops to think that, actually, being self-employed is a nightmare. I never know how much money I'll be earning from one month to the next; I never know if my last contracted book might be my last ever book. And then there's the fact that, no matter what is going on in my life, I pretty much have no choice but to work. No matter how messed up my head feels or how unwell I am – times when being creative is the hardest thing to imagine – I know that I have no choice but to make myself work. And there are no bank holidays, no maternity leave. Just me, alone, knowing I've got to get this work done, no matter what. No one has my back.'

I take a deep breath, because I think I said all of that on an exhale.

I look at Freddie's furrowed brow and realise I got too gloomy too quickly.

'I understand why you feel so stressed,' he replies.

'Thanks,' I say. 'I think I just needed to spit that out.'

'Well, my plan has completely backfired,' he admits. 'The idea wasn't to get you thinking about work at all – this was just my convoluted way of getting you to look at the date.'

'The date?' I reply. It's my turn to furrow my brow. I look at my watch. 'It's the 10th.'

Freddie stares at me blankly.

'The 10th,' I repeat. 'The... oh, my God.'

Freddie just laughs.

'Well, I feel like an idiot,' I confess, feeling my cheeks start to flush with the fire of a million suns.

'Don't beat yourself up,' he says. 'We've all forgotten our own birthday at least once.'

'Really?' I ask.

'Erm...' Freddie laughs awkwardly. 'Look, you've been through a lot and no one knows what date it is when they're on holiday – no one even knows what day it is. Let alone whether it's their birthday.'

I nod thoughtfully until something occurs to me.

'Wait, how do you know it's my birthday?'

'I had a peep when I hid your passport,' he jokes. 'Or maybe Ali told me.'

I smile. The idea of celebrating my birthday here by myself was one of the main things that gave me pause when I decided to run away.

'I see,' I reply with a smile.

'So, we're going for brunch,' he says. 'You, me, Ali and Marty – it was Marty who organised it. We came up with a plan together. He made the arrangements last night.'

We might've got off on the wrong foot, but Marty doesn't sound all that bad. I'm not sure how happy Ali will be – I hope she doesn't think this is a double date that I'm sneaking on her. I am blown away though – brunch sounds amazing.

As I get ready, there's a real spring in my step, which is surprising, given how much my thigh muscles are aching. It's a good ache though, like the kind you get after you've been to the gym. It's uncomfortable, sure, but I know that it's because I've been having a great time.

I never really thought Daniel and I were boring in the bedroom but now that I've got this spark with Freddie, it's easy to see what was missing between the sheets before.

I'm walking on air today. Just very carefully.

It isn't just things with Freddie and my birthday plans that are making me giddy – today is also the final day of Mr & Mrs Valentine Island and I've got a good feeling about it. We've done so well so far, I think we might just be able to do this. I've never won anything before – not even one pound on a scratchcard – and, given that this is skill-based, I feel especially proud of myself for coming so close. Even if I go home a loser, telling myself it's the taking part that counts, I know that I've done well. With a 'winner takes all' final round, if I do lose it will be both comforting and frustrating to know that Freddie and I won every other round.

As we step out of the villa and into the sunshine we come face to face with Ali and Marty, kissing in the doorway of my suite.

'Good morning,' Marty announces with a boastful yawn.

'Morning,' I reply, before turning to Freddie and lowering my voice. 'I'll just go ask Ali what she was thinking.'

'Yeah, send similar regards from me,' he says through the gritted teeth of a fake smile.

I hurry past Marty, ushering my bestie back inside. I close the door behind us.

'What are you doing?' I ask her.

'Kissing,' she says simply. 'By the way, happy birthday! Your present is at home.'

'I meant in a more general sense,' I clarify. 'Don't change the subject. You said you didn't fancy him... but thank you very much, that's very kind of you.'

I struggle to maintain the sternness in my voice.

'I didn't,' Ali replies. She hugs herself thoughtfully. 'I kind of don't but... I don't know. He was right, I guess. He is charming sometimes. He's got good banter, he kept me on my toes all night.'

'Yeah, that's definitely what it sounded like from next door,' I joke.

'Sorry,' she says. 'I don't know – you know when you meet someone and you're just like "that's a bit of me, that is"?'

'Yeah. You said that about Max a matter of days ago,' I remind her.

'That was physical,' she says. 'Physically Marty is maybe not my type, I guess, because he's a little older... but...'

I see something in Ali that I don't think I've ever seen before. She shuffles awkwardly on her feet, her cheeks blush slightly... she's embarrassed.

'You actually like him,' I point out. 'Sometimes I'm not even sure if you like me, and I'm your best friend, but with this guy... you just like him.'

'Please don't tell anyone,' she insists. 'Definitely don't tell him. I don't know what to do with it yet.'

'Of course, I won't,' I tell her.

'This is your fault,' she tells me, sounding a little pissed off all of a sudden. 'You caught feelings for Freddie and now you've passed it on to me. I've caught feelings for Marty.'

'You can't catch feelings,' I tell her. 'But... if you could... yeah, I've definitely caught them for Freddie. What the hell am I going to do?'

'He's clearly into you,' she assures me. 'And he's such a good person. He doesn't have a secret wife or keep a mini tripod in his pocket for making X-rated home movies...'

'I really hope you're not talking about Marty, but I'm almost certain you are.'

'You know, he actually is separated from his wife,' Ali tells me in hushed tones. 'We had a chat last night, about how they're not together, how he misses his kids. He got really emotional and normally that would turn me right off but, I don't know, all I wanted to do was comfort him, stop him sobbing.'

'It wasn't sobbing I heard last night,' I insist.

'No, what you heard was what happened after,' she admits. 'It's the only real way I know how to cheer men up.'

I feel better, seeing my cheeky friend rear her head. I worry so much about Ali because she's not as tough as she seems. This bravado is all an act, to try and stop herself from getting hurt. She's fashioned herself as some sort of man-eater to give herself a fail-safe, so that if things go pear-shaped or if someone tries to break her heart, she has this shield, this out – she acts as if she doesn't care, but she does.

Ali made me swear that I'd never tell anyone – in fact, she made me swear I'd never so much as privately think about it again – but one night a few years into our friendship she confessed something to me: that she was married. I damn near spat my cocktail all over her when she told me, and I'm pretty sure she only told me because she was drunk, but she had been married and divorced by the time she hit her mid-twenties, and the reason is her husband cheated on her. That's why she puts up this front now; that's why she didn't want me to marry Daniel. She isn't a fan of marriage because she thinks it's the biggest mistake she's ever made. For her to have hit it off with Marty like this, she must feel something strong.

'Okay, then, feelings expert, what do I do about Freddie?' I ask.

'Talk to him,' she tells me. 'Tell him how you feel. I'll bet you anything he feels the same way.'

'Hmm,' I say thoughtfully.

What have I got to lose by telling him? If I don't say something, I'll always wonder what might have happened if I were only brave enough.

I can't do it right now because we're off for the birthday brunch I had no idea about, and I don't want to ruin our chances in the competition this afternoon... Maybe I'm stalling, but maybe I just need a little more time to prepare myself.

I'll do it, tonight – hopefully after we've won Mr & Mrs Valentine Island. I will tell Freddie how I feel about him. If he feels the same, great. If not, well, it's not as if I ever have to see him again, is it? Not unless I turn on the TV.

36

Before my failed wedding, I knew that I was going to be on my honeymoon for my birthday and I was so excited about it. I wondered what we would do to celebrate, whether we'd go to a restaurant or we'd shop for authentic Italian ingredients before making our own food together. Perhaps we'd go for a walk on the beach or cuddle up under the stars and fall asleep in each other's arms. Whatever would happen, I was excited for my first birthday as a married lady. I don't need to remind you how that played out.

I suppose, when I arrived here, never mind that it's hard to keep track of the date when you're on holiday, I just put all thoughts of celebrating out of my mind. Even when things turned around for me and I started enjoying myself, I suppose I just... forgot to let my birthday back in.

I was already blown away by the gesture, before I knew what it was. None of this would be happening without Ali, Marty and Freddie, and I can't thank them enough for making an effort to make my birthday special. I'm sure that, in context, my first birthday with my new husband on my honeymoon would have been hard to top, but this... this is something else.

As soon as we were all dressed in our best (and I'd had my birthday FaceTime call with my family back home), carts arrived to drive us down to the dock, where we boarded a small private boat. I had no idea where we were going, which only added to the excitement. I asked if we were going back to the mainland or to visit Capri, but my friends just smiled at me, refusing to ruin the surprise in the last moments leading up to it.

You'd think I might be disappointed, when the boat didn't actually take us away from the island at all. Instead it simply transported us to the other side, but it was nice to see it from a little distance, during the day. To admire the shifting scenery, from the beaches to the trees to the cliff faces.

After docking at a tiny jetty, that you would absolutely miss if you didn't know it was there, we are walking up a narrow path, leading us gradually up the cliff face.

I do everything I can to try and pretend I'm not absolutely knackered from the walk. It's not that it's especially long or steep, I'm just incredibly unfit, it turns out. I am absolutely not getting back on my diet when I get home – my days of starving myself to squash into a dress for a man are a thing of the past – but I probably do need to start going to the gym more, so that I can walk up hills without dying and use my muscles without them aching for days afterwards.

'Ladies and gentlemen,' our boat driver/guide starts. 'Welcome to Grotta Biancofiore.'

As we reach the top of the path and are ushered inside our destination, I feel my chin hit the hard floor. We're inside the restaurant Freddie told me about, the one built inside a cave in the side of a cliff.

Inside it is nice and cool and kind of dark but, looking outside the cave, it's like peering into another dimension, a portal to a hot and sunny place with an ocean, crashing against the rocky shore far below us.

There is just one table set up in the vaulted limestone cave, which somehow just looks exactly as you would imagine a cave to look, but also manages pulling off looking like an absolutely stunning restaurant too.

There is no music playing, no noisy air con, just the sound of the waves and the gentle breeze to keep us cool. Our table is right by the edge of the cave, looking out to sea. Only a small fence stands between us and a sheer drop.

'This place is incredible,' I say as I sit down. 'Are we the only ones here?'

'We hired it out for your birthday brunch,' Marty tells me. 'The place looks even better at night, with all the lights everywhere, but it was fully booked tonight and we were working at short notice so, I guess, you give people enough money, they'll open a restaurant whenever you want.'

'Not that the money matters,' Freddie quickly adds.

'I just... I can't believe it... Is this real life?' I ask as I look around. 'Seriously, I think I might be in heaven.'

As waiters cover our table with a variety of sweet and savoury dishes – more food than I can imagine the four of us being able to eat – I realise that I must be right.

'Yep, I'm dead.'

'I'm okay with it,' Ali says. 'If this is the afterlife, I'm happy to live here for eternity. I always thought I'd go, y'know, downstairs.'

'We all did,' I tease with a laugh.

To drink there is a variety of fruit juices – the peach one is my absolute favourite – and the waiter takes our coffee orders. I honestly don't think I'll ever have another birthday as incredible as this for as long as I live.

'Guys, I honestly can't believe you've brought me here,' I say after swallowing a mouthful of sfogliatella, a flaky lobster-tail pastry absolutely bursting with Nutella. 'This is just... this is perfect.'

'You are the love of my life,' Ali tells me, leaning over to squeeze my shoulder. 'You deserve the world.'

'I am so lucky to have you,' I tell her, before turning to the men. 'Freddie, you've not even known me a month and, Marty, we met *yesterday*, and you organised my birthday party!'

'Ah, forget about it,' Marty said through a mouthful of frittata. 'Any friend of Freddie's is a friend of mine.'

I raise my eyebrows for a split second.

'Yeah, okay, I know yesterday wasn't a good start, and I knew you weren't a hooker, I was just being cute, trying to scare you off so this one would come home and get back to work.'

'Apology accepted?' I reply. It sounds more like a question than a statement, but I'm not actually sure whether or not he's apologising.

'Seriously,' he says. 'You seem like you're having a great time together, and I got to meet Ali, so I'll drink to all of that.'

Marty lifts his espresso cup.

'To Lila,' he says. 'The birthday girl.'

Everyone joins Marty in toasting me with their drinks.

'So, did he nearly scare you off?' Freddie asks me.

'Nah,' I reply casually. 'I was tempted to take his money though.'

'Hilarious,' Marty replies. 'You know, I thought it might work, make you think that Freddie was a bit of a bad boy, but as clients go, man, he's a bit of a nightmare.'

'Gee, thanks.' Freddie laughs sarcastically.

'Nothing wrong with him, he's a great guy, but... as far as a client goes...'

'I'm boring,' Freddie spits out. 'That's what he's trying to say. I'm a boring guy. I have no crazy exes. I haven't had any wild affairs with the actresses or models he tries to set me up with. I'm just a dull guy who likes to watch movies and play video games and occasionally star in the odd BDSM movie.'

'I mean, that last part doesn't sound boring at all,' Ali chimes in. 'But, if it helps, the fact that there's a complete lack of information about you out there – no skeletons, or exes, or skeleton exes – it may well be because you're just a dull, average, normal guy. But to people like me, you seem mysterious. It makes me wonder about you. Question what dirty secrets you must be hiding.'

'Is that good for business?' Freddie asks Marty.

'Erm, I guess, yeah,' he replies. 'I'd rather have people wondering whether or not you were into swinging than know you spent evenings on Red Dead Online.'

'Then I'll take it,' Freddie says happily. 'Another toast. To being boring.'

'To being boring,' I reply, clinking mugs with him. 'It's always served me well.'

'Well, now we get to be boring together, don't we?' he says.

Gosh, I hope so.

'You know, I think we might be lost,' I tell Freddie as I look left, then right, holding my compass out in front of me, as though I even have a clue what I'm looking at.

The final round of Mr & Mrs Valentine Island is a treasure hunt, following clues around the island, picking up more clues, moving on to the next.

Each couple has a different set of clues so that we can't simply follow each other around if we're struggling. That means this round can only be won on hard work and teamwork alone, but the competition is much smaller now, we found out earlier. There is just us and two other couples left. For reasons undisclosed, Daniel and Eva have dropped out. And do you know what the best part of all is? I don't care. I'm not bothered about beating them any more. All I care about is having fun with Freddie, and making the most of my last proper day on the island.

It's proving to be a nice distraction for me, from 'the talk' – the one I'm going to have with Freddie later, where I tell him exactly how I feel about him and hope he doesn't laugh in my face. Of course, he won't laugh in my face though; he's too amazing. That's why I can't imagine him being as into me as I am to him.

We are three clues deep, with just two more to go.

We're in the woods. Not the ones near the villa, the much bigger ones where the bicycle and hiking trails are, much deeper into the heart of the island, away from the built-up area where all the shops and villas are.

I imagine we'll all wind up out here at some point during the treasure hunt, but right now it's just us.

'So, we're looking for a distinctive tree,' Freddie says as he walks around, scanning the tree trunks for something unusual. 'But they all look the same.'

'And we're lost,' I remind him.

'*You're* lost,' he corrects me. 'I know where we are.'

'You do?'

'Yeah... we're in the woods.' He laughs. 'Things happen when we're in the woods.'

'That's right, they do,' I say with a smile. 'I'd completely forgotten about the last couple of times.'

Freddie stops in his tracks.

'The last couple of times?' he asks curiously.

'Yeah, the other night and...' Oh, God, I've just realised my mistake. 'Sorry, yeah, just the one time.'

Why didn't I just pretend I was referring to our lunch date?

'Who was the other time with?' he asks curiously. 'It was a first for me.'

'Unless your movie counts,' I reply.

'My movie doesn't count. Don't change the subject,' he says with a laugh.

Freddie has stopped looking at the trees. He's looking at me now. He might even be looking through me because he knows I'm hiding something.

'It was a first time for me too,' I insist. 'Never done anything like that without a ceiling.'

I cringe.

'Lila,' Freddie says calmly as he approaches me. 'Are you okay? You seem... skittish.'

'Pff, I'm not skittish, I'm not I... I do sound skittish, don't I?'

Freddie nods.

'Okay, well, I'd like to start by saying that this is your fault.'

His eyes widen.

'This ought to be good,' he replies. 'It doesn't pre-date me if it's my fault.'

'I had a sex dream about you,' I blurt. 'I watched your stupid movie and that scene must've given me ideas because I guess I took them to bed with me. And then you took me for a picnic the next day, and I started getting flashbacks.'

'Oh, wow, is that why you were so weird? I thought I'd come on too strong with the romantic lunch.'

'No, no, no,' I say quickly. 'Lunch was amazing. I just couldn't stop thinking about you pinning me up against a tree.'

Freddie looks around, only this time he's not looking for clues, he's looking for spectators. Satisfied we're alone, he steps towards me.

'Like this?' he asks as he presses against me.

'Exactly like that,' I reply.

As Freddie kisses me passionately I decide that we can take a short break from the treasure hunt.

'It's not exactly like the dream, though, because in the dream my legs were wrapped around your waist,' I say when he pauses for breath.

'That is easily arranged,' he replies.

As he grabs hold of my bum in his big, strong hands I glance over his shoulder and see Daniel standing behind him. His face is red and blotchy, his eyes dark. He looks as if he's been crying. Seeing him standing there is like something fresh from a horror movie, both because of how he looks and because he has just turned my favourite dream into my worst nightmare.

'Daniel,' I shriek, as if I've just seen a ghost.

'Okay, that's awkward,' Freddie says, putting me down. 'You know I'm not Daniel, right?'

'No, he's behind you,' I tell him.

'What?' Freddie turns around and sees Daniel standing behind him. 'What the hell are you doing here?'

'I just...'

'Did you follow us?' I ask him. There's no way he could've just found us.

'Yeah,' he replies. 'Lila, I need to talk to you.'

'Now?' I ask.

'Yeah,' he says again, his voice breaking a little. 'It's important.'

'No,' I reply firmly. 'We're in the middle of the competition.'

Daniel drops to his knees in front of us and bursts into tears. It is the scariest thing I have ever seen in my life because the most emotion you can expect from Daniel usually comes from his football team winning or losing. He doesn't usually cry. I didn't even think he was capable.

'What do I do with him?' I ask Freddie quietly.

'Take him back,' Freddie insists, before quickly backtracking. 'I mean, take him back to his room. Maybe Eva can help him.'

'I told Eva to get lost,' Daniel sobs. 'I should have never brought her here in the first place.'

It's nice to see a little remorse – even if it doesn't come with a sorry, and it's not exactly his biggest crime he's seen the error of his ways over, is it?

I don't even know what to say to that. I look at Freddie.

'Take him back anyway,' he tells me. 'We can't just leave him crying in the woods.'

'What about the competition?' I say.

'I'll keep going,' he tells me. 'Just hurry back, okay? Call me when you're done.'

I kiss him on the cheek.

'You're a good man,' I tell him.

'Hurry back,' he says again with a smile.

I walk over to Daniel and, while the urge to help him is still there – I'm not a monster, after all – I'm so angry at him for turning up like this and ruining my day.

'Come on, let's go,' I tell him. 'I'm pretty sure if we just head back down the hill, we'll come out near the villa.'

'Okay,' he says, hurrying to his feet. 'Thank you.'

For the first ten minutes, we walk in silence. I don't think either of us knows what to say but at least he's stopped crying. I am all for men crying, showing their emotions and sharing their feelings, but this just isn't how Daniel operates. He didn't even cry when his granddad died – not that I saw, anyway.

'Thank you, Lila,' Daniel says before sniffing to try to clear his nose.

'Don't thank me,' I tell him. 'I'm doing this because I feel sorry for you.'

'You're a good woman,' he replies. 'The best I know.'

'What about Eva?' I ask as we walk down the path towards the villa.

'I told her to get lost,' he says. 'We had this huge row and she said she didn't think I was over you, and I realised I wasn't. She was upset, she was angry. She said she wasn't willing to share me with anyone so I told her to go home.'

Daniel stops in his tracks so I stop too. It's too hot to stand still right now and it makes me impatient.

'Am I supposed to care that you sent her home?' I ask. 'Because, honestly, I don't care any more. I hope the two of you are really happy together.'

Oh, my God, I really mean it. No brave face, no one-upping. I really don't care.

'When we were going behind your back, we'd spend a few hours together, here and there,' he starts but I don't let him finish.

'Oi, I might not care, but you can spare me those details,' I say.

'No, listen,' he insists, taking me by the hands. 'It was fun and exciting and I thought she made me happy. But being with her on this holiday, with her around me day and night, oh, my God, she's been driving me mad. She's so vapid and stupid.'

I weirdly feel sorry for her but he's not exactly wrong. What he's saying, in a rather hurtful way (the way I was talking about her, when I was at my most upset) is that they're not on the same wavelength. They don't share interests. She won't talk about politics with him or sit around doing nothing while football is on. I don't suppose, while they were having their dirty little affair, she had to put up with him screaming at a football match whilst intermittently ranting about Brexit. Similarly, he won't have had to put up with her talking about her beauty vlogging work – I doubt Daniel even knows what an S-curl is, but during one particularly boring conversation, I once listened to Eva talk about the 'art form' for twenty minutes.

I can't say I'm shocked to learn that a couple who had an affair actually have nothing in common other than sex, and it just makes me all the more angry that he threw our relationship away for it.

But not that angry. Not any more. I'm angrier that he's taken me away from Freddie.

'Well, I'm sorry to hear that,' I tell him. 'Maybe, once you get back home, you can work it out.'

I tune out a little, perhaps because I'm thinking about Freddie or because it's just so damn hot out here.

'About that,' he says with a snivel. 'I was thinking me and you could work things out.'

'Wait, what?'

He has my attention now.

'Lila.' Daniel gets down on one knee. 'Will you do me the honour of being my wife?'

I stare at him.

'You cheated on me,' I tell him. 'Up to – and on – our wedding day. What makes you think I'm keen to relive that?'

'Okay, don't marry me,' he says. 'But let's go back home and work on our relationship.'

'Get up,' I insist, pulling him to his feet. 'Daniel... I'm with Freddie now.'

Well, I sort of am... kind of... we need to talk, obviously, but I haven't got round to it yet. But I want to be.

'He's just a holiday fling,' Daniel tells me. 'You're just a holiday fling to him.'

'It's more than that,' I insist.

'So what happens next?' Daniel asks me. 'You go back to your life, he goes back to his. You're living with me in our house in London. He's shagging models on Hollywood Boulevard. You're working on our sofa in your onesie. He's working on movies thousands of miles away for months at a time. Tell me how that works long term.'

I stare at him for a second. I don't have an answer for him.

'He won't cheat on me while we're apart,' I tell him. 'What else even matters? We'll make it work.'

'How do you know he won't cheat on you?' Daniel asks.

'Because he wouldn't do that,' I reply.

'Okay, did you think I would do that?' he asks me.

I wipe the sweat from my brow with the back of my hand. I'm so warm I feel as if I'm going to be sick.

'Well, no,' I admit.

'I was cheating on you for months,' he reminds me. 'You had no idea. Freddie is going to be in other countries, with girls throwing themselves at him – he's paid to film movies with romance and sex scenes. He's going to be kissing other girls and you're going to be watching him on TV, wishing it was you, and you can't even call him and tell him because of the time difference.'

'Daniel, he's an actor. He has to kiss other people – all actors do.' I stop trying to justify my relationship to him. 'I cannot believe this is your big speech for trying to win me back.'

'No big gestures,' he says – other than his second, half-hearted proposal, I imagine. 'No games. Just honesty and common sense. We belong together. He's just some guy you shagged on holiday because you were mad at me – and I get it.'

'I'm so glad you get it,' I reply sarcastically.

He's the one who doesn't get it. Trying to win me back without so much as an 'I love you' or an 'I'm sorry'.

'Look, no more tears,' he says, wiping his eyes. 'No more begging. We've got our original tickets for flying home tomorrow so let's just take some space now, talk on the flight tomorrow, figure out what happens next. You can't run away from the fact we have a life together. I might have made a mistake, but I'll never do it again. You can keep tabs on me forever. But with Freddie, won't you always be worried, wondering? Every time he kisses a co-star or you see him on a red carpet with some dolly bird. Every tabloid article saying he's shagging some Spice Girl or other.'

'All right, all right, all right, all right,' I rant. 'Jesus Christ, you've made your point.'

'Just... think about it, okay?'

Right now all I'm thinking about is how Daniel still thinks the Spice Girls are relevant. No wonder he and Eva had nothing to talk about. She'd talk about Little Mix for hours if you'd let her.

Suddenly much more composed, Daniel retreats back to the villa, leaving me out here by myself. I find some shade underneath a tree and sit down, fanning my face with my hand, not that it does much to cool me down.

I don't think much of his non-apology, but he's given me a lot to think about. Not as far as he and I are concerned, but with Freddie... I hate to say it, but he's right. And it's so cruel and unfair because it's all thanks to Daniel that I will never just blindly and happily trust another man again. I'm always going to wonder. And he's also right about how hard it's going to be, seeing Freddie kissing other people, filming sex scenes, hearing the rumours about who he is romantically linked to. It's going to drive me mad, and I'll be observing it all from home where I'm all alone, maybe in my own house or maybe in some tiny flat because Daniel forced me out and that's all I'll be able to afford.

It isn't fair on Freddie either. He's an A-lister; he should be living like one. Not flying to London to visit me between movies. He lives in LA, I live in London. It's never going to work.

I do still need to talk to Freddie, but it's going to be a completely different conversation. I need to break things off with him before I get carried away – for my own good as well as his.

38

Rather than go find Freddie, I've spent my afternoon packing my suitcase – most notably, taking all my things from Freddie's suite and moving them to my own. I might not be going home until tomorrow, but I can't stand the thought of packing my things in front of him, moments after telling him that this is where we say goodbye.

I'm sitting on the veranda outside the villa. It's starting to get dark now and the bugs are beginning to come out. I swat them from my face as I wait for Freddie to show up. I could wait inside but I don't want to miss him. I need to tell him asap or I'll lose my nerve.

Eventually, I spot him walking up the driveway, all smiles as he approaches the arches. By the time he reaches me he notices the look on my face and his smile falls.

'What's wrong?' he asks.

'Sit down,' I say. 'We need to talk.'

'Well, this doesn't sound good,' he says as he sits down next to me. He takes my hand in his and squeezes it. I can't believe he's comforting me, even when I'm about to ditch him. 'You want to go inside?'

'No, I could do with the air,' I tell him. 'I've just been thinking, you know, because I'm going home tomorrow.'

'Me too,' he replies.

'You've been thinking or you're going home tomorrow?' I ask.

'Both,' he replies. 'I just spoke to Marty. He says Ali is going home tonight?'

'She is,' I reply. 'I said goodbye to her not too long ago.'

'That's our leverage gone,' he jokes. 'He's booked us both on a flight tomorrow morning.'

'The party's over, then,' I say. 'I just wanted to thank you for everything you've done for me. Seriously, you've gone above and beyond.'

'I'd say you were welcome, but I'd be lying if I said there wasn't anything in it for me,' he replies. 'So thank you too.'

God, this is so hard. I thought it was going to be hard telling him I had feelings for him but now that I've had my reality check, the alternative is even harder.

Telling him how much I like him might've been scary but at least it would have been honest. I would have been being true to myself. But this... this is just me being practical, and it sucks.

'It's been a fun holiday romance,' I say. 'The most fun I've ever had. But it's back to reality now, right?'

'Back to reality,' he echoes. 'What do you mean?'

'You go back to your life, I go back to mine.'

'And that's that?' he asks.

'Well, yeah.'

I feel like such a cow but I don't know what else to say. Can I tell him the truth? That I'm so scared he's going to hurt me, and not because of anything that he's said or done, but because I know the world he lives in, and I can't compete. I can't compete with the women – I certainly can't compete with the lifestyle. Freddie would be so hurt if I told him that I didn't want to be with him because I'd just be scared and jealous every second I wasn't with him. My blood boils at Daniel for getting in my head and planting all these seeds of doubt.

'Are you going back with Daniel?' Freddie asks me simply.

If he thought that, would he take this news better?

'I'm flying back with him,' I reply. 'Obviously, we already have tickets.'

'And when you get home?'

'Well, we do live together...'

'You're actually going to take him back?' Freddie asks in disbelief. 'Because he cried?'

'I don't know what I'm going to do,' I reply honestly. 'But I do know that, whatever we've got going on, it's not going to work, is it?'

'We could make it work,' he tells me.

'It's okay for you, with your easy life. But I've got a mortgage and a job that I have to keep doing so I can pay my bills and eat. I have plants that need watering and a grandma who I take shopping every Wednesday. I have an entire life waiting for me, with or without Daniel. And I have to go back to it.'

Freddie shuffles in his seat. I don't think he knows what to say or do but there's nothing he can do.

'Come inside,' he says. 'Let's pack while we do this.'

'I already did,' I reply.

Freddie exhales deeply.

'Why do I feel like my wife moved out while I was at work?' he asks with an awkward laugh.

I give him a half-smile.

All I want to do is grab him and kiss him and beg him to make this work no matter what it takes, but I know that it can't. I'm sure he would try, but it just can't.

'What if I loved you?' he asks. 'What would you think?'

It feels as if every organ in my body has stopped working all at once. I feel weightless, suspended in mid-air, unable to do anything. I love him. I'm sure that I love him. But I just can't be in another complicated relationship. My brief dice with Daniel's extracurricular activities has left me petrified.

'I'd think I was relieved you never told me that,' I reply.

Freddie's eyebrows shoot up.

'Okay, then.' He coughs, clearing his throat. 'Looks like I've massively misunderstood the situation.'

'Come on,' I start. 'You were acting. We were both playing a part.'

'Lila, I am not that good an actor,' he replies. 'All of it was real for me. The attraction was there from the moment I met you. Perhaps you're a better actress than you think.'

He turns around and heads for his door, stopping just before he gets there. As he lingers, I want more than anything to tell him that I love him too. His pause gives me pause; perhaps it doesn't have to be this way.

'Oh, before I forget,' he says, tossing an envelope towards me.

'What's that?' I ask.

'We won Mr & Mrs Valentine Island,' he says with a laugh. 'That's your cheque. Have a nice life.'

And with that, he goes inside and slams the door behind him.

I head into my suite alone, about to end my holiday the way it started. Sad, lonely and with the realisation that I won't be spending my life with the man I love.

39

DAY 13

I've made a mistake.

In hindsight, I knew I was making it even while I was making it. I went to sleep with it on my mind, just chipping away at me, but when I woke up... the second I opened my eyes the reality of what I had done really set in, and all I could think about was making it right.

I jumped out of bed, hurried down the stairs and ran next door, ready to spill my guts, to right my wrongs, to tell Freddie that I love him.

But he had already checked out. I realised this after banging on the front door and peering into the back, but there was no sign of him.

So I guess that is that, then.

I finished packing my bags and made my way to the boat that will take me from the island back to Naples, where I can catch a plane back to my shitty life.

I sit on the side of the boat that looks out to sea. When I arrived it was so dark; at least this time I'll be able to take in the views.

Another big difference is that I'm not by myself this time. I have Daniel next to me. On the way here I wished he were with me. Now that we're on the way back I desperately wish he weren't.

I've asked him not to talk to me and so far he has obliged.

We're just about to set off when one last couple gets on. It's Kevin and

Jen, but they seem different.

'Lila,' Jen squeaks as she sits down opposite me. 'Where's Freddie?'

'He has to catch an earlier flight,' I say.

Kevin sits down next to her.

'All right?' he asks, but then he looks confused. 'You two were with other people. Don't tell me you're together now.'

'Kev, don't be cheeky,' Jen says, kissing him on the cheek.

'Sorry, boo,' he says, turning into her kiss, bombarding her with pecks.

'You too seem great,' I tell them.

'We had a turning point,' Jen explains. 'It was the night of the storm and we had this huge row. I wound up telling him I wanted a divorce and he said he wanted the same. I flounced off, in a proper huff, and that's when the weather got worse and I slipped on some wet grass, fell down, twisted my ankle – lowest point of my life.'

'Then what happened?' Daniel asks curiously.

'Just when things seemed at their worst, Kevin appeared. Never mind your guy, he was like something out of a movie,' Jen says. 'He picked me up and carried me back to our villa.'

'It was just like when Samwise carried Frodo up Mount Doom,' Kevin adds.

'Don't ruin it, babe,' she says with a laugh.

I can't believe how much lighter they seem.

'But, yes, if you love someone, no matter what happens, everything just figures itself out,' Jen says.

They kiss again.

It's so great to see them work things out, especially because they've been together for so long and because they have kids.

Freddie and I might not have been together for very long, and we might not have any kids or major ties to each other whatsoever, but what we had was real, and Jen is right. If you love someone, you work it out. We could've worked it out.

But no, instead I let Daniel get in my head, I let my insecurities run amuck, and I pushed him away.

As we finally board our plane and take off, things finally feel real. I blew it. And now it's back to real life, or whatever will be left of it, once Daniel and I figure out how we're supposed to split everything we own.

'Oh, love, before I forget, I'm going to need my golf stuff washing for tomorrow,' Daniel tells me as he reads his newspaper.

'What?'

'My golf stuff,' he repeats, but slower this time, so it's easier for me to understand. 'It needs washing. Maybe stick it in with our holiday stuff when you wash that.'

I stare at him, unable to do anything but blink. Eventually, he feels my eyes on him. He stares at me blankly.

'What?'

'I'm just trying to work out whether you're high or you've lost your mind,' I reply.

'What are you talking about?' he asks rudely.

'I'm not doing your bloody washing,' I tell him. 'And I'm flabbergasted this doesn't go without saying.'

'Why not?'

'Because we're not together any more,' I reply, frustrated. Did he really think I'd keep doing his washing?

'I thought we were giving it another go,' he insists.

I don't know what I find more disturbing, the fact that he thinks I'd give him another chance or that he thought we were getting back together and the first thing he asked me to do was his dirty washing.

'Why would you think that?' I ask.

'Because you're coming home with me,' he says with a smile. Because a smile makes everything okay, right?

'These are our pre-booked seats,' I tell him. 'We'd already paid for them.'

Now I'm beginning to wish I'd paid the extra money for a different flight, or at least exit seats so I could take my chances with a parachute.

'Wait, so if you haven't picked me, why did you bin off Freddie?' he asks. 'I was outside the villa this morning, he was outside too, talking to his American friend. Sounded to me like he'd been dumped. Why would you dump him?'

I honestly have no idea, but I really, really wish I hadn't.

40

FIVE MONTHS LATER

'Cast your mind back five months ago,' Ali demands. 'Back when we were in Italy.'

'Wow, was that five months ago?' I reply.

Where the hell has the time gone?

If it's five months since we got back, then it's pretty much five months since I moved back into a flat-share with Ali.

I was adamant that I didn't want to give up my house and thankfully Daniel wasn't precious about keeping it. But going back there after everything that happened, I somehow just knew things would never be the same. It was like walking around a graveyard of our life together. How was I supposed to get up every day and look into a bathroom mirror that Daniel put up, before eating breakfast in the kitchen we chose together? And then there were those awful hallway tiles that he chose, that I hated, that we ended up with because he won the game of Rock, Paper, Scissors – our last resort when it came to decision-making.

What was I going to do? Spend thousands of pounds having work done? Work that we'd spent thousands on already. In the end, we decided just to sell the place and split what little money we got from the sale after the mortgage was paid off. A clean break for all involved.

A clean break, but not a new beginning. I'm off the property ladder and back to renting a room, living with Ali like the good old days. In some ways, it's exactly like the good old days because Ali isn't here most nights and on the nights when she is here, she's quite chilled out and quiet. I am yet to hear any unnecessarily loud sexcapades, but you're not going to hear me moaning – so I guess that makes two of us.

I'm glad that Daniel and I were able to sort things out amicably. I didn't have any energy left for fighting with him. I think he's happy now; he's also living in a flat-share, with someone from his work. Things between him and Eva didn't work out – in fact the last I heard she was moving away to start afresh somewhere else. I don't think she ever wanted to be an 'other woman' – or, at the very least, to be known for it.

'Do I remember the holiday we were on five months ago?' I ponder out loud. 'Oh, you mean my honeymoon, that I went on alone, but then my ex, his new bird/my ex-friend, and my best friend turned up. Oh, and I fell in love with a movie star, won 5,000 Euros, but still managed to come home heartbroken and depressed – that holiday, or a different one?'

'All right, sarky,' she replies. 'Well, remember when you asked me to go on a date with that guy and you said you'd owe me a double date in return?'

'Oh, Ali, no, please,' I say. 'I'm still not over Freddie. The last thing I want is to be the person who gets lumbered with your latest "special friend's" boring, weirdo friend. And I have so much promo work to do.'

'How's promo coming along?' she asks.

'Good,' I reply, although, truth be told, it's a little strange reliving it.

When I got back from my holiday, after a couple of days of wallowing and feeling sorry for myself, I decided the best thing to do would be to throw myself into my work, and, just as Freddie suggested, I wrote a story based on us. Of course, in my version, the end is a little different. When you read romantic fiction, you are here for the 'happy ever after' – nothing else will do. In fact, readers feel cheated if they don't get one.

So around the time where, in my real-life story, I sat Freddie down and told him that things weren't going to work out between us, that's where my book goes off in a completely different direction. Instead, I give my characters the ending that I wish I'd been brave enough to go for myself. My leading lady confesses her love for the handsome actor character. He tells her that he loves her too. He's about to jet off, to film some movie, when he asks the leading lady to go with him. She can do her job anywhere, after all. So the pair fly off into the sunset together, full of hope for their future. When it comes to writing the final scene of a book, I like to keep things realistic; I don't lay it on too thick. My love stories always end at the beginning – the beginning of the couple's happy ever after, because that's the most exciting part. At that point, there are years and years of a happy life on the horizon and that's the positive note you should end a romance novel on. Not too far down the line because, in real life, that's when things start to get difficult. Cut your audience off at the hopeful sweet spot, rather than when your couple starts arguing about whether or not their first romantic holiday in years should be to visit the set of *The Lord of the Rings*.

It was nice, to give my book the ending I never got. Well, not nice. Perhaps bittersweet is closer to the mark.

'What did you think of it?' I ask her. I gave Ali an early copy to read, eager to get her opinion. I've always written stories with real-life inspiration in mind, but nothing as close as this, and Ali was actually there.

'I haven't read it yet, I'm sorry,' she replies. Ali is currently removing heated rollers from her head. She's wearing a slinky red dress that lightly skims her enviable figure. 'I think I lost it. Can you get me another, please?'

'Sure,' I reply. 'I guess, even if you think it's dumb, it's too late to change now anyway.'

'That's true. In that case, go put your best dress on. That black one, with the mesh at the front.'

'The one you got me for my birthday, that I feel wildly self-conscious in?'

'That's the one,' she says. 'It's hot!'

'Are you really going to make me do this?' I whine. 'I'm so comfortable in my pyjamas and it's winter out there.'

'You're too comfortable in your pyjamas,' she corrects me. 'So go get ready and I'll bang what you're wearing now into the washing machine so that we can wash the tea stains out whilst you're distracted. You can put them back on again when we get back, and keep them on for another five months if that's what is going to make you happy.'

'It is,' I reply with a faux seriousness. 'I'll go on the double date – because I do owe you one after forcing you to go out with Marty – but I will be counting down the seconds until I can put my pyjamas back on.'

'Atta girl,' Ali says enthusiastically. 'I just need to go do my make-up.'

'Seriously? You look like you already have. Any more make-up and your date won't recognise you.

'I just want everything to be perfect,' she replies.

I eyeball her suspiciously. Sure, Ali takes a lot of pride in her appearance, but only ever for herself, never for a man.

'Come on,' Ali orders. 'I'll do yours too.'

'Oh, I'm not so sure about that,' I reply.

'Why not?'

'Because the last time you did my make-up someone asked me what my drag name was.'

'That's a compliment for us both, so I'm doing it.'

'Oh, joy,' I say.

'That's the spirit,' she says.

'Do we know anything about this guy?' I ask.

'Mine is someone I've dated a couple of times, and it's going very well. Your guy has been single for a long time, so we're trying to get him back out there.'

'Yay,' I say sarcastically. 'It doesn't sound like there is anything wrong with him at all.'

'You've got to move on at some point, you know,' she says.

'I know, I know,' I reply.

I know that I should force myself to get dressed up and go out; it's just hard to find the will. When I got back from my holiday I had a whole book to write, so it was easy to keep myself distracted. Now that's out of the way I need to fill my life with something. It might as well be squashing myself into tiny clothes and forcing myself to go out with people I have no interest in. That's what single people do, right?

41

Imagine the team from Babestation going out for their work Christmas party. Basically naked, overly made-up girls walking through the city in sky-high heels, with only bravado to keep them warm.

That's what Ali and I look like right now. Well, Ali certainly does. I look like the work-experience girl who is trying too hard.

I think it's funny, that my try-hard look has come from a complete lack of effort on my part. I let Ali do whatever she wanted, and what she wanted to do was give me big curls, bold make-up, and I wore the black, revealing dress she insisted I wear.

As we walk into San Carlo restaurant the shift from the freezing-cold weather outside to the toasty temperature inside is very welcome. It smells amazing too. I can't say that, at least by reviving my social life, I can go back to enjoying food in my favourite restaurants, because I have absolutely been ordering food from here, brought to me in the comfort of (not) my own home by the wonderful people of Deliveroo.

Ali checks her phone.

'We're here first,' she says. 'So shall we sit in the bar?'

'Okay,' I reply cautiously.

'What?' she asks.

'We're early,' I point out. 'And you're never early. You have rules, on how late you need to be, depending on what you want to achieve. And the extra effort getting ready...'

Ali smiles at me but, in her attempt to appear blank, she just looks shifty.

'You sit down,' she insists. 'I'll get the drinks. Porn star martini?'

I nod cautiously. It's a good attempt at a distraction, offering to buy me my favourite drink, but I'm on to her.

I anxiously mess with my phone, keeping myself distracted. I fire up Instagram and do what I always do: meaningfully scroll through my newsfeed, as though that's why I'm there, before punching Freddie's name into the search box. I don't even have to go to much effort; he's always a suggestion now.

I creep on his profile and see a photo of him posted an hour ago, standing in what I'd guess is his massive, pristine kitchen, brandishing a plastic flask full of some protein drink. He's smiling, looking straight into the camera. I always feel as if he's looking at me, as if he knows I'm looking at his photos, and it amazes me that he's able to get in my head without even trying.

I know I shouldn't even be looking but I just can't help myself. We've all stalked people we've had crushes on or ex-boyfriends online – the problem with Freddie is that there is simultaneously a ton of information about him on the Internet, but at the same time never quite enough. I want to know how he is; I want to know what he's up to. I spend far too long trying to work out if he looks happy, looking for signs that maybe he misses me. A picture of him with his shirt off and a caption promoting protein shakes is nice, but it doesn't satisfy me.

I give up, feeling frustrated at myself for even looking. I imagine being an old woman, telling my story to my grandkids as Rose does in *Titanic*... except somehow 'Granny banged a movie star on holiday and then ruined the relationship for no real reason' isn't quite as epic or as romantic as Jack and Rose's tale.

I look over at the busy bar to see some guy talking into Ali's ear. I can tell he's older than she is, even from behind. He has his hand on the small of her back – I'm surprised she hasn't given me the signal yet. Usually, if one of us wants the other to swoop in and save them from unwanted attention, we place our right hand on our left shoulder.

I watch as the man's hand slides further down her back, grabbing hold of her arse. I jump up from my seat and hurry over.

'You okay?' I ask her, whispering into her other ear.

'I'm fine,' she says. 'Here's your drink.'

'Where's yours?' I ask, noticing only one on the bar in front of us.

'We're going elsewhere,' she says.

'What, you and...' I'm about to refer to the random man next to her, except he isn't random at all '... Marty?'

'Lila, how you doing?' he asks me. He pulls me in for a hug, as if we're old friends and not just people who have met twice and on one of those occasions he tried to pay me for sex.

'Shocked,' I reply. 'What about our double date?'

'This is my date,' she says.

'What?' I reply. 'I'm so confused.'

'We're a couple,' she tells me.

Marty lifts up his right hand and dances like Beyoncé does in 'Single Ladies', showing me that there are no signs of his wedding ring.

'A couple?'

'We've been seeing each other long distance,' she explains. 'I was, well, sort of embarrassed about it. You know me, I don't really do relationships...'

I remember, back when we were in Italy, Ali saying she really liked him, but she never mentioned it again after that, so I never really gave it much thought. I just assumed it was a similar deal to Max, who she was also really into... until she wasn't.

Marty looks great. He seems happier and way more relaxed, and he looks as if he's been working out too – either that, or Ali has been working him out.

'I can't believe it,' I say.

'Where did you think I was last month when I went away for a week?' Ali asks giddily, clearly so very proud of herself for such a well-executed con.

'Well, I could tell you were being kind of secretive about wherever you were going. I just thought you were going to the Czech Republic for more breast...' Ali stares daggers into me, so I reroute my sentence '... cancer charity fundraising.'

'Nope,' she reveals with a cackle. 'I was in LA, hanging out with this guy. And he's here for work now, so we'll be seeing a lot more of each other.'

'Well, I'm really happy for you,' I tell her – and I mean it; it's nice to see her so happy. 'Both of you. And I'm even happier that there isn't actually a double date lined up. I was dreading it. I suppose calling that favour is the only way you could think to get me out of the house.'

'I can't believe they've put your champagne shot inside your porn star martini,' a voice says behind me. 'What do they think this is, a Jägerbomb?'

His voice paralyses me. All I can do is stare ahead at Ali and Marty who are both grinning like idiots.

'He's behind you,' Ali mouths at me.

After a moment's hesitation, I finally turn around.

'Hi,' Freddie says.

'Hi,' I reply.

'Okay, we'll leave you two to it,' Ali says.

She hugs me from behind, squeezing my shoulders.

'You're welcome,' she whispers into my ear.

Freddie, who already has a glass of something in his hand, offers to carry my drink over to our table. A table for two. I can't believe how well Ali has played me.

'You look...'

'Like Ali,' I say, finishing his sentence. 'Ali dressed me.'

'I was going to say you look amazing,' he replies.

We sit down at the table and for a moment we just laugh.

'I can't believe you're here,' I blurt.

Freddie looks so different from the last time I saw him. I don't know if it's because I've missed him or if it's true, but he's better-looking than I remember. His hair is neater and much shorter. He looks bigger, as if he's found new places to store new muscles. He's wearing trousers and a shirt appropriate for winter – I guess the version of Freddie that I knew had a tan and was always wearing summer clothing.

'In London, or having dinner with you?'

'Oh, are we having dinner?' I ask, my voice getting higher and higher as my sentence goes on.

'If you want to?' he says.

'Yes,' I reply. 'Of course. I... Oh, boy.'

When I first got here I welcomed the heat. Now I feel as if I'm sweating. I know I should be playing it cool now but I can't. I can't believe Freddie is here, sitting across the table from me. I honestly didn't think I'd ever see him again.

'It's okay,' he reassures me, giving my hand a brief squeeze on top of the table. 'I'll talk for a while, if you like? Sorry, I think... Marty and Ali thought this might be a good surprise.'

'I am definitely surprised,' I reply.

A young waitress places a bottle of water down on our table. She notices Freddie and smiles at him. Then she looks at me.

'It's okay,' she whispers into my ear. 'I used to get starstruck too. Just try to remember that famous people are just like you.'

Freddie laughs.

'Remember, I'm just like you,' Freddie jokes once we're on our own again.

'I just... can't believe you're here,' I say for probably the millionth time. 'I just saw you on Instagram. You were at home...'

'So, you've been looking at my Instagram, huh? Those sponsored posts are planned way in advance – that picture might have been taken before we met.'

So much for wondering if he looked happy or as if he missed me in his photos.

'What are you doing here?' I ask, changing the subject from my Insta-stalking. I suppose it's a much better way to get answers, by asking questions. It beats trying to read between the lines of his image captions.

'I'm in London for a few months, filming the second *Eden* movie,' he explains. 'That's why I look so neat and tidy. And why I'm drinking diet soda. I had to get back into shape to play Edward. I feel like a dork.'

'I can't believe the you I met on holiday wasn't in shape,' I say. 'You look great.'

'So do you,' he replies. 'How are things?'

'Erm, not bad,' I start. 'I'm living with Ali now, which is exactly as I remember it – apart from the screaming orgasms, but I suppose that's because she's been having a secret affair with Marty.'

'I'm sorry things didn't work out with Daniel,' he says. 'You were right to give it a try. I'm sorry if it seemed like I was trying to get in your way. God, I've wanted to say that to you for months.'

'We didn't even try,' I tell him. 'We were never going to.'

'Oh,' he replies. 'Sorry, I thought you said...'

'Yeah, I did. I didn't know what else to do. I was planning on saying something completely different to you that night but...'

I don't know how to finish my sentence. Everything just sounds so stupid.

'Well, I have a confession to make,' Freddie says.

'Oh?'

'I read your book. Your new one.'

I feel my cheeks flush with embarrassment. It never occurred to me that he might read it.

'Wait. It's not even out yet,' I say.

'Yeah, my manager knows a woman who had a copy,' he jokes.

Ali! So much for her saying she lost it.

'I liked the ending,' he says. 'The book seemed pretty accurate up to then.'

'I have to write happy endings,' I reply. 'And I really messed stuff up with us.'

'You know you said you were going to say something different that night,' Freddie starts. 'Do you mind me asking what it was?'

'Would you like to hear our specials?' our waitress interrupts.

'Can we have a few more minutes, please?' Freddie asks her hurriedly.

'Oh, okay, of course,' she replies, clearly realising we're in the middle of something.

'You've read the book,' I say when we're alone again.

It makes it easier, that he's read it. It saves me having to own up to the fact that I was going to tell him that I was falling in love with him.

'Can I ask what changed your mind?'

'It was Daniel,' I reply. 'But not like that. I just got scared. I couldn't see how we could work, living so far apart, you travelling a lot...'

'It's funny, isn't it, that this is the first time I've travelled since, and it's pretty much to your doorstep?'

'Yes, that is a strange coincidence.'

'When you think about it, coincidence is all we know. It was a coincidence we both wound up alone at the same hotel – a hotel for couples – at the same time. It was a coincidence that I used to be a bartender and you asked me to make you a drink. Everything just seemed to bring us together and work out in our favour.'

'That's true.'

It's strange, we can only talk back and forth for a few sentences before the conversation falls flat.

'So, how's the sequel going?' I ask, changing the subject.

'Lila, I love you,' he blurts out. 'I love you and I've missed you and I haven't stopped thinking about you. There. I said it.'

'I love you too,' I reply.

There they are, those three little words that I was too scared to say five months ago. Today they come out so easily.

'Phew,' Freddie says. 'We did it.'

'So, what happens now?'

'Pizza?'

'I'm serious.' I laugh. 'Is it really that easy?'

'A very wise person once told me that relationships are as easy as you make them.'

'Which *The Lord of the Rings* movie was that from?' I joke.

'God, that day was funny, wasn't it?'

'You know, they worked out their differences,' I tell him. 'I met them on the boat, on the day I left, and they were so loved-up. That's when I knew for sure that I'd made a mistake.'

'That's great. If they can make it work, anyone can.'

'Can we make it work?'

'I know that you're worried,' he starts. 'But I'm here for a few months – we can just hang out and see what happens.'

'I'd really like that,' I reply. 'I have no idea what happens after that, but I feel like we could work it out.'

'I think you've already worked it out,' he points out. 'In your book... she's a writer, she can work from anywhere. They decide to travel the world together, shooting movies, writing books.'

God, that sounds wonderful.

'I feel like we just sat down and figured this out like adults,' I say.

'We did. I know it's not very romantic. The grand gesture was me turning up unannounced. If we could have done it the other way round, I would have. I could've had Marty negotiate our contract.'

'He wouldn't have stood a chance against Ali,' I reply.

Freddie thinks for a moment, a smile creeping across his face. I've missed those dimples and that little glimmer in his eyes when he's up to something.

'I can salvage this,' he says. 'Give me five minutes and then join me at the bar, okay?'

'Erm, okay,' I reply.

I watch as he dashes off. I wonder what he's up to...

Our waitress comes back.

'Oh, no, has he gone?' she asks. 'I'm sure it wasn't anything you said.'

'Thanks,' I say with a smile.

I head back into the bar, scanning the room for Freddie, but he's nowhere to be seen. I don't think I'm far from assuming that he has done a runner when I spot him behind the bar.

'What are you doing?' I ask him.

'Did you just ask me if the bar was open?' he replies. 'Yes, it is. It's always open.'

'What?' I laugh. But then I realise – he's recreating the night we met.

'Can I have a porn star martini, please?' I ask, playing along as best I can. 'Are you allowed behind there?'

'It's great, being famous, people pretty much let you do whatever you want,' he whispers. 'Now stay in character.'

'Okay, sorry.'

'What's your name?' he asks.

'Lila,' I reply. 'What's yours?'

'Freddie,' he replies as he finishes making my drink. 'I knew what you'd order so I got a head start making it. Here we are, one porn star martini.'

Rather than place it down on the bar, he walks out from behind it, carrying it with him. Then he places it down next to me.

'What are you doing?' I ask him.

'I'm doing what I should've done the night we met,' he replies. 'This.'

Freddie hooks an arm around my waist and pulls me close before planting a kiss on my lips, all in one swift motion.

'God, I've missed you,' he says as he releases me. 'I just want to kiss you all night.'

'You know, they do food to go here,' I point out with faux innocence.

'Oh, really?' he murmurs, kissing me again. 'Let's do that, then. Just warn me if there's going to be a sex toy on your coffee table.'

My entire body goes rigid in Freddie's arms.

'What's wrong?' he asks.

'The sex toy... the one that Ali put in my suitcase, the one you saw on the coffee table. People kept seeing it and thinking it was mine so I threw it under the sofa in the villa. I never got it back out.'

'Oh,' he smiles. 'Ah, well, we probably don't need it tonight.'

'No, I'm sure we don't. We probably don't need to eat either.'

'My appetite has shifted,' he says, kissing me again.

Suddenly I feel very aware of the fact we're in the middle of a bar, and Freddie is a celebrity.

'Let's go,' I say, leading him towards the door.

It's a strange feeling, not knowing where we're going. I mean, we know where we're going now, we're going back to my flat and we're not leaving again until one of us absolutely has to, but, in a more general sense, I have no idea what's on the horizon.

I planned my wedding down to the last little detail and look how that turned out. No amount of planning could've saved it.

If the best-laid plans always go awry then perhaps it's time I start winging it. We can write our happy ever after a day at a time.

ACKNOWLEDGMENTS

Thank you to Nia, Amanda and everyone behind the scenes at Boldwood Books for all of their hard work on this book.

A massive thank you to Joey, James, Kim and Aud for all that they do for me.

Thank you so, *so* much to Joe, for absolutely everything.

Finally, thank you to everyone who reads and reviews this book. I really hope you enjoy it.

MORE FROM PORTIA MACINTOSH

We hope you enjoyed reading *Honeymoon For One*. If you did, please leave a review.

If you'd like to gift a copy, this book is also available as an ebook, digital audio download and audiobook CD.

Sign up to Portia MacIntosh's mailing list for news, competitions and updates on future books.

http://bit.ly/PortiaMacIntoshNewsletter

Discover more laugh-out-loud romantic comedies from Portia Macintosh:

ABOUT THE AUTHOR

Portia MacIntosh is a bestselling romantic comedy author of 12 novels, including *It's Not You, It's Them* and *The Accidental Honeymoon*. Previously a music journalist, Portia writes hilarious stories, drawing on her real life experiences.

Follow Portia MacIntosh on social media here:

facebook.com/portia.macintosh.3
twitter.com/PortiaMacIntosh
instagram.com/portiamacintoshauthor
bookbub.com/authors/portia-macintosh

ABOUT BOLDWOOD BOOKS

Boldwood Books is a fiction publishing company seeking out the best stories from around the world.

Find out more at www.boldwoodbooks.com

Sign up to the Book and Tonic newsletter for news, offers and competitions from Boldwood Books!

http://www.bit.ly/bookandtonic

We'd love to hear from you, follow us on social media:

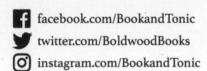

facebook.com/BookandTonic
twitter.com/BoldwoodBooks
instagram.com/BookandTonic

9 781804 261705